Also by Luiz Alfredo Garcia-Roza

The Silence of the Rain

December
Heat

December
Heat

Luiz Alfredo
GARCIA-ROZA

Translated by Benjamin Moser

Henry Holt and Company
New York

Henry Holt and Company, LLC
Publishers since 1866
115 West 18th Street
New York, New York 10011

Henry Holt® is a registered trademark of
Henry Holt and Company, LLC.

Originally published in Brazil in 1998 under the title *Achados e perdidos*
by Companhia das Letras, São Paulo.

Library of Congress Cataloging-in-Publication Data

García-Roza, L. A. (Luiz, Alfredo)
    [Achados e perdidos. English]
    December heat / Luiz Alfredo Garcia-Roza ; translated by Benjamin Moser.
        p.   cm.
    ISBN 0-8050-6890-2
    I. Moser, Benjamin.   II. Title.
PQ9698.17.A745 A6313   2003
869.3'42—dc21   2002038825

First American Edition 2003

Printed in the United States of America

1   3   5   7   9   10   8   6   4   2

December
Heat

PART 1

It wasn't the nasty words that woke the boy up late at night—he was used to sleeping with noise—but the banging on the cardboard box, a discarded refrigerator container someone had tossed onto the sidewalk a couple of days before and that had now become his bed and home. He didn't want anyone to fall on top of him. He lay motionless, silent, ears pricked, heart pounding, until he could be sure, from the kinds of noises he could make out, that the banging wasn't meant for him. Poking his neck out of the box, he looked around. He was careful not to make any noise: the strategy of a survivor. A drunken man was emerging from a restaurant, trying to help a bejeweled woman into a car parked little more than two meters from the box. In fact, she was the one helping him. The man, already advanced in age and in alcoholism, threatened to totter onto the box. With great effort, he lodged himself into the passenger seat, his leg dangling out the door. The woman slid behind the wheel to start the engine, at which point she realized that the key was in her companion's pocket, and that furthermore his door was open and his leg was halfway out of the car.

The boy was growing bored and was about to return to his sleep when he noted that the man's wallet was dangling precariously from his back pocket, ready to be plucked. He stayed vigilant and waited. The man was vainly attempting to collect his leg; his shoe had become wedged between the car and the curb. With every movement he made to free it, the wallet trembled; the body shook, dangerously threatening to crumple onto the pavement, while its owner, huffing and puffing, tried to extricate the keys from his pocket. Unable to locate them in his left pocket, he sought them in his right; that wobbling movement caused the wallet to fall noiselessly between the sidewalk and the car. The man found the keys at last; the parking attendant arrived to offer assistance and the leg was placed inside the car, but the door could not yet be closed because the man's body was still protruding. The attendant gently pushed against the passenger's shoulder and, not without some physical exertion, managed to secure the door. The boy thought the man would notice his missing wallet when he tried to give some money to the attendant, but before the woman could even turn the key he had his chin on his chest and was murmuring disjointed words while drooling on his shirt.

The car rattled off, leaving the attendant in its wake. The boy waited for him to depart, made sure no one was approaching along the sidewalk, and darted out of the box like a cobra. He could have crossed the two or three meters separating him from the curb with a normal stride, but the films he watched on the televisions in the windows of electronics stores had taught him that commandos always attack low to the ground. He retrieved the wallet and returned to the box, head still down, the wallet hidden beneath his shirt. Though it was night, there was still enough light to examine the contents. He counted the money. Three fifties, five or six tens (he couldn't tell exactly), one five, and two or three ones. In the other parts of the wallet there were credit cards, a checkbook, and a small plastic object upon which, with difficulty, he made out the word POLICE, in red. He was paralyzed by surprise for a few seconds. His first impulse was to get rid of everything immediately. Everything except the money. He wasn't fool enough to walk around with a policeman's I.D. in his pocket, but neither was he crazy enough to throw money away.

Even at that hour, there were plenty of people on the block;

if he discarded the wallet someone would find it soon enough. He waited for the right moment, emerged from the box, and tossed the wallet just far enough away that he would be able to see who picked it up. People coming out of the bars and restaurants on the Avenida Atlântica, couples, groups of kids: all walked by without noticing it. The boy wondered whether it was too dark on that part of the sidewalk. He came out again and nudged the wallet out to where it was more visible. He went back to the box.

When he saw the man approaching, he had no doubt that he would be the one; he walked and looked like someone with nothing to lose. In fact, he saw it long before a normal passerby would have; he stepped up his pace, glanced around, bent over skillfully and gracefully, grabbed the wallet, and stuck it in his pocket without examining it.

The boy didn't like it. After all, the wallet was a little bit his: he was the one who had thrown it back there, and he didn't like that it had been picked up by this particular guy. He left his box and followed him, maintaining his distance. The man walked toward the Avenida Atlântica, the direction he'd come from, turned the corner, and sat on the edge of a long cement bench that was empty at that hour. He pretended to be tying his shoe while he looked around. When he was sure he wasn't being watched, he took the wallet out of his pocket, glanced around once more, dumped the contents out on the bench, and examined them one item at a time. He looked carefully at the checkbook and the credit cards before happening upon the police I.D. He attentively scrutinized both sides of it, placing it in his own wallet. He put the checkbook and the credit cards in his pants pocket. After sticking his finger into every compartment of the wallet, he tossed it underneath the bench, got up, and walked away. His stride had changed.

There had been a woman, but he didn't remember what happened to her. He was lying in his own bed in his underwear, the shirt he'd been wearing the day before, socks, no shoes. How he had gotten there, and who had taken off his pants and shoes, he had no idea. He could have come back by himself, taken off his clothes, lain down in bed, and fallen asleep immediately. And the car? He didn't remember driving home, just like he didn't remember the woman. It wasn't the first time this had happened. Alcoholic amnesia, they called it. He had nothing against it, except that it blotted out the good times. He didn't remember the woman, or what happened— the good part, in fact—and he didn't know how he'd ended up back home. He couldn't have been brought back by a stranger, since his wallet didn't list his address anywhere. His wallet. He looked around for it and saw his pants crumpled at the foot of the bed; when he bent over to pick them up, his neck could hardly support his head. Things were a little fuzzy, and only with great effort did he manage to reel in his pants. He checked the pockets, but there was no sign of his wallet. He sat at the edge of the bed, his head throbbing horribly, and looked around, examining the dresser, the bedside table, the floor, the chairs: nothing.

He tried to stand up, managing it only by holding his head with both hands, grumbled, and noticed that his mouth was stuck shut. With great effort, he walked to the living room, only a few steps away from his bed. He didn't know what he was hoping to find. In any case, he didn't find anything, or at least anything different. He went back to his room, crossing in the direction of the bathroom. His effort to urinate into the bowl was a disaster. He looked at himself in the mirror above the sink, passing his index finger along his doughy face. He took off his clothes and got in the shower. The cold water didn't help his headache; it only added a little thermal shock to his body's general distress. He hadn't yet recovered enough balance to be able to dry himself standing up. He returned to the bed, supporting himself by pressing one of his hands against the wall while the other dragged the towel along the ground. He sat down and remained motionless while waiting for his head, which seemed to have stayed behind in the bathroom, to rejoin his body. He sat long enough to dry off without resorting to the towel.

He was almost certain that it was Saturday, or maybe Sunday; he was sure that it was the weekend. After a lengthy hesitation, he went to the door to get the newspaper. It was Saturday. The clock in the living room read twenty past twelve. He knew it was twelve noon and not twelve midnight because of the awful light coming through the window. The minute hand of the clock moved quite a ways before he reached a decision between lunch and breakfast; the latter seemed more prudent. When he was getting dressed, he noticed that he didn't have a belt. It wasn't on the pants he'd worn the night before, and he couldn't find it anywhere in the room. Maybe he'd been in a motel; where else would he have left his belt? He got another one from the wardrobe, finished dressing, took the money he kept in case of emergency—and this was an emergency—made sure he had the key to the apartment, got to the door, and only then noticed that the key to the car was also missing.

Drinking his coffee at the corner bar, he tried to summon some recollection of the night before, but the most he could scrape together was a hazy image of Magali and the restaurant. Though the image was unclear, he thought it could only be Magali. He had to transform the supposition into certainty, however; the wallet could be with her, though he couldn't imagine why. Besides the money, the checkbook, and his professional identification, there were the credit cards he'd have to cancel as soon as possible, in case Magali didn't have the wallet. This, however, he only managed to determine with some modicum of clarity after the second cup of coffee, a cheese sandwich, and two aspirin. He had to go back to make the call. He hoped desperately that the woman was Magali.

Back in the apartment he rummaged around one more time, without success, before making the call. The phone rang fifteen or twenty times. He hung up and called the credit card companies to report his lost cards, hoping that no one had bought a refrigerator or a color television or a fresh wardrobe for the next season. He called the woman again. No one answered. It occurred to him that he could look for his wallet in the car. Maybe he'd been in too much of a hurry to cancel the cards. What if the wallet had fallen onto the floor of the car? He didn't remember where he'd parked; he didn't even remember taking the car. He looked out the window. The street was narrow and curved just beyond his building; the car wasn't visible, but perhaps it was parked past the curve or on the next street; spaces were tight in the area and the building didn't have a garage. He left the apartment, walked down the street, went around the block, checked out the next few streets. No sign. He couldn't forget to call the bank about the lost checkbook, which couldn't have had more than ten checks left, but the credit cards, the car . . . his head started to throb again. He returned home and took another aspirin; he would have to wait till Monday morning to tally up all the damage and losses. He called and ordered a pizza that he didn't manage to eat; when the delivery boy rang up from downstairs, he was fast asleep.

He woke up in late afternoon, dazed from sleeping so much but free of his headache. He lived on the border of Copacabana and Ipanema and Magali lived near the Túnel Novo, at the other extreme of the district, at the border of Copacabana and Botafogo, but he was determined to find her and try to figure out what had happened. Since she wasn't answering the phone, he assumed that she was just as bad off as, or even worse off than, he was.

The vibrations of the taxi had his stomach churning; a cheese sandwich was no substitute for a proper lunch. While he was crossing Copacabana, he reflected for the umpteenth time on the possibility of giving up drinking. Eating, drinking, and fucking: the three best things in life, although not necessarily in that order, as he liked to say. If he eliminated one, there would still be two left; narrowing it down to one would suggest that his days were numbered. He knew that giving things up went along with aging, but he wondered why he would bother living without life's main pleasures. If you could call that a life.

As soon as the taxi pulled up to Magali's building, he had his first pleasant surprise of the day: his car was parked a few feet away. Intact. He got in the elevator, confident that he would find his wallet with his checkbook, credit cards, and documents. It was a seedy, rundown old building of almost two hundred efficiencies. At least the elevators seemed to work. He rang her bell so many times that the neighbors started to complain. He went down and sought out the doorman. No, he hadn't seen the woman from 918 since the previous day, and no, he hadn't seen her come back this morning, the night doorman was someone else, his shift started at ten, it wasn't even eight yet. He asked for a piece of paper and wrote down his name and phone number.

"Hold on to this and give it to the night doorman. As soon as she gets back, tell her to call me, no matter what time it is." He reinforced his request with a ten-*real* bill. Even though his car was parked at the door, he still had to take a taxi home.

He ate in a pizzeria near his house, the same one that hadn't been able to deliver the pizza he'd ordered for lunch. He tried to pay for both of them but the manager wouldn't hear of it; they had known each other since the place first opened. He went back to his apartment before ten, just as a film was coming on television, a police flick he'd seen a few times but wouldn't have minded seeing again. Watching television was one of the few activities that didn't put his physical limits to the test. The film was almost over when the phone rang. He answered immediately, assuming it was Magali.

"Hello!"

"Vieira?" A man's voice.

"Yes."

"It's Espinosa."

It took him a few seconds to get his mind off the woman and the film and focus on the phone call.

"Espinosa?"

"Yes."

"Espinosa! My God, it's been a long time! How are you doing, old man?"

"I'm fine. And you, buddy?"

"Never as good as you, but I'm getting by. Where are you these days?"

"After the police evaluations I was transferred to the Twelfth Precinct, right near my house."

"You deserved it. But what's up, old man?"

"Vieira, are you going out with a girl named Magali?"

"I am, or at least I was until yesterday. I'm not sure if she got rid of me or if I got rid of her. I still haven't managed to find out. Why? Is something wrong with her?"

"More than that. Can you come to her apartment?

"Now?"

"Now."

"Damn, Espinosa, what's going on?"

"I'd rather talk about it face-to-face."

He had made up his mind to follow the man and find out where he lived. The clock on the corner showed 2:06; the temperature was twenty-five degrees Celsius. Leaving the Avenida Atlântica, the man went back up the Rua Santa Clara, walking a little hurriedly, hand in his pants pocket, probably caressing his find. The boy followed at a careful distance. He didn't need to walk far; at the next intersection the man turned right onto the Avenida Copacabana and entered a building whose ground floor had a little bar and a few small shops, all closed at that hour. The entrance to the building lay behind a grate, squeezed into a corner right next to the neighboring building. The man used his own key; the building didn't seem to have a night doorman. The boy crossed the street and looked up, checking to see if a light would come on in one of the windows. Nothing happened. At least he knew where he lived, and that it wasn't an apartment that faced the street. He went back to his box.

It wasn't a good idea to stick around; they could come back, ask around, and eventually turn him up. The earlier he left, the better. He didn't need to move far; he didn't even need to go to a different neighborhood, just a different spot. People couldn't tell street kids apart. He made sure he had the money in the pocket of the shorts he was wearing beneath his pants; he picked up the piece of canvas he placed on top of the newspapers he slept on, took one last look at his box, and abandoned his bed and home.

He walked on the Avenida Atlântica toward Leme until he reached Fernando Mendes, a small street near the Copacabana

Palace with old buildings, ample doorways, and generous marquees, great to sleep under. The Italian café, open until the morning hours, was a good resource for food during the night. He had hung out there when he was younger, waiting by the cars in front of the restaurant for a group of four or five customers; as soon as they went in, he'd take advantage of the open door to slide in between the people, slipping past the watchful owner and waiters. Once he was inside, he'd crawl up, practically on hands and knees, to the biggest table and ask for food. Almost always, before getting kicked out, he'd manage to get his hands on bread, olives, salami, and if they took too long getting rid of him, he could even get a piece of meat or a dessert. When he'd gotten a little bigger he'd had to modify his strategy: a plate of food in exchange for not disturbing the restaurant's peace or letting some friend do the same—which hadn't been that hard, since he didn't have any friends. Now he was back. He knew the place well. He tried to hide the change of clothes he had brought and once again made sure the cash was stashed in his shorts.

The apartment wasn't much more than a room with a little kitchen and a bathroom, with the added luxury of a shower with an aluminum-frame door. In addition to the closet, there was an old dresser made of wood and pink marble with a little beveled mirror; on the shelf was an enormous variety of glass bottles, jars, boxes. A peacock feather was stuck between the mirror and the backboard. In the corner next to the window, there was a clothes rack with purses, hats, necklaces, and colorful neckerchiefs. There was also a little *bergère* in need of new upholstery; on the wall, two reproductions of famous paintings; and, occupying the majority of the space, a big cast-iron bed, upon which rested Magali, entirely nude, save for the plastic bag over her head. Her arms were tied to the head-board with articles of clothing (the dresser drawers were open and had been rummaged through), and her legs were tied together with a big silk scarf that had itself been attached to the foot of the bed with a leather belt.

From the threshold of the door, the man looked at the bed, perplexed; at Espinosa; at the bed again; at Espinosa again; until he heard the question:

"Is that your girlfriend?" Espinosa had to repeat the question, which he did while moving closer to his old colleague and touching his arm.

"Is that your girlfriend, Vieira?"

"Damn it, Espinosa, of course it is . . . you already knew that when you asked me on the phone. Who was the son of a bitch who did this?"

"We don't know. The night doorman had gone out when she got back last night; everyone in the building has their own key to the entrance. The neighbors didn't hear anything out of the ordinary; no screams or sounds of a struggle. In any case, there are no marks on her body. It looks like she let herself be tied up without resisting, and the bag must have been put on her head without her having time to scream. The body was found less than an hour ago by a friend who had the key to the apartment and who thought it was funny that she hadn't answered the phone all day, even though they had lunch plans. Nobody's touched anything. The doorman said that you had come looking for her, that you left a note for her, and that your car is parked almost directly in front of the building, unlocked."

Espinosa spoke as if he were making a report. He didn't usually talk so mechanically, especially in front of somebody he respected. The two of them were alone in the apartment.

"Sorry, Vieira. I could have warned you, but the only thing

I knew was that you two had gone out last night. The lab tests haven't come back yet; we don't know if she was drugged before being killed, but I found this on the floor of your car." He showed a little plastic lid. "It's the top of a can of Mace that was sitting next to your car key on the bedside table."

"What are you thinking? That I did this?" The ex-cop's voice was filled with suffering and indignation. "Espinosa, I'm an old man, and I'm not rich; this girl was one of the few joys I had left."

Espinosa had known Vieira for a few years; they had worked together in the same precinct, long enough for him to know that Vieira had never been a violent cop. He had bad manners and used a lot of obscenities and was perfectly at home dealing with all kinds of undesirables, but he had never been one to beat people up, and he wasn't corrupt. Espinosa couldn't see him pulling off a crime like this.

"Did you know her friends? Any ideas about who could have done this?"

"Magali, originally called Lucimar, was a hooker; anyone could have done this. She thought she owed me something. A little more than two years ago, before I retired, I got rid of a violent pimp who was stealing her money, and she wanted to return the favor. There was real affection between us. What happened here doesn't have anything to do with me."

"I didn't think it did, but I needed to talk to you." After a brief pause, still somewhat uncomfortably, Espinosa asked, "Where were you last night, and what time did you get home? I'm going to need that information."

"I know. That's where the fuckup is. I don't have the slightest idea what I did or where I was; I only know that I was out with Magali. I must have had too much to drink. I got up this morning around noon. I was in my bed, wearing the clothes I had on last night. Or at least almost. I was missing my underwear, and my wallet had disappeared. I'm pretty sure that we went to a restaurant where we go a lot; I could be confusing the days, but it's easy enough to find out. The Mace was a present from me. I don't know how it ended up in my car. Actually, I don't know how my car ended up here. She probably dropped me off at home and drove over here. That's happened before. She was a good driver and never got drunk. Thanks to her I could drink."

Vieira looked at the bed for a few seconds, in silence, his face twisted in pain.

"And one more thing, Espinosa. The belt tied to her legs is mine, and I was wearing it last night."

It was after two in the morning when they left the building and went to the station to make their statements. Vieira was wide awake, and all the external signs indicated that he would stay that way until he could shed some light on the shadows of the previous night. He knew that officially he was a suspect. In any case, as far as he could tell, he was the only one. But that didn't bother him as much as the fact that he couldn't remember a damned thing. What if, in a moment of insanity, he *had* murdered Magali? But even in that absurd event, he wouldn't have killed her like *that*; he would have killed her passionately. If he'd had any reason to kill Magali, and he couldn't imagine any, he could only picture entering the apartment and firing quickly and repeatedly, so she wouldn't have to suffer. Suffocating someone with a plastic bag, though clean and quiet, inflicts a lot of pain. What did the son of a bitch do after sticking the bag over her head? Did he sit on the *bergère* and watch as she turned red? Imagining the scene on the way to the station, he shivered slightly while recalling the feeling of the cheap brocade of Magali's armchair on his arm. He had sat in that chair dozens of times while she got ready to go out or tried on a new dress for him to admire. He was certain, however, that he had not been sitting there for that final scene.

What he couldn't understand was how the belt he had been wearing last night ended up in Magali's room. He could explain away everything but that.

Back at the station, the statements were taken bureaucratically. The morning temperature was pleasant, and the sky soon began to clear up. He was tired, emotionally exhausted, sad about the death of his friend and lover, frightened at himself. The car was being examined; he walked home. He hoped that over the course of the three or four kilometers some image would come to him, and that he could find a twenty-four-hour stand to buy a sandwich down on the beach. He ate a hot dog with coconut milk, which didn't go together very well. He reached home without any reliable recollections, his head full of ghosts. Sitting on his bed, he felt like crying.

He slept in fear. It would have been better never to have picked up the wallet. It would have been even better never to have seen the wallet fall from the man's pocket. The money guaranteed him food for many days, but he didn't like one bit the fact that it had come from the wallet of a cop; that complicated things. When they wanted to, they could track down anything. All the guy would have to do was return to that restaurant, question the waiter, the doorman, the parking attendant, and the latter would recall where the car was parked, right in front of the cardboard box where a street kid slept. If anyone was guilty, it was clearly him.

He slept in fear of the cops and the thief. He was more scared of the cops, or whoever did their dirty work. He didn't think it would do much good to seek protection with other kids; when they wanted to liquidate one of them, they liquidated all of them. Street kids were all the same. And besides, if he wasn't being chased by the police, there was always the risk of some lowlife getting wind of all the money he was carrying; he hated beggars and winos more than the cops. It was safer to sleep in a different place every night. He didn't want to leave the district. It was his territory and he knew every inch of it; he knew where to go to get out of the rain and the cold, where to get food and clothes, where to swap things, where to take a bath, and where to go to the bathroom. Copacabana was his workplace; he spent a lot more time wandering its streets than at his own house in a distant slum, where he went once a month to contribute the money he picked up (not always in the most honest way) on his travels. He would leave the area around the Avenida Atlântica for a few days; a week should be enough. No one would spend any more time than that looking for a wallet.

He found a place protected from the street by a newspaper kiosk; someone driving by in a car wouldn't be able to spot him. He didn't like to sleep by himself—he felt exposed and didn't have much chance of escaping attackers—but for a few days he'd have to manage. The night was pretty warm; he lay down under the awning, took a little wrapped-up piece of bread from his pocket, and began eating it slowly.

He rose before dawn; he hadn't slept more than three hours. He rubbed his eyes, peed next to the curb, patted his shorts to confirm that the money was still there, and looked around to see if anyone was nearby. On the sidewalk, right near the place where he'd slept, he managed to pry open, with the help of a piece of wire, the iron cover of an electricity box measuring about fifty centimeters square. He removed a few pieces of clothing—shorts, T-shirt, tennis shoes—he had stuck there the night before and put everything in a plastic bag before replacing the cover of the box. He stuck the wire into a smaller box a few feet from the first. If he was going to spend a few days away, it was best to bring some clothes.

It was still too early to get his hands on any breakfast. He went back beneath the awning. He had about two hours before people started to appear on the sidewalk. He rested his head on the plastic bag and thought about the man emerging drunk from the restaurant the night before. He kept his eyes open until dawn, when the street began to receive its daily serving of pedestrians.

It was Saturday, and the beach crowd got going early. The first to arrive (and the last to leave) were the slum-dwellers, who wanted to have as much time as possible because they could come to the beach only on the weekend, and the weather wasn't always so nice.

When the movement started to pick up, he got up and looked for a little bar. Breakfast wasn't a problem; in Copacabana people usually had their coffee in the nearest bar or bakery. All he had to do was wait for the right moment to slide between two people and order bread and coffee with milk. The money he had hidden in his shorts was enough for lots of breads and coffees, but that was no reason to pay for something that other people could buy for him. His strategy was to eat whenever he could.

He didn't drink every day, but once he started he didn't stop. He was a fun kind of drunk: he talked, told jokes, laughed, sang. He was never mean or violent. At most, he became slightly annoying. So he got drunk every once in a while, trusting in his good nature. He wasn't an alcoholic.

Magali had been his companion and protector for the last couple of years. He liked her. She was caring; she looked after his
money, shielded him from dubious hangers-on, and dropped
him off at his house at the end of the adventure. When they
went out to dinner, it wasn't with the hooker Magali; it was
with Lucimar. Why would he have killed her? They had gotten in countless arguments, but they were just shouting
matches, not real fights. The biggest misunderstanding they'd
ever had was when she'd tried to pay him that first time.
"Damn it, Magali, that's the reason I got rid of that pimp, and
now you're trying to give me money?" Magali had cried, pure
tenderness. "Magali wasn't something you killed; Magali was
something you'd plant to see if more would grow," he said in
his deposition. Now he could do only two things for her: give
her a decent funeral and track down the son of a bitch who
killed her. The first wasn't a problem; as soon as they released
the body he would take care of the burial. The second was a
little more problematic: he had lost his police I.D., which he
had hung on to even after retirement, and he couldn't get
another one. That made him even more dependent on Espinosa. And policemen didn't usually like ex-cops sticking their
noses into their investigations.

Sunday afternoon. Like everyone who lives alone, Vieira
knew that it was the worst day of the week, and the afternoon was the worst part of it. When he'd become a widower,
he'd thought that weekends would become more tolerable; he
could stay home, like now, in shorts, slippers, and a T-shirt,
deciding between putting on the air-conditioning or opening
the window, without his wife complaining about his choice.
She hadn't been a bad person, Maria Zilda, but she had been
insufferably annoying. She'd probably died because she
couldn't stand to be around herself anymore. The fact was,

weekends hadn't improved. For other reasons, to be sure. But at that moment Vieira wasn't thinking about his wife, he was thinking about recent events, about Friday night. He thought, since he could no longer remember. He even wondered if his amnesia was caused only by alcohol. His words from the deposition kept coming back to him. "Magali wasn't something you killed, Magali was something you'd plant to see if more would grow." Wasn't that exactly what he was trying to do? Bury Magali? His head began to ache; confused images, like fragments of a dream, began to flash like paparazzi lights around a celebrity. He felt dizzy, nauseous; he ran to the bathroom and puked.

He was scared. He had often been scared in all kinds of different situations, but now it was different: the threat was much closer and he couldn't make out exactly what it was. He didn't vomit because he'd been drinking; he hadn't touched liquor since Friday night. Nor had he eaten today, but he wasn't hungry. He looked for something in the fridge, but found only a few bottles of water (some empty, some almost) and a carton of sour milk. He made instant coffee, even though he knew that on an empty stomach it would only add heartburn to the list of his discomforts. He turned on the television, but there were no movies on; Sunday television was shitty. He went out to take a walk through Ipanema. On the corner of Praça General Osório he managed to eat a sandwich, which he washed down with some orange juice. The crafts fair in the square was enough to distract him for an hour, no more. He went back to the apartment at the end of the afternoon. The final and most melancholy part of the weekend had begun. He was about to go down to the street again, just to wander, when the phone rang.

"Vieira?"

"Speaking."

"It's Florinda."

"Florinda?"

"Yeah."

"...?"

"Flor, Magali's friend. We had dinner once together."

"Right...Flor..." He vaguely remembered a black girl who looked almost Thai, with a slender figure and firm muscles, who had gone out with them a few months ago.

"Vieira, I'm sad and scared."

"Where are you?"

"I'm in Magali's building. I came by to pick up some things I'd loaned her but I couldn't get into the apartment. I'm really scared. I had your number so I called. Could you come over?"

"Flor...I'll be there in twenty minutes."

Flor had everything to succeed in the profession—beauty, sensuality, and charm—in just the right proportions. She had managed to stay independent thanks to her contacts from a job she'd had at city hall. She'd never understood exactly what she was supposed to be doing, so with time she ended up using the job (or function; she was never sure which) for her own benefit. She recruited her clients but didn't overdo it: she kept their number modest and didn't crowd her schedule. She didn't earn a fortune, but when she added this money to her income from the city, she pieced together enough to guarantee more than her mere survival. She lived a few blocks from Magali, in a mixed residential and commercial building, very convenient for her line of work. When they met, she still hadn't turned twenty-five, but she knew the ropes; her first classes had been in the streets of Recife, before she moved to Rio de Janeiro as a maid in the service of a family with considerable estates in Pernambuco. She'd been fourteen at the time, but she was no virgin. The boss didn't take long to recognize (and get a taste of) Flor's charms and the need to bring her to Rio "to take care of Junior." Not long after the move, the boss's wife figured out that Florinda wasn't only taking care of Junior and kicked her out. The boss felt sorry for the poor girl, who couldn't just sit on the street and beg—"And besides, she's a minor, we're responsible for her"—and arranged a place for her to live and a job to support herself. Without the wife knowing, of course, and without anyone doubting that she was of legal age. From that day on, Flor was on the street only by her own choice, or at her other job. The friendship with Magali had begun while waiting in line at the supermarket. Magali, just as she was about to pay, realized she had left her wallet at home. Flor offered to loan her the money—it wasn't much—without accepting the I.D. card the other woman insisted on leaving as a guarantee. Just after she got home, she received a visit from her new friend, paying her debt and bringing a bouquet of violets. "Flowers for a flower." They became sisters.

Flor remembered that period as she paced back and forth across the building's entry hall. Without realizing how absurd the situation was, she had brought her dead friend a little bunch of violets, which she clasped with both hands. She had said something to the doorman, in an attempt to justify the anomaly, but he couldn't even make out what she was saying, her voice was so choked up by tears. When Vieira got there, she threw herself into his arms, flowers and all.

"Vieira . . ."

"Flor, you shouldn't have come here by yourself."

"Vieira, I lost the only friend I had . . . I lost my sister."

"Let's go, Flor. There's nothing for us to do here."

On the street, people had their Sunday-night faces on. The two walked in silence. Flor clutched the flowers with one of her hands and took Vieira's arm with the other. They looked like they were walking behind a hearse.

After he chose the place where he would spend the next nights and hid his change of clothes, he decided to follow the new owner of the wallet. He wasn't entirely sure why, but something told him that it was a way of protecting himself. Since he was so young, they knew he couldn't use the credit cards or the policeman's I.D., but they could accuse him of selling them to someone. He was only three blocks away from the man's building and had the whole Sunday ahead of him. Not that it made a difference if it was Sunday or a weekday; he was sure that, like him, the man didn't have a job. He had seen him a few other times on the streets of Copacabana. One occasion, around the time that he'd found the wallet, stood out in his mind. He had seen the man hit a woman, and someone who hits a woman wouldn't hesitate to hit a child.

Later, he'd been the one to find the wallet. The boy felt like he had handed it to him, and every minute the idea tormented him more. When he tossed the wallet onto the pavement, he thought it didn't matter to him who picked it up, but now he knew he was wrong. When he'd thrown it onto the street he had been gambling on who would find it, and now he was paying the price. As he saw it, he had to get it back or render it useless. Not out of a sense of justice. He knew only his own justice, which could be described simply: what was good for him was just. And this whole thing had been bad for his soul. He decided to stick behind the man and follow him all through Copacabana, every bar, restaurant, dive, crack house, gambling parlor; to make a note of every person, man or woman, he met up with. This was betting that he wouldn't leave the district, where both of them spent all their time.

The afternoon was starting. The man had clearly slept during the day in order to be awake and operate at night. Maybe he would go out to eat something nearby, maybe one of those chickens that spin around in the windows in front of luncheonettes, and take it home to eat. He thought that, just like him, the man must eat by himself.

Sometimes an insignificant event can prove to be the beginning of a crusade. For the boy, the discovery of the wallet had been such an event: that man simply could not be allowed to benefit from his discovery. Before the afternoon ended, the idea had assumed epic proportions, occupying his entire brain, transforming it into a holy war, the existence of which he alone was aware. The war was nothing more than a struggle between two people, but it had attained cosmic dimensions. It didn't matter that one of the two people involved had no idea he was in a battle at all.

"Vieira, I want to say something. . . . Magali always said she had a debt of gratitude toward you. . . ." A couple of seconds passed. "Now that she's no longer here . . . the debt is mine."

Her voice was as solemn as the silence she had broken. Vieira didn't say anything; they kept walking, Flor with one hand on Vieira's arm and the violets in the other. There was no visible reaction on his part, but she felt a slight increase in tension in his arm and an almost imperceptible reduction in their pace. Even though they hadn't stopped walking and life went on around them as always, they felt that they had somehow stepped out of time.

"You are a flower."

They found themselves walking from Magali's building to Flor's. It wasn't far, and they were already close when Vieira suggested they get something to eat in one of the nearby restaurants. They chose the one with the fewest people. While they ate, Flor talked about the time when she'd lived in Recife.

Her business sense had shown itself early, before she turned fourteen. She lived with her mother and three siblings, two older brothers and a nine-year-old sister, in a stud-and-mud house in the poor section of town. Her mother worked late into the night as a cook in a greasy spoon; the two brothers worked during the day and, when circumstances permitted, studied at night. She took care of the house, cooking and babysitting her younger sister. The street where they lived was (or so she thought) right on the way to the Jesuit boys' school in the next neighborhood. The boys said her street was a shortcut. When she noticed that the path didn't shorten the distance in the least and was, to the contrary, the cause of repeated tardiness at the school, Flor realized that she was the real reason for the changed itinerary. The realization didn't do much for her vanity (they were a bunch of brats), but it did open her eyes to the possibility of an innocent but lucrative business. She let a few of the boys know that for a small fee, no more than the price of a soft drink, they could watch her change clothes through her bedroom window. All they had to do was stop by the window—one at a time, so as not to arouse suspicion in the neighborhood—put their money on the windowsill, and witness the quick scene of Flor taking off and putting on her clothes. Soon she had to establish a schedule, so that the boys wouldn't all show up at the same hour on the same day.

The little shows were a big success. But soon enough the boys were no longer content to watch; they wanted to touch. One Sunday, when the family went to the beach, Flor began to envision wider possibilities. The job as a nanny and the subsequent move to Rio were on the new paths she saw open before her.

Vieira thought it was surprising that Flor didn't blame the world or anyone else for her misfortunes. Moreover, she didn't consider herself unfortunate; she saw her early poverty as something entirely accidental and fleeting, which in fact it was. She didn't think prostitution was a job like any other. She thought it was better. "Look at all these maids, washer-women, supermarket checkout girls: they're slaves. I work at home, whenever I want to; I don't have a boss and I don't have to please anyone." She concluded, "Besides, they say it's the oldest profession in the world, and if it's been around for so long it must be good." Vieira, fascinated, looked at her silently, contemplating her beauty just like the boys in Recife.

Magali's death was fresh, and he was still confused. He left Flor at home and walked back to his own apartment. It was the second night in a row that he'd crossed all of Copacabana on foot. This time his steps were a little lighter.

As soon as the chief had finished reading the file on the crime, his thoughts had turned to Espinosa. At least that's what he said when he interrupted Espinosa's weekend rest with a phone call.

"I thought of you for two reasons: because you live nearby and because an ex-cop you know is involved." Espinosa didn't really like Vieira's manners, but he knew Vieira was an honest fellow; all he had to show for himself upon retirement was a one-bedroom apartment on a rundown street in Copacabana. This second quality amply made up for the first, if only because they didn't have to see each other socially.

So Espinosa had his weekend interrupted, which didn't imply much of a sacrifice, given his aversion to Sundays.

He recalled the bedroom scene, and saw Vieira paralyzed in the doorway, eyes glued to the horrifying mask of the suffocated woman. Unshaven, wearing the same clothes he'd had on the day before, his few white hairs askew, belly spilling out over his waist, posture beaten down by emotional and physical shock, Vieira was the second victim in that room. The circumstances—the car parked in front of the building, the can of Mace—plus the alcoholic amnesia put him in a delicate situation. Though the scene was at odds with Espinosa's image of him, the clues he had to work with weren't at all to Vieira's advantage. The main thing in his favor was his lack of a motive. There wasn't much to support the hypothesis that it was a crime of passion; it didn't have the characteristics of that sort of murder. Espinosa didn't doubt that Vieira was capable of committing a crime, but he doubted that he had committed *this* crime. The suffering he showed during his deposition wasn't the desperation of someone passionately in love or the chilliness of a pervert but the pain of someone who had lost something dear to his heart. In an age usually marked by little daily pleasures, Magali had appeared in his life like the promise of the thousand and one nights. He knew she was a prostitute, and he knew that no man could hope to control her. Vieira had taken care of the only one who had tried to exploit her. So at first glance he didn't seem to fit the role of the murderer. What Espinosa didn't understand, though, was how his belt had ended up around the dead girl's legs.

It was almost four in the morning; the officer on duty hadn't paid much attention to the crime (a hooker's murder doesn't make it into the news), and the next day the chief would hand the file to Espinosa with only one comment about Vieira: "He's a good guy."

The exhaustion that had overflowed from Vieira invaded the beginning of Espinosa's Sunday as he walked home. After taking the deposition, he didn't feel like going to bed. More than his sadness, the ex-officer's loneliness struck him. While he tried to force himself to go to sleep, at five in the morning, he was overcome by images of himself in the not-too-distant future being courted by young prostitutes hoping to be protected from the rigors of the law—which was rigorous only when it was looking after someone's personal business. He tried to convince himself that in his case things would be different; he wasn't a fat boor like Vieira, he liked books, he had good taste, he wouldn't end his life running after hookers. But this reflection—which he thought was fair—notwithstanding, he couldn't fall asleep. He knew that he couldn't force it, and since he didn't use sleeping pills he just let his imagination quiet down, which happened when the sun was already in the sky. He fell asleep without having rid himself entirely of the image of Magali.

When he woke up, half of Sunday was already behind him; but the other half still loomed, and while he had his coffee, he thought about ways to try to shorten it. Vieira had given him a list of the restaurants he frequented. There weren't many, and he had told Espinosa which ones were the most likely. The first was on the Rua Santa Clara, a few blocks from Espinosa's apartment; a walk there could be a pleasant way of passing the afternoon.

He usually spent entire days interrogating people in the hope of getting a single bit of useful information, so he was delighted to hear from the manager that he knew Officer Vieira and that on Friday he had been here with a blond girl, departing around one in the morning.

"Were they here by themselves?"

"They were."

"Was he agitated, aggressive, rude?"

"No. Officer Vieira is an old customer. When he drinks the

only thing that happens is he talks too loud, but he never gets aggressive."

"Do you remember how he paid?"

"With a check, but she filled it out. He just signed; his hand wasn't very steady."

"He didn't forget anything on the table?"

"What do you mean?"

"His wallet disappeared; he could have left it behind here."

"If that had happened, you can be sure we'd keep it for him and let him know."

"Do you know if they met anyone when they left?"

"That I can't tell you, but maybe the parking attendant might remember."

"Is it the same one every day?"

"Yeah. He should be out there now."

"Thanks. If you hear anything about the wallet, call this number."

Since he'd arrived on foot, the parking attendant hadn't paid him any attention. There weren't many people in the restaurant and accordingly few keys in the lockbox. When Espinosa flashed his badge, he thought he perceived a subterranean tremor in the man. He pretended not to notice. The attendant remembered perfectly well the back-slapping policeman who gave good tips. On the night in question he had been so full of whiskey that he'd almost fallen on top of the boy who slept on the sidewalk and had to be helped into the car. It was just him and the woman; no one had met up with them. The two of them left in the car by themselves, with her at the wheel. He hadn't seen a wallet; the officer had gone straight from the door of the restaurant to the car parked right across the street, and if anything had fallen he would have seen it. Espinosa reminded him that the wallet could have fallen out when Vieira got into the car.

"I personally helped get him into the car and can promise you that no wallet fell out."

"There was nobody else around?"

"It was already late; at that time the only other person on the street was the boy."

"What boy?"

"The one who sleeps under the marquee sometimes. On that night, he was inside a refrigerator box someone had left on the sidewalk."

"And where is the boy now?"

"He hasn't shown up since that night."

"Does he always sleep here?"

"Sometimes. He waits until the restaurant's closing to get his hands on a plate of food."

"If he comes back, try to keep him around and call me."

Espinosa left thinking that this Sunday hadn't been so bad. Instead of taking the same route home, he walked a few feet to the Avenida Atlântica. There was still a little bit of light left in the sky. The ocean was a mixture of green, blue, and gray, with the white of the waves giving light to the colors; the mountains were bluish masses, living curves against the sky. Espinosa thought that if the world had been created by God, he had used his best material and all his inspiration to create that landscape. He went back home convinced that some Sundays were better than others.

There wasn't much to do until tomorrow. He called Vieira but there was no answer. Maybe if he knew which restaurant he had been to that night it would help jog his memory. Unless it wasn't in his best interests to remember anything. He had heard of traumatic amnesia as well as the alcoholic amnesia Vieira alleged; what he didn't know was whether you could recover the lost memories. Espinosa felt sympathy for his ex-colleague; he wouldn't like to see him accused of Magali's murder. But he recognized that there were a few details pointing in that direction and that the alleged amnesia was awfully convenient. He decided not to leap to conclusions.

A cup of coffee and a slice of toast was not enough to keep him on his feet all day. Rather than resort to the frozen lasagnas at home, he decided to eat on the street, in spite of the parents and little kids who invaded the restaurants at that hour on Sunday.

The Peixoto district is really an enclave of Copacabana, one block square with a plaza in the middle, surrounded by mountains on three sides and facing the beach on the fourth. It was a survivor of the old Copacabana, before the area had been transformed into a compact mass of buildings squeezed between the ocean and the mountains. The buildings, mostly three or four stories high, are of simple design; the only architectural variations consist in the presence or absence of little balconies. Few buildings have a garage or an elevator. Espinosa's apartment, on the top floor of a building of only three stories, had French windows and a wrought-iron balcony with a view onto a little square that wasn't quite pretty but couldn't be considered ugly, either; in any case, it was one of the trademarks of the neighborhood.

He didn't inhabit this privileged locale because he longed for the bucolic. Espinosa was actually drawn to big cities, even to the point of wondering, when he stopped to think about it, whether his urban ideal wasn't something out of *Blade Runner*— a fact that struck him from the rosters of normal, healthy people.

He hadn't chosen the place, at least not at first; he'd inherited the apartment from his parents. He had decided to stay

on after their deaths, when he was fourteen, and his grandmother had come to keep him company, remaining until he
turned nineteen. Why nineteen, and not eighteen or twenty-
one, he had never quite understood. He owed his taste for reading to her. At first, with the hunger of the dispossessed, he'd
read anything and everything. Slowly he'd begun directing his
interest toward English-language writers. In spite of his intimacy with books, he didn't much care for intellectuals. He
liked to read, but he nurtured a secret disdain for criticism and
literary theory. His reading included not only Melville, Chan-
dler, and Hemingway but also a healthy serving of authentic
pulp fiction. This interest often led him to abandon Copacabana for extended visits to the used-book stalls downtown. It
was important to him to draw out these expeditions, to create
a whiff of adventure that doubled the pleasure of the find.

When he was transferred from the downtown precinct to
Copacabana, he gained something priceless: a commute he
could cover on foot in no more than ten minutes. He had two
different routes, one down Tonelero and the other down Barata
Ribeiro. They were the same distance, but the Barata Ribeiro
option took a little longer because he was always distracted by
the shop windows, the pedestrians, and the cars. He was not
interested in window-shopping because he was a compulsive
consumer; he was simply in the habit of memorizing every
environment—a room, a segment of a street, a shop window.
He noticed even the slightest alteration: the habit, refined over
the years, had earned him the reputation of being a meticulous
observer. Depending on the hour he returned home, he sometimes took a third way: leaving the station, he went down the
Rua Hilário de Gouveia and turned right on the Avenida
Copacabana, following the human masses streaming down the
sidewalks; after a little more than two blocks, he entered the

Galeria Menescal, which connects the Avenida Copacabana to the Rua Barata Ribeiro, in order to enjoy a kibbeh at the Arab's stand in the middle of the Galeria.

His familiarity with the neighborhood was like the intimate knowledge older people have of their childhood gardens. It was with this feeling of intimacy that he left his house on Monday morning and headed for the station. He took the route least likely to distract him inadvertently; he had to attend to a few matters relating to what he had started calling the "Vieira case." The first was taking the deposition of the dead woman's friend. He entrusted a young detective on his team with bringing her to the station. Then he called Vieira to tell him that he had found the restaurant where he and Magali had eaten on Friday night. Vieira took the news as a confirmation. The fragments of his memory suggested that place; what he hadn't been able to determine was whether the fragments referred to that night or some other time. "Thanks, Espinosa, but unfortunately that information doesn't do much for my memory, which is still a complete blank." When Espinosa told him that no one knew anything about the wallet, he replied that he had reported the loss of the credit cards and would cancel the checks as soon as the banks opened.

It was almost eleven in the morning when Flor arrived, accompanied by the detective. She didn't look like a typical prostitute. She wasn't made-up, and her clothes—jeans, untucked shirt, and tennis shoes—were discreet. But it was obvious she wasn't a nun or a college student by the easy way she walked into the police station and answered their questions. Right away, she hastened to point out that she was Officer Vieira's girlfriend.

"What?" asked Espinosa. "Wasn't Magali Vieira's girl-friend? And weren't you her friend?"

"Exactly. He inherited me." Seeing Espinosa's surprise, she added: "Nothing like that. When Magali was alive, there was nothing between us. Magali always told me that if anything ever happened to her, I was supposed to take care of her man, Vieira."

"Why did she say that? Did she think anything was going to happen to her?"

"No, it was just an idea."

"What do you mean 'it was just an idea'?"

"It was just an idea. You know that in our line of work things can happen. We never know who our customer is: he can look like a monster and be as delicate as a flower or he can look like a kid and be capable of anything. We're always a little scared, which is why we look for protection in men like Vieira."

"I know, but men like Vieira don't just stand there and watch you when you're with a client."

"Of course not, but people hear about it and don't dare get violent."

"Let's get back to Magali's idea, that someone was going to kill her."

"I never said she thought someone was going to kill her. I just said that she had the idea that something could happen to her."

"Flor, don't try to play all innocent with me. It's not going to work. If Magali told you to take care of her man in case something happened to her, it could only be in case she died or disappeared. Otherwise she could take care of him herself. So that's exactly what I want to know. Did she ever mention any specific threat? Did anyone say they were going to kill her?"

"She never named names, but she thought it could happen."

"And why would it happen to her specifically and not to anyone else?"

"Because she was thinking about herself."

"And you think that the simple fact that she was worried about herself could have made her murder come about?"

"They say that frightened people draw out the evil in others. It's like when you walk near a dog: he could be sweet and harmless, but if you walk by him trembling he's going to bite."

"Any idea who this client was who killed her because she was scared?"

"No. I know she had a few regulars, but I didn't know any of them, and a regular wouldn't do something like this. I think it was probably someone who went for the first time, couldn't get it up, and decided to avenge himself on her. The most dangerous thing in the world is a man like that: they either turn into crybabies or they want to kill everything in sight."

"And you? How were your relations with Magali?"

"We were sisters. I mean, not really, but it was like we were."

"And even real sisters fight every once in a while."

"We never fought; we got along perfectly."

"So perfectly that you ended up with her man."

"What does that have to do with it? She asked me herself."

"That's what you're saying."

"What are you trying to say?"

"I'm not trying to say anything; you're the one saying it all."

"I don't understand where you're going with this."

"Maybe there's nothing to understand: that's the way of the world. Or maybe you don't want to understand, which amounts to the same thing."

Flor was clearly beginning to feel uncomfortable and wary. She clammed up. Espinosa didn't think it would help matters to prod her any further; better simply to let her think about what had been said, and especially about what hadn't been said. He let her go, telling her not to leave the city, and sat thinking about why Vieira hadn't mentioned that Flor had become his lover so quickly. Unless it was all in her imagination, or a shield for the interrogation.

He hadn't expected the vigil in front of the building to be so agonizing. He couldn't distract himself by looking at the latest car models or imported tennis shoes or the pictures on T-shirts; any slip could coincide with the man's exit. Around ten at night, the man left the building and walked unwaveringly in one direction; a more experienced observer would have realized that before he'd gone out he must have spent some time choosing his target, going over the route, thinking about how to proceed. The boy, however, was worried about action, not preparations. As soon as the man's feet touched the sidewalk, he shot out of his shelter on the sidewalk across the street and started walking parallel to him until he managed to cross the street and place himself at a safe distance. They walked toward Leme, and since the man didn't appear to be looking for a taxi or a bus, the boy inferred that they wouldn't have far to go. He had to take two steps for every one the man took, and occasionally he had to run in order to keep up. They went through the Praça Serzedelo Correia; the man didn't change his pace or stray from his path; he never looked back. Even if he had, he wouldn't have deemed the boy worthy of notice. One block after the Copacabana Palace, the man slowed down, narrowing the distance between them. When they reached the Praça do Lido, the boy guessed where he was heading: to the sleazy little dives around the square.

The man went first into a gay club. The boy had to wait outside and guess what was going on. The little street beside the square was closed to traffic; the boy sat on the curb and waited.

He was paying so much attention to the door of the club that he didn't even notice the two boys sitting next to him. He knew them both from the shelter, where they got a bed and food when things got complicated on the streets. There was no dialogue, just some hand slapping and a few mutterings. At first the boy was annoyed by the interruption, but then he decided it could work in his favor; three boys sitting on the curb wouldn't attract the man's curiosity. After a few minutes, they made some comments about the death of a transvestite who had been a protector and occasional mother to them. They asked him what he was trying to figure out sitting there on the pavement; they had seen him arrive, sit on the curb, and stare across the street. He responded that he was following a man who had stolen a policeman's I.D. The two got up and left. He maintained his solitary vigil. Almost an hour went by, and he began to doubt that the man was still in there; maybe he'd left when he was talking with the other kids, or maybe the people in the bar had figured out what he was really up to. Another half hour. He could have sworn the man hadn't come out of the club, and there was only that one door. Staring at the same point for so long, his mind started playing tricks on him: had the man really gone in that door? He remembered others who had come out, any one of whom could have been his man. He was about to give up when the door opened and he saw him leave the building, walk toward a light, take something out of his pocket, examine it at length, put it back into his pocket, and start walking toward the Avenida Atlântica. The boy had no doubts: the man's operation had been a success. He thought that the man would be content with one victory that evening, but then he saw him cross the square and go into another club. He re-emerged in less than five minutes. Either he'd recognized a cop or had seen someone who could identify him. This time he left the area a little faster, once again walking toward the Avenida Atlântica. He went up to two men who were then approached by a third who was obviously selling drugs, but the group broke up before anything happened. From there he went home. He got back to his building at one in the morning. The boy felt that he'd had a full day.

It was time to take care of himself. The afternoon watch, on top of the chase and vigil at night, hadn't left him any time to find something to eat, and he was hungry. Restaurants closed early on Sundays, but he would try a couple, not far from there, where the doorman knew him and would rummage up something. At the first restaurant he was badly received by the security guard, but at the second the attendant recognized him and interceded with the waiters on his behalf. While he ate a few strips of meat with bread, he reflected that the man hadn't gotten money in that little dive. He hadn't looked at whatever he'd left the club with like someone counting money. Though he had only been watching from a distance, the boy could have bet that what he had taken out of his pocket were little bags of powder.

Before going to sleep, he decided that in order to continue his mission he would need to take a few precautions. The next day he would find Clodoaldo, who knew the cops in the area and could tell him who was trustworthy. If the man was dealing with drugs and money with the clients of those bars, things could get out of hand. In that case he would need to be able to count on some kind of official protection.

While he was talking to the bank manager about canceling his checks, Vieira tried to imagine what had happened to his wallet and, consequently, to his credit cards and checkbook. It was almost Christmas; even an honest housewife could have interpreted the find as a gift from heaven to underwrite the holidays. She could refresh her husband's and kids' wardrobe and maybe even buy a color television. He started getting annoyed and threw angry looks at the women clutching their deposit slips and checkbooks and waiting in line for the cashiers. He thought about Flor. It wasn't really a conquest; after all, he had done absolutely nothing to make her fall into his arms, or into his lap. He complained to the manager about the cost of canceling each missing check; it was almost worth risking letting someone use them. From an aesthetic point of view, he had traded up—Flor was prettier and more sensual than Magali—but from a personal viewpoint he had unequivocally come up short. It takes a long time for people to understand each other, he thought; he would have to wait for that comprehension to grow between him and Flor. It was like waiting for a new sapling to spring up where a tree has fallen. His trust in Magali had been boundless. Not that he didn't trust Flor—there hadn't even been time for that. It was just that she had come along so suddenly, out of the blue, without the slightest warning, announced only by the death of her friend. They'd have to get to know each other. All he knew about her he had learned during the first dinner, after they'd left Magali's building. It wasn't much, but she did have many charms.

He left the bank and decided to stop by the station. He wanted to help, even though he knew he was in a delicate position: not only was he *a* suspect, he was the *only* suspect. He reformulated the statement: he was a suspect only because there wasn't anyone else. At least that's how he saw it. More than anything he wanted to talk to Espinosa. It was too far to walk; he preferred to take the bus. Since he'd retired two years ago, his time had been his own, but he still wasn't used to it, and during the day he was ashamed to look at people. At night it was different; he didn't need to pretend to be doing anything after hours. On the packed bus, seated next to the window, he could quietly enjoy the urban landscape; everyone would think he was on his way to work.

Espinosa received him politely but unenthusiastically. He informed him that Magali's body would probably be released at the end of the day; he had spoken with the man who'd conducted the autopsy, but there was nothing to add to what they already knew: the only marks on the body were around the wrists and ankles, which indicated that there had been no struggle and that she hadn't been bound forcibly. There was no sign of recent sexual intercourse; she had a modest amount of alcohol in her bloodstream and had probably been exposed to the Mace from the container found at the scene. She had most likely been tied up while still unconscious and had the plastic bag tied around her head before she came to. She woke up to die of suffocation.

Vieira didn't know what to say. On the one hand, he was devastated by Magali's death, but on the other he was in the position of being the sole suspect. It would be contradictory to kill her and feel sad about losing her. Logic dictated that if his sorrow was real, he couldn't be the killer. But that logic didn't apply to him; the point would be moot if he had killed Magali and then blacked out. His embarrassment mounted as Espinosa informed him that his car had not yet been freed up; forensic examiners were still going over it. The examination of the automobile and its possible role as a piece of evidence in the investigation were concrete signs that he was officially

implicated in Magali's death. Espinosa's next question eliminated any doubts as to who was the cop and who was the
suspect.

"You didn't tell me you were dating Flor."

"Damn, Espinosa, what're you talking about? How could I
have told you that?"

"She said you were when she was here at the station."

"I don't know what she said. I only know that I only saw
that girl a couple of times before she called me."

"And that's when you started going out?"

"What the fuck, Espinosa? We're not teenagers. We don't
talk about 'going out.' Anyway, we're not going out. The only
thing that happened is that we went to dinner last night."

"And you want me to be satisfied with that? Let me help
you go over the facts: a girl is found dead in her own apartment, naked, tied to the bed, with a plastic bag tied around
her neck. This girl is your girlfriend and went to dinner with
you the night she was killed. On the bedside table, along with
your car keys, is a can of Mace, the top of which was found
on the floor of your car. As if that weren't enough, the girl's
feet were tied with the belt you were wearing on the night of
the crime—and that you can't recall how you lost. And as a
finishing touch, you show up, the day after the murder, on a
date with the dead girl's only friend. Damn it, Vieira, the only
reason I'm not arresting you is because I don't think you're
stupid enough to accumulate so much evidence against yourself. The only thing missing is the dead girl's will naming you
as the only beneficiary of the small fortune she accumulated
in the business."

Vieira looked at Espinosa in silence. There was a lot he
wanted to say. He wanted to explain himself; he wanted to
say that Flor had dropped into his lap without his lifting a
finger; he wanted to say how much he'd cared about Magali.

But he didn't say a word because he knew Espinosa was right. He knew from his own experience that the more excuses he tried to make, the guiltier he would look. He also knew from experience that at that moment silence was golden. He limited himself to a single sentence:

"If we manage to find whoever got their hands on my wallet, we might be able to figure out what happened after Magali and I left the restaurant."

Espinosa accepted the first-person plural, once he had made clear who was in charge of the investigation.

He was interested in what had happened after dinner. According to the parking attendant, the two had left the restaurant with Magali behind the wheel. She could have left Vieira at his place and taken the car back to her own apartment, finding the murderer there, which would, in fact, justify the car's location in front of her building and the keys on her bedside table. The murderer could have been waiting for her inside or could have arrived just afterward. If things had happened that way, two things would still be left unexplained: how Magali had managed to get Vieira, completely drunk, probably half-asleep, up to his apartment without anyone else's help; and, second, how Vieira's belt had found its way into her apartment. That is, if you believed he was drunk. The exit from the restaurant, complete with obscenities and stumbling, could have been a farce, which would imply a cold sense of premeditation seemingly at odds with Vieira's personality.

The conversation took place in what they called the visitors' room, on the second floor of the station. The staircase leading to the second floor ended in a spacious kind of reception room, complete with two sofas and two easy chairs, all in need of new springs but unstained and clean enough that people with light-colored clothing could sit down fearlessly. It wasn't the most appropriate place for a private conversation—the room was en route to every office on the floor—but Vieira seemed less worried about privacy than about Espinosa's decision as to the direction the investigation would take.

They said their farewells with a mixture of politeness and mistrust, Espinosa promising to keep Vieira up-to-date, which Vieira heard as a cordial recommendation to keep his distance. The rest of the day passed unremarkably. Espinosa's attention was on the autopsy report and the results from the car; he thought about how uncharacteristically thorough it all was for an investigation into the death of a prostitute. The afternoon was consumed by memos and reports.

Espinosa chose to walk back home along the Avenida Copacabana. The sheer number of people on the street at six-thirty reminded him of an Oriental metropolis. He went into the Galeria Menescal with the intention of buying some kibbeh to reinforce the spaghetti Bolognese he planned to defrost for dinner. As he neared the Arab's place it occurred to him that he was being followed. While he was waiting for the meat-balls, he looked around but couldn't pick anyone out. He decided to try again a few feet ahead, at the traffic light on Barata Ribeiro, where there weren't as many people. He stopped in front of one store window, then another, taking advantage of the reflection to glance across at the other side of the street, but there was nothing. He put it down to the touch of paranoia present in every policeman.

The boy thought it was especially lucky that the cop lived only four or five blocks from the man. It would make it easier, if necessary, to go from one to the other. This was the cop Clodoaldo had said you could count on. He really didn't seem dangerous; he seemed distracted and inoffensive; but the boy knew that an inoffensive policeman was like a white vulture.

He wasn't in the habit of confiding in anyone, but occasionally you had to, like the time Clodoaldo saved him from a lynching when someone mixed him up with another kid who had slashed a woman's face at a stoplight.

Seated on the bench in the square, he saw a light come on in the window. He thought the cop must live alone; if there was someone else, the light would have been on before he got home. He probably didn't have a wife or kids. Actually, he realized then that he never thought of any cop as having a wife and kids; when he heard the phrase "policeman's family" he thought of brothers and sisters, mothers and fathers, but never imagined the cop himself as the head of the family. He kept his eye on the illuminated rectangle. He didn't know why he was sitting on a park bench watching the window of a cop's apartment, but that was probably all he could do: watch, snoop, follow, just like he was doing with the other man.

The square started to empty as the kids went home to take their baths before dinner. While a few mothers and nannies took the little ones away, other moms shouted at the older ones from the windows. It had been nearly a month since he had last been home. His mother had stopped worrying about him and eventually learned that he always dropped out of sight when things in the city were more threatening than usual. He thought about taking her half of the money he'd found in the wallet, or even all of it, since that money worried him more than it helped him; but he might need it when he was following the man.

After a short while, the venetian blinds opened, revealing a silhouette. The silhouette stood up and stretched his arms, yawning, before immediately heading back toward the interior of the apartment. The boy didn't see any reason to keep sitting there watching someone for no particular reason; in any case, the idea that people were going home to eat made his hunger more acute. He got up and stretched out his arms, imitating the silhouette, then turned toward the Avenida Copacabana; along the way, he would get a roasted chicken at a luncheonette. He walked away thinking about the cop's funny name; he'd never heard of anyone named Espinosa. Before long he'd have to take up another vigil; the man tended to begin his nocturnal wanderings around ten.

"If it's to eat and not for drugs, fine," said one of the ladies in the luncheonette, "though I should think a whole chicken would be a lot for a kid like you."

"Don't put the money in his hand," said the other one. "Pay the cashier so he can't use the money for anything else." She spoke like someone deeply versed in the most intimate corners of the human soul, not to mention the world of street kids. He wondered if they'd examine the chicken to make sure it wasn't stuffed with pot or cocaine.

At ten, after he'd devoured the chicken, he was sitting on the sidewalk across the street, waiting for the man to come out. Maybe the old lady was right: it was a lot of chicken for a small body, and it was weighing on his stomach. After a while, he started to get a little stomachache. If it got any worse, he couldn't stay there on the sidewalk. The man appeared at the door of the building at a quarter to eleven. He looked around as if trying to decide where to strike next and fixed his eyes on the kid sitting across the street. He seemed to be searching his mind for a bit of information while his eyes memorized the face. By the time it looked like he'd remembered something, the kid had already gotten up and disappeared.

The boy knew the look. He'd come across others like it, and he didn't intend to wait around to see if the consequences would be the same. That man would do anything to get rid of anybody who got in his way, and he would stop at nothing to take personal advantage of anyone or anything. The boy knew that for that kind of man there was no line between legality and illegality: robbing and killing were activities as normal as breathing, eating, and living. The boy could be sure of only one thing: the man knew of his existence.

The hearse left the coffin at the gates of the cemetery as if dropping off a package sent through the post. Besides Vieira—for whom death had long been contaminated by bureaucracy—and Flor—who attempted to cry—there was no one in the way of friends. Before closing the coffin into a drawer in the concrete wall, they waited awhile for the night doorman from Magali's building, who had kept track of her comings and goings, but he didn't show up. The body was buried (or drawered) without anyone bothering to make a note of the number of its location. Flor and Vieira left the cemetery arm in arm, like relatives. They split up in Copacabana, planning to meet again that night. Vieira headed for the restaurant where he had dined with Magali.

"Sir, great to see you here again."

"Thanks, Chico."

"Is it true what they say? That Dona Magali died?"

"She didn't die, Chico. She was killed."

"And who did that, sir?"

"That's what I want to know, and in order to find out I need to find out other things. One of them is what happened to my wallet."

"Here in the restaurant nothing happened, sir. I waited on your table; when I brought the check you got your wallet out of your pocket and handed over the checkbook for Dona Magali to fill out; then you signed and put the checkbook and the wallet back in the back pocket of your pants."

"Are you sure I put the wallet in my pocket?"

"Absolutely. You'd had a little to drink and it took you a while. I was waiting to pull out the chair to help you up."

"And outside? Who was the parking attendant?"

"The same as always. If you'd like, I'll have him come over."

"That won't be necessary. I'll speak to him on the way out."

Vieira knew there wasn't necessarily any link between the disappearance of the wallet and the death of Magali, but without interfering in Espinosa's investigation, it was all he had to start with. The fact was, he couldn't sit home watching TV while the police were gathering evidence against him. He declined the drink he was offered on the house and went to talk to the attendant.

"Yes, sir, I was the one who helped you into the car. You were on the other side of the street when I saw you almost fall on top of the kid, and I ran to help."

"What kid, damn it? I didn't have a kid with me."

"The kid wasn't with you, sir. I'm talking about the kid who usually sleeps there on the sidewalk, right in front of where your car was parked."

"And what's the deal with the kid?"

"Nothing, sir. It's just that you were a little tipsy and almost fell on top of him; maybe the noise woke him up."

"Noise?"

"From the box."

"What goddamn box are you talking about? What does a fucking box have to do with it?"

"The refrigerator box, sir." He hastily added: "He was sleeping inside a refrigerator package someone had left on the sidewalk; you almost fell on top of him."

"And where's the kid now?"

"I don't know, sir. Since that day he's disappeared. The

other gentlemen also asked about him; one of them told me to call them when he shows up."

"What other gentlemen? Who the fuck are you talking about?"

"Your colleagues, sir. They also asked me about the wallet, and I told them the same thing."

"What was the number they gave you?"

"Only one of them gave me a number. The one who was here first left his card." He stuck his hand in his pocket and extracted several bits of paper that looked like they'd been there for years: sports betting tickets, a doctor's prescription, and, in the middle, Espinosa's card.

Vieira didn't know whether to be satisfied or scared. And he didn't know what had put Espinosa onto the kid. What excuse could he give for arriving after someone else from his team had already come? He looked at the man, at the place on the sidewalk where the boy had been, at the place where he must have parked his car, forcing himself to try to recall anything about those scenes. Useless: it was as if nothing had happened, and he was sure it would stay that way.

Monday, late afternoon: the only pleasant feeling in his soul was the promise of Flor's body. He wasn't in a hurry. The memory of Magali, with time, had become softer and softer, until only random fragments remained. He missed her, but he knew that as the years went by he would miss her in ever smaller degrees, until even remembering his old suffering would cease to pain him. But maybe that wasn't how Flor felt, and he didn't want to rush her. He needed, moreover, to protect himself from Espinosa's suspicions, and Espinosa wouldn't be sympathetic to a romance between the only two people linked to the dead woman, especially if one of them was the prime suspect. On the other hand, he and Flor were free, unattached adults; no one needed to know what went on between them, even though Espinosa might not see it that way.

His first night with Flor deserved a special celebration. They would eat at a restaurant by the beach; the moon wasn't bright and the sky was overcast, but at least it didn't look like it was going to rain. He still didn't have his car. After dinner they'd go to her place; he didn't like to take women to his apartment because he felt his ex-wife's ghost still spying on everything. Besides, he liked to preserve his personal space. The only woman who had entered his apartment since Maria Zilda's death was Magali.

He decided to take a long bath; he would use a cologne Magali hadn't given him, and he would wear white pants, white shoes, and a colored shirt, though he wouldn't unbutton it too far, so as to cover the white hairs on his chest. He had learned that hair goes gray from top to bottom, and nothing was more pathetic than white body hair. He had thought of dyeing his hair light brown to produce a color something like mahogany, but he'd never gotten around to it.

He arrived home out of breath; it had been a nice walk. Before getting in the bath, he laid out his clothes. He still hadn't decided between the colored shirt and the white linen guayabera with white embroidery. Dressing all in white, like a groom, would really impress her. He decided not to take a bath: too much work. He took off his clothes and lay down in bed to relax.

When he awoke, it was two-twenty in the morning.

The news didn't take long to arrive at the station: an unknown police officer was shaking down homosexuals, prostitutes, drug addicts, drunks, and foreigners. His description didn't match that of any known officer, and the general opinion was that he wasn't from another precinct, either: in other words, that he wasn't a cop. Espinosa concluded immediately that someone had found Vieira's I.D. The first reports came from the managers of bars and clubs located around the Praça do Lido; the next, from the beachside, suggesting a route down the beach toward Ipanema. If the guy was smart, he'd only stick around for a few days, then lie low before defensive measures were taken, not starting up again until a few weeks later, once everybody had forgotten about him. Espinosa doubted this first wave would last more than five days, which gave his team only a couple of days to intercept him—if the people he was robbing didn't intercept him more definitively. Judging from the order of events, Espinosa figured the next place he'd hit would be a club that used to be mixed but was now a gay cruising ground. The plan was simple: two young detectives would serve as bait. He didn't want to go himself or send more experienced detectives, because they might be recognized. His goal, more than simply recovering Vieira's I.D., was to get the man. If he showed up, the detectives had orders to grab him as soon as he completed the first transaction.

At ten-forty, Espinosa sat watching the partygoers' movements attentively from a car parked almost directly in front of the club. He wanted to be one step ahead of the detectives inside and identify the man before he could go in; or, if he managed to get in, to protect the exit in case anything went wrong inside.

He didn't like stakeouts. He had a lot of trouble concentrating on a single point: he could focus his gaze, but his attention would wander; his eyes would stay fixed on the scene, but his mind would stray so far that he might as well be blind. Watching a door, he would fall into intense imaginary dialogues with someone he knew, often talking to his ex-wife about their son, losing track of time, completely unaware whether the suspect had come or gone. Other times, the shine off his bumpers would evoke the '52 Chevrolet Hydra-Matic that his father had kept in perfect condition until the day he'd died. The three of them had died together: mother, father, and car. He was the only survivor. The presence of his grandmother had been a crucial factor in his life, but a grandmother wasn't the same as a mother and father.

He concentrated on the movement around the door again. Though names and fashions had changed, he could still see, shining on the facade in red neon, the name Bolero, evocative of the mysterious interiors like those he had seen in American films. Twelve-fifteen. The mist, almost imperceptible when they'd arrived, now formed a compact mass that blocked his view of the waves on the other side of the street behind him. Maybe the man had decided to interrupt his forays—he'd been too active in the first couple of days—or maybe he'd chosen another bar. The description they'd been furnished didn't help much. At one o'clock, Espinosa saw the two detectives come out of the club and walk toward the car.

"Chief, we don't think he's coming. There aren't a lot of people in there, and it's thinning out. It's not a good night." Both pairs of eyes were red with smoke and beer.

"Let's keep at it another half hour; after that we'll go home."

It was almost two in the morning when they called it a night. They'd try again the next day. All they could do now was go home and sleep.

Stretched out in bed, Flor looked at her own feet and examined what little there was of her apartment beyond her big toe. The bathroom had the necessary equipment, but it was all so crammed together that even lathering up her hair in the shower required synchronized arm movements: if one arm was bent upward, the other had to remain flat against her side.

Though she received very few clients at home, and though these were all carefully selected, Flor figured it would be hard for her to move up in the world while living in that cubicle. She couldn't even offer them a proper chair; the client opened the door and bumped immediately into the bed. Neither could she invite them to enjoy the view: the only window looked out at a narrow space surrounded by hundreds of similar windows. The rent and the maintenance were paid by her Pernambucan benefactor. "Only until I can afford it myself," she'd said to him at the time, but she'd never had to worry about that detail. As for improving her situation in life, she knew she'd moved quite a long ways up from the stud-and-mud house in Recife, but not enough: from TV she'd learned that an artist could do much better, and she considered herself an artist. "Josias could hook me up with a bigger apartment, one compatible with my future." She was still looking at her big toe when it occurred to her that it wouldn't be long before Josias would show up with Junior and say: "I want you to make him a man, Flor." She switched the position of her legs. Now the other big toe moved into focus. The view of the room stayed the same, but the toe was different. She liked her slender, elegant feet; she hated puffy feet with clubby toes. Josias didn't like for her to paint her nails. "I hope Vieira doesn't like it either; I can't walk around with the nails painted on one foot and not on the other." She considered herself taken care of. On the one hand, there was the financial security Josias offered, which would certainly be enhanced when Junior arrived on the scene; on the other hand, she had a new protector in Vieira. The fact that he was retired didn't change anything; once a cop, always a cop—the only difference was that the older ones needed more love. She wouldn't have any problems if she could handle these two. She liked Vieira; she thought she even liked him more than Josias, which she attributed to his not being afraid to walk arm in arm with her on the street. Josias had only taken her to dinner once, but in a restaurant so far away, on the side of a highway, that it felt like they were in another state. Magali had told her that once she had gone to visit Vieira in the hospital when he was recovering from an operation. When she entered the room, he was with two colleagues from the precinct and a third man she figured was a relative. He introduced her to all of them as an old and dear friend. When he complained about his cold feet, she got a pair of socks out of the wardrobe and put them on him, in front of everyone, a clear proof of their intimacy. The scene she described became Flor's paradigm of all loving relationships. Flor imagined the scene and the almost sacred intimacy of the gesture of putting on someone's socks for them. She looked back at her own feet. And once again she was happy to find them thin and elegant. Her hands, with long, narrow fingers, matched her feet. She didn't wear rings because she thought they distracted from her own beauty. She avoided all kinds of accessories. "Only ugly girls need baubles" was one of her favorite sayings. She thought, moreover, that the only function of clothing was to reinforce forms and allude to whatever was hidden. All her considerable wisdom was placed at the service of her body's powers.

That was the body Vieira was thinking about when he called.

"Flor, my dear, I'm so sorry about last night; I went to rest before our date and fell asleep. I didn't wake up until the middle of the night."

"Don't worry about it, love. We can go out tonight; I don't have plans." And even before Vieira could think about what her plans might entail, she went on: "Because now I'm your flower and you're my gardener." As usual, the phrase produced the intended effect.

PART 2

He got to the station after the beginning of the morning shift and had to hear the news secondhand: a street kid, sleeping underneath the awning of a building in front of the restaurant where Vieira had gone with Magali, had been burned alive. The building's garage attendant was washing the cars when he heard the screams; he reached the garage door in time to see the boy, in flames, take a few steps and fall onto the sidewalk; by the time the fire department's ambulance got there, he looked like a charred doll. He died before the ambulance reached the hospital.

The garage attendant couldn't identify the boy. A group of beggars sleeping a hundred meters away hadn't seen anything and didn't know the boy. Espinosa knew that street kids and beggars were enemies; they must have been scared, because the boy had been killed the same way delinquents killed beggars. He waited for the restaurant to open before heading over there; maybe the parking attendant could help.

"Sir, from what you're telling me, I was long gone at the time it happened."

"I know. The garage attendant across the street told us what time the crime took place, so what I want to know is if you were still parking cars when the boy lay down to sleep underneath the awning."

"I was, and I saw him lie down. He talked to me; they almost always ask me to get my hands on something for them in the restaurant."

"Was it the same boy as when the other officer was here?"

"No, sir. It was another one."

"Are you sure? He usually slept in that very same place."

"I know, but it wasn't him, it was another one. I know the boys around here; I don't know their names, but I can tell them apart."

"Let's go to the Forensic Institute to—"

"Sir, we don't need to go to the Forensic Institute. I know it wasn't the same kid. I got him some bread and sausage; when I ended my shift and went home he was already sleeping."

"While you were parking the cars, did you see anyone suspicious around?"

"Sir, after a certain hour in Copacabana either everyone looks suspicious or no one does." Espinosa provided the description the managers of the bars had given of the man posing as a police officer. "No, sir, I don't remember anyone like that. And, if you'll pardon my French, a son of a bitch who would do something like that—we ought to be able to tell when someone like that's around." Espinosa left thinking how wrong the parking attendant was on that last point.

He was sure the two crimes were linked, which didn't mean the same person was responsible for them, only that they were related events. Setting fire to a victim was the way urban predators worked—but that could be precisely the reason the murderer had used that method.

The news of the boy's death had raced through the streets of Copacabana long before it made its appearance on the evening news. What didn't show up on the news, Espinosa reflected, was the fact that the murderer thought he had eliminated his target but had actually gotten the wrong person: the kid had died because he'd slept in the wrong place on the wrong night. The reporters discussed the extreme violence of the act. A sleeping person was completely helpless, incapable of self-defense; in the case of a child sleeping on a sidewalk, such helplessness was an expression of trust in the people around him. Someone who took advantage of that trust to throw gasoline on a child and set him on fire was a monster. Some channels interviewed psychiatrists, psychoanalysts, and psychologists in search of an explanation.

The event scared the kid but didn't throw him off his investigation. He knew who had committed the crime, but the criminal didn't know he'd killed the wrong boy. That was a big advantage. If he went to the police, no one would pay him any attention; the story was too extraordinary. Better to shut up and make the most of his supposed death. He'd have to become invisible, which wasn't much of a problem for him. Now, more than ever, he needed a guarantee of safety. He thought about Clodoaldo's suggestion again. He'd keep following the cop and would talk to him at the right time; he just didn't know when the right time would be or what he would say. No story he came up with would make sense without allusion to the wallet episode, and if he talked about that he'd have to give back the money. He could forget about the whole thing, even forget about the man himself, and live his life the way he'd always lived it. But if he did that, he risked running into the man someday—and being killed for the second time.

When he'd worked at the Praça Mauá, he'd usually—at the tensest moments, while trying to solve a problem—left the building and sat on one of the benches to watch the movements of the cranes at the docks. In Copacabana there was no port and no cranes, and the Peixoto district wasn't on the beach. The only thing to watch there was the assemblage of

four-story buildings built at the same time as the neighborhood itself, with doors and windows outlined in colors ranging
from colonial green and blue to, more unusually, canary yellow
or wine red. So it was that, on Thursday afternoon, as he was
on his way home, Espinosa stopped in the square in front of
his building, looked for an empty bench, and sat gazing at the
dusky light on the hills surrounding the Peixoto district. He
didn't miss the cranes; the curiosity they elicited in him was
nothing more than what he felt for prehistoric animals in
fictional films. Kids ran screaming around him, which didn't
stop him from starting a little when he heard a voice close to
his ear:

"Officer." A child's voice, which calmed him down even
before Espinosa turned his head. The child tried to smile, but
his eyes examined Espinosa meticulously.

"Hi. What's your name?"

The boy didn't respond. He walked around the bench and
stopped in front of it, watching, sizing him up. Espinosa could
tell that he wasn't a kid from the neighborhood.

"Do you want to have a seat?" He wasn't sure of the kid's
age, but he was certainly older than he looked. That much he
could read in his eyes.

"How do you know who I am?"

"I followed you, sir."

"From where?"

"The station."

"And how did you know to follow me?"

"Clodoaldo told me."

"Clodoaldo?"

The boy shook his head affirmatively as he sat down next
to Espinosa.

"And who is Clodoaldo?"

The boy stretched his arms out to the seat of the bench, as

if he was going to get up, a frightened look in his eyes. Espinosa thought he would run off.

"Sorry, but I know a lot of people—which Clodoaldo are you talking about?"

"The Clodoaldo from the beach." And in a final, desperate gasp: "Clodoaldo, the street teacher, said we could trust you." That was when the picture came together for Espinosa.

"Of course! How stupid of me not to have thought of him right off the bat! So Clodoaldo told you to come find me? And why didn't you go straight to the station instead of following me around?"

" 'Cause I was scared."

"Scared of the police?"

"Scared of getting killed."

"And why did you think the police were going to kill you?"

"Not the police, the man."

"What man?"

"The one who burned up my friend."

Espinosa looked at the boy for a long time, glanced at the children playing, then looked back at the boy. He spoke slowly, as if trying to break a spell.

"Listen. That luncheonette on the corner has great ham sandwiches. How about I order two for each of us, get us some soft drinks, and come back over here . . . and then you can tell me the story from the beginning."

With the living room in the dark, the lights from the street came through the venetian blinds, projecting stripes onto the ceiling. The little red and green lights on his answering machine contrasted with the surrounding darkness. Espinosa didn't always immediately answer their call; nor did he always turn on the lights as soon as he came in. While he was crossing the room, he threw an almost disdainful glance toward the machine, contemptuous of its two-tone blinking. Without paying it any more attention, he went straight to his room and then to the bathroom before listening to the messages. For two days he'd felt compelled by purely external forces, emptied of desire, mechanically going through the motions at the station. The week was over and he really couldn't think of any reason to be proud to have lived through it. It didn't help that it was less than a month to Christmas, a time when he became sensitive; this susceptibility had nothing to do with his religiousness but with a story by O. Henry he had read as a child, and with Hollywood films. Ever since then, Christmas had always moved him, though he thought it would move him a lot more with snow.

He had long since abandoned the fantasy that Friday night was the prelude to a weekend rich with worthy accomplishments. And he hadn't needed many of these to realize that this night was different from other nights only because of the illusion that all tasks interrupted (or never even begun) during the week could be completed on Saturday. This included regluing loose floorboards or—one he had initiated over a year ago—constructing a bookshelf for all the loose books in the apartment or—on the intellectual level, one offering equal numbers of variations—embarking on a letter to a distant friend, even beginning the epic narrative of his adventuresome life. But he'd lost the friend's address; as for the adventures, he knew they were more story than fact.

This was his state of mind when he went out to look for a restaurant, tired of eating frozen spaghetti Bolognese. The shops of Copacabana had already been deeply infused by the Christmas spirit, staying open late, with music wafting out of the stores and so many trees for sale that it seemed someone must have emptied out Lapland. He walked a few blocks to a trattoria near the beach. The height of his adventures that night was a chocolate cake with cream on top.

The emptiness of the previous night made him awake on Saturday like a demiurge, ready to instill order into chaos. A while before, in the spirit of entrepreneurship, he had, in lieu of a shelf, piled up the books he had accumulated—bought or inherited—over the last twenty years, arranging them vertically, like plates in a dish rack. Instead of shelves he laid books horizontally on top of the vertical row and, on top of them, began another vertical row. The result of this improvisation was a bookshelf-without-shelves that was already more than a meter and a half tall and occupied the entire length of one of the walls in the living room—without employing any wood. Espinosa was proud of this piece of domestic engineering, but it was time for a few remedies. The reason was twofold: the first, and most important, was that the housecleaner he had used for many years had subtly suggested that she and this arrangement were not compatible; the second, less important reason was that the shelving had reached a point of precarious balance. The situation required energetic action, and that usually implied lengthy reflection, even with that morning's otherworldly inspiration. Once he was through with breakfast, he took some paper and a pencil and began the project of creating a proper set of shelves for the living room. The first step was to make a design and calculate the exact measurements for the wood he needed to buy; the second was to find a workman. The first part took up his whole Saturday, or almost all of it: he still had the night free.

The TV movie was halfway over. The star seemed to think that acting consisted of making expressive faces, but there wasn't much else in the guide. He was about to change the channel or turn the TV off entirely when the doorbell rang. As soon as he went out on the balcony to see who was there, the two figures moved away from the door and looked up, attracted by the noise of the blinds. The streetlamp illuminated a boy and a young woman. He immediately recognized the boy who had approached him in the square and to whom he'd given his address. He didn't know who the girl was. He gestured for them to wait and went down. It was twenty minutes to midnight.

As soon as he opened the door to the street both of them started talking at the same time. He asked them to calm down and tell him what had happened. The boy didn't say anything; she started talking.

"A man tried to kill him," she said, looking at the boy and the street, as if the kid were there to confirm what she was saying.

"Why don't you come in and tell me the details?"

"I can't; I left my canvases in the street."

"Your canvases?"

"I'm a painter. I sell my canvases on the sidewalk on the Avenida Atlântica—that's where the man tried to kill him."

She said everything in one breath. Espinosa calculated that she must be about twenty-five and noted that she was very pretty, as angry as she was scared.

"So let's go get your canvases. On the way you can tell me what happened."

"Are you coming with us?"

"I am. Don't worry. He won't be there anymore. Wait a second while I go lock up."

He took a little more than a minute to get his weapon, his wallet, and a jacket. He had his car parked in front of the building; besides concealing them from the eyes of the thug, it would give them more mobility. The boy sat in the back seat and the girl sat up front, next to Espinosa.

"What's your name?" asked Espinosa as soon as they drove off.

"Kika. K-i-k-a. That's how I sign my paintings and what everyone calls me. My real name is Cristina. The kid says your name is Espinosa."

"That's right. What else did he tell you?"

"That you're a police officer and that we can trust you."

"Then tell me what happened."

"Okay." She paused, as if organizing her thoughts, then began her story while the boy, leaning on his elbows, nodded his head affirmatively, underscoring certain points of the narrative. "Me and the other painters show our work on the island dividing the lanes of traffic on the Avenida Atlântica. It was after eleven and I was trying to get the attention of a group of tourists when I saw the man running after the boy on the sidewalk across the street. Suddenly the boy crossed the street, almost getting hit, and hid behind me, shouting that they were trying to kill him. The man stopped on the other side and folded up what looked like a switchblade or a penknife. He stared like he was photographing us, turned around, and went away. The boy told me afterward that that same man had burned another boy, thinking it was him. I asked someone I knew to watch my paintings; we went around the block in the opposite direction from the one the man had taken, and I was ready to go to the police when the boy told me about you. Since it was close, we decided to come here."

"You did the right thing. Let's go get your pictures."

It took them less than ten minutes to get from the Peixoto district to the Avenida Atlântica, long enough to establish a climate of trust. While she was talking, Kika gestured and stretched her legs, occupying most of the car and almost reaching Espinosa. They managed to park two blocks from the place the two had indicated. They got out and walked past the kiosks selling all sorts of tourist junk. The boy walked between them, wary and attentive. The friend who had stayed behind to watch Kika's canvases breathed a sigh of relief when he saw Kika coming; he had gathered up and wrapped all of his own pictures and was visibly yearning to get home. He made a quick comment about someone who'd seemed interested in one of her pictures. Then Kika thanked him for watching her things, they said their farewells, and he left. No questions about what happened; no interest in the boy; no curiosity, which Espinosa thought strange. Later, Kika made it clear that he wasn't an artist or a painter. He just sold the pictures, a mixture of *marchand* and street hawker. Kika's pictures were exhibited on an aluminum stand, where they were hung unframed. The colors suggested Matisse and the forms Gauguin. They looked nice to Espinosa, though his knowledge of painting was limited to reading books with titles like *Masters of Painting*.

While taking the pictures down and disassembling her stand, Kika explained that she painted with acrylic, which dried quickly; at first she'd used oils, but since she didn't have the patience to wait days on end for the colors to dry completely, she had gone over to acrylic.

"I'm hyperactive—I need my paint to correspond with my personality."

"Your paintings are really pretty, which corresponds with you."

It was a gallant thing to say. At least Espinosa hoped it would be received as such. Kika looked at him questioningly, as if hesitating between asking for a clarification and thanking him, but Espinosa had already turned to the boy, making an unimportant comment.

While they were waiting for Kika to take down her stand, Espinosa made an effort to focus on the man, not on Kika; but no matter how intently he looked around for someone he'd never seen, he couldn't keep his eyes off the girl for more than a couple of seconds. Next to him, the boy stayed alert, aware that he was being forgotten. Kika gathered up her paintings, rolling them with corrugated plastic and making a big but transportable package. The metal structure was taken apart and tied with a nylon rope. They crossed the street, Kika carrying the pictures and Espinosa the stand, which she stored in a garage in exchange for a weekly tip for the doorman. It was twelve-thirty in the morning. It was hot, and the bars on the sidewalk were packed. Men in shorts and women wearing next to nothing strolled in both directions down the avenue, enjoying the light sea breeze.

After storing the metal stand, they walked two blocks toward the spot where they had parked the car, occasionally having to maneuver their way around the tables that were steadily taking over all the available sidewalk space. When they crossed the street, almost directly across from their parking place, Espinosa moved to grab Kika's arm as he glanced toward the boy. But he wasn't there. Espinosa looked around, holding his breath, his heart racing, his eyes trying to focus on an absent object. He studied the cars pulling out, glancing in every direction for a man grabbing a boy by the arm. Nothing. He retraced their steps, peering inside the restaurants, inside the doorways of buildings, inside passing cars and vacant lots, then returning to the other sidewalk, with Kika running behind him until they reached the car.

The boy had disappeared.

He felt completely useless; he felt that the two of them had come to find him at home simply to verify the skill of a man who could snatch the boy out from under his nose. While he looked around indiscriminately at everything and everyone, he reflected that the whole time they'd been together he'd been so charmed by the girl that he'd forgotten the most basic norms of witness protection. Instead of calling for backup from patrol cars in the area, he had believed he could master the situation by himself. But his eyes had been much more focused on Kika than on the boy and his supposed persecutor. The boy had vanished while he was practically holding his hand.

They got into the car and started scouring the area. Their assumption was that the boy had been kidnapped and that the kidnapper had been on foot; he couldn't have gotten too far from the scene of the crime. They drove around all the nearby blocks, scrutinizing all men and boys, together or not. After half an hour, Espinosa returned to the place they'd started, giving up the search; it was no use. To pacify his conscience, he called headquarters to ask for an alert and provided a detailed description of the boy, along with a less precise sketch of the alleged kidnapper.

He parked his car in the same space he'd first left it; then he and Kika walked toward Leme down the Avenida Atlântica, in a last stab at remedying their failure. Of the two of them, only Kika had seen the man, and Espinosa glanced at her every time he saw a man who looked like the one she had described. He was frustrated, angry, and tired. The bars on the beachfront were almost all still open. During the search, he didn't say a single word. When he decided to give it up, he suggested having a beer and a sandwich before taking her home. They didn't pick a bar; they just sat down in the first one they came across.

"You're feeling guilty for no reason. I didn't see him disappear either, and I was as close to him as you were." Kika put her hand lightly on Espinosa's arm, touching only the material of his jacket, as if there were a great distance between it and his skin.

"True, but you're not a police officer; there was no reason for you to pay as much attention as me. It was incompetence."

"Why do you sound like you're mad at me?"

"I'm not mad at you."

"Of course you're mad. Just look at your face."

"What does my face have to do with it?"

"The way it looks, the waiter won't come near us."

Espinosa was trying to picture the state of his own face when the waiter came up to take their order.

"The kitchen's already closed, but we can do sandwiches and snacks." He spoke in the impersonal tone of a supermarket checkout girl while running a towel across the wet table.

Until seconds earlier, Espinosa had thought of the boy like a cloud of uncertain density but clear form, while Kika looked like a strike of lightning in the middle of the night, fascinating and disturbing. When they sat at the table, the picture changed and the boy's shriveled face was the only thing he could think about. He didn't want to chat, and certainly not about anything personal.

He made a few comments about the boy's disappearance, raising all the possible explanations, and quickly exhausted every conceivable reason. The awkwardness was shared, and any conversation was destined to fall into the void. He tried a few questions about painting. Kika said she studied painting at the School of Fine Arts, mentioned her favorite painters, and then went from aesthetic considerations to economic ones, discussing the cost of materials and her difficulties in selling her work. When the sandwiches arrived, they ate heartily, despite the circumstances. Two beers were enough to impress on both of them their fatigue and frustration, and made perfectly clear that for them the night was over.

"I'll take you home. Where do you live?"

"In Catete. That's where we found a good deal on an apartment."

"We?"

"Me and some girlfriends; three of us share an old house on the Rua do Catete."

On the way, she pressed her head against the window and wordlessly pushed her legs against the front of the car. Except for her pretty brown eyes, focused on the windshield, she looked like she was asleep. She didn't accept Espinosa's help in taking her pictures upstairs, saying only, "I do it every day." They said good-bye with a kiss on each cheek, like two schoolmates. While she went up the staircase leading to the third floor of the little building, Espinosa was struck by the contrast between the modernity of Kika and the antiquity of the old colonial house on the Rua do Catete. He sat for a few minutes, the deafening noise of his motor throwing the quiet of the night into relief, and stared at the empty street, beneath the serious gaze of the venerable Catete Palace across the way.

He woke from his hangover. Failure, too, intoxicates, he thought, looking at himself in the bathroom mirror. While the coffeemaker made its usual gargling noise, he called the station. The officers on duty hadn't heard any news about a kid. The Forensic Institute hadn't received any dead children.

The two cups of coffee contributed little to his sluggish mood. During their meeting, before they had lost him, the boy had mentioned a building on the Avenida Copacabana, between the Rua Santa Clara and the Rua Siqueira Campos, with a shop on the ground floor and a small entryway bordering the next building. The description was good. It wouldn't be hard to find it.

Sunday morning under a cloudless blue sky. Local residents were sleepily walking toward the beach, alone or with children, tents, rafts, balls, rackets, mats. Moving against this tide, Espinosa didn't have any trouble finding the building. It was a little after ten when the doorman answered the insistent buzzing of the bell. He was wearing shorts, a T-shirt, and sandals and carrying a twisted wet rag. He arrived saying that today was Sunday so the cleaner had the day off and he had to do everything himself and couldn't sit around in the lobby and . . . Espinosa flashed his badge.

"Good morning, I'm Inspector Espinosa from the Twelfth Precinct. I'd like to ask you a few questions."

"What happened?" The voice softened and sounded frightened.

"Nothing to do with you, I hope. I'm looking for information about a resident of this building. A white man, around thirty, skinny, straight black hair, well dressed, lives in an apartment at the back, goes out at night."

"Sir, the building has eighty apartments. I can't know everyone."

"But you know this guy. Think about it. We're not talking about a retired gentleman. He's relatively young, good looking, a nocturnal Copacabana crook. He probably doesn't talk a lot and probably lives by himself. I'm not sure about the last part. But maybe the police have come for him before."

"You say he goes out at night. I wasn't here last night; I just arrived this morning."

"I'm not talking about last night. I just want you to give me his apartment number."

"I don't know . . . I don't remember anybody like that."

"Well, maybe back at the station? Maybe that would refresh your memory?"

"Hold on a second. It might be the guy in 607."

"Great. And does the guy in 607 have a name?"

"I don't know, sir. He never said."

"And the guy in 607 doesn't pay his maintenance or get any mail or bills or anything with his name on it?"

"No, sir. It all comes in the name of Mr. Elói."

"And who is Mr. Elói?"

"The owner of the apartment."

"Very good. Let's have a word with Mr. Elói."

"He doesn't live here; he's a rancher in the state of Rio. Sometimes he doesn't show up for a whole year. The one who uses the apartment is the guy you're looking for."

"Whose name you don't know, even though he lives here."

"He lives here but he's not always around. Sometimes he doesn't show up for days and weeks, and then suddenly there he is—he stays a few days and then disappears again."

"And you don't know if he's home?"

"No, sir."

"Do you have the key to the apartment?"

"No, sir. It's against the rules. I prefer it that way. Something goes missing and they blame us."

"Like you said, there are a lot of apartments; you can't pay attention to all of them. I'm going to go see if he's there."

"We can call him on the intercom."

"That's exactly what I don't want you to do. I'm going to go up and you're going to sit still and not touch the intercom."

"No problem, sir."

During the conversation, the doorman had been wringing the wet rag he had in his hands, which Espinosa interpreted as a sign of nervousness. Maybe he wanted to wring 607's neck; maybe he wanted to wring Espinosa's neck; maybe he was thinking about what 607 would do to him. Espinosa concluded that something that can be interpreted in so many ways probably didn't have any meaning at all. He went up.

The apartment had only one door. He rang the bell, then tried the knocker. The door didn't seem to have been bolted. He tried to pop it open with a credit card but only managed to mangle his card in the process. A lady opened the door to one of the neighboring apartments and surprised him at the moment he was removing his card from the door frame. She scowled at him, frightened; Espinosa replied with his best ambiguous smile and then, imagining she'd be too uncomfortable to ride down with him in the same elevator, waited for the next one. When he got down, he found her warning the doorman, who was still squeezing the rag. When Espinosa walked over to them, she scurried off.

"When the man shows up, call me immediately," he said, giving the doorman his card. "I don't have to tell you not to say anything to him."

"Of course, sir." Espinosa left with the absolute certainty that he would not be alerted when the resident of 607 reappeared.

Once he was back home, he opened an Italian wine to accompany some pasta he had made himself. It wasn't the best lunch of his life, but neither was it the worst.

The fact that no body had been found corresponding to the boy's calmed him down a bit. He was already coming to accept the idea that the boy had run off when he'd seen the man nearby; he would have hidden, and when he felt less threatened he would come find Espinosa again. At least that's how Espinosa hoped things would turn out.

He hesitated for a while between doing the dishes from breakfast and lunch or letting them pile up in the sink in expectation of Wednesday, when Alice, the cleaning lady (who didn't think the apartment was a wonderland), would arrive to restore order.

He decided to get the Conrad he had bought a month before in a used-book store downtown. It was a translation of *Lord Jim* dating to 1939. The former owner had written on the first page, "I began reading this book on 22.2.40 (Thursday)," and on the last page, "I finished it on 24.2.40 (Saturday) at 23.30. A little monotonous..." Just below, in a darker ink in a different blue, were the words "21.3.54 (Sunday)—I've just reread this book and now I think it's one of the best I've ever read." Fourteen years later. Had he changed? Had his reading changed? Had he become more condescending? More mature? Seduced by the extra ingredient introduced by the former owner, Espinosa began reading, his mind made up to be the referee between the two readings, considering himself within his rights to add a decisive stroke. But it still wasn't time to enter the world of Tuan Jim: he couldn't concentrate on the words; images of Kika and the boy kept invading the story. Joseph Conrad deserved a more attentive reader. He put the book aside for another, better occasion.

At some point the man would have to come home to take a shower and change clothes, unless he had really fled, which would be an admission of guilt. There was no evidence that he was the murderer of the sleeping boy, and he couldn't be sure that the boy he had lost had anything to do with the wallet found in the street. One thing, though, was indisputable, no matter who had killed the first boy: if he had killed the wrong kid, he would have to hurry to rectify his mistake. Espinosa decided to go back to the building. He waited until five for a possible phone call from Kika, at which point he left and headed toward the Avenida Copacabana. Since it was summer, the sun was still shining brightly. There was a new doorman, who promised that the resident of 607 hadn't come through the door of the building in either direction. "Some-times he goes for days without showing up," the man said, adding that he didn't know why. From there Espinosa walked to the point on the Avenida Atlântica where Kika showed her pictures, but her colleague was the only one there and Espinosa didn't feel like approaching him. He retraced his steps from the night before several times but still couldn't see how the boy had disappeared. His few suppositions didn't hold together. He walked down the sidewalk by the beach, wandered through the streets of Copacabana, and ended the night eating a piece of pizza, standing up, in a snack bar as inelegant as the pizza. The third part of the Sunday only added a feeling of dejection to the first two-thirds.

Monday morning. Chaves, a new detective bursting with eagerness, had been placed in charge of monitoring the building on the Avenida Copacabana to make sure the man hadn't returned. No sign of the kid, but at least he hadn't turned up at the morgue. An NGO who worked with street children buried the incinerated boy. Espinosa devoted great mental effort toward convincing himself that the kid he was looking for hadn't met with the same fate. He considered the idea that the kid had fled not only from the man but from Espinosa himself, from Kika, from everyone but his peers.

He felt incredibly uncomfortable that Kika had witnessed his failure, all the more because that bothered him more than the boy's disappearance. He thought about dropping by her house with the excuse that he needed a better description of the man to compare it with the boy's, or even to suggest that she use her drawing skills to produce a portrait of the man. Or, he thought, he could find something useful to do instead of giving himself over to adolescent fantasies.

The chief asked for his help in reducing the mountains of paperwork accumulating on his desk. It was a dull, strictly bureaucratic job, which is why he thought it matched his mood perfectly. They worked at neighboring tables in the chief's office. His difficulties in concentrating on the work stemmed not only from his situation but from his fear that at any moment the door could open to reveal someone with a problem that had nothing to do with what he was reading. For the rest of the morning and most of the afternoon he worked through the piles, an activity as exciting as standing in line at the bank.

Right before four o'clock, Chaves came in to report that every time he had gone by the building he had been told that the man was not there. The doorman might be protecting the man, more scared of him than of the cops. There was also the possibility that the man lived in several different places, which would explain how he could regularly stay away for days on end. It was even more probable that he didn't have a fixed residence, moving according to the moment and the circumstances.

The description of the kid that Espinosa had given to the radio patrollers turned up no new leads. The same description matched no known body at the Forensic Institute, though it was possible for people to die without their bodies ever being recovered.

Early that evening he went home, hoping the boy was tailing him as he had before. He took the longest and busiest route in order to be followed more easily, stopping in front of several stores, pretending to examine things on display, in the hopes that he would capture the face of his stalker reflected in the glass, but he didn't see a thing. He arrived home feeling heavy, ascended the three flights of stairs with difficulty, and entered panting, as if he'd been running. The answering machine was blinking. He hit the playback button and heard

Kika's voice regretting that he wasn't home; another call with no message; and the voice of Kika once more, promising to call again at nine that night. It was seven-ten; he had time to think of something not off-putting to say to her. He imagined the emotions of younger people as being like a light switch, on or off, while his own seemed more like those dimmers that adjust the light intensity on a spectrum from weaker to stronger. He thought the thesis was ridiculous, but it was all he could muster before his bath.

Kika sounded less anxious than she had earlier; her tone was friendly, almost caring. She wanted to know if there was any news of the boy; she too felt guilty about it. But that wasn't the real reason for the call; Espinosa felt clearly that she was extending the offer of conversation in the hopes of an invitation. He wanted a little more time. Not for her, but for himself. Fifteen years of difference was enough to create lots of static on his communication channels. At the end of the message, she had left her beeper number—"In case you want to talk to me, of course."

He had gotten used to living alone. The freedom of having full run of his space and time and not having to explain anything to anyone was seductive. Marriage and separation demanded difficult decisions, but it was just as tough to decide whether to *stay* married or separated. Ever since he and his wife had separated, he'd been noticing this—and noticing that people like Kika threatened (but also contributed to) this state of affairs. This was how he had spent the last decade—with some moments more intense, some less.

He tried not to think about Kika. He tried to pick up *Lord Jim* again. Conrad versus Kika. After half an hour, he had to grant Kika the victory. It was impossible to keep reading with her image stamped on every paragraph. He put down the book, opened a beer, and threw a frozen dinner into the microwave without bothering to check what was written on the box.

As persistently as Kika's face, the emptiness left by the boy's disappearance forced itself into his thoughts. It seemed impossible for the boy to have been snatched so close to him and Kika without either of them noticing and without his making the faintest sound. Espinosa was starting to believe that he had disappeared of his own volition. He knew the basic principle of all street kids: "A boy on his own is a dead boy." A group provided the minimal conditions for security; an isolated boy was easy prey. Perhaps he had decided that he couldn't count on anyone's help and had fled to seek protection with his group. That was what Espinosa wanted to believe.

The verdict from the Forensic Institute was clear: Magali had been asphyxiated by the plastic bag after breathing Mace. There were no marks on her body except those found on her wrists and ankles, and there were no signs of recent sexual intercourse. Putting together the postmortem, the medical report, and his own on-scene observations, Espinosa came up with the following picture: Magali was with someone who had made her breathe the gas while she was sitting or lying on her own bed. Her clothes had been found on the chair; her pants were folded on the seat and her shirt hung from its back; her panties and bra were in the bathroom: a clear indication that none of her clothes had been torn off quickly or violently. Tough to say whether she'd stripped or been stripped before or after she'd been stunned. A cold-blooded murderer could have arranged all her clothes. Once she was undressed, still dazed, her ankles had been bound with a silk scarf and her legs secured to the footboard with Vieira's belt, while her arms had been tied to the headboard with T-shirts from her dresser drawers. From the way the sheet was twisted, it seemed she'd regained consciousness before dying. The detail of the panties and the bra in the bathroom suggested that Magali had come into the room completely naked, probably after having washed up in preparation for a sexual encounter, or simply to go to sleep. The lack of semen could be due to the use of a condom or to lack of penetration.

Espinosa had heard of cases of men reacting violently to impotence. But this reaction seemed a bit over the top. If a man couldn't get it up, the most common response was to make excuses. Or, ashamed, he could beat a hasty retreat. In some cases he might even attack the woman, in extreme cases with a knife; but the common denominator was that these were all immediate emotional reactions, timid or enraged, but always in the service of momentary impulses. Whoever had attacked Magali had done so in three distinct stages, and that couldn't be considered impulsive. The aggressor had applied the gas. He had carefully tied her arms and legs to the bed, then stuck her head into a plastic bag and tied it around her neck. Espinosa couldn't conceive of this as an out-of-control emotional reaction. It was more like the behavior of a meticulous pervert. It didn't match Vieira, or at least not the Vieira Espinosa knew.

He preferred not to tell Vieira immediately that his wallet had been located, though not recovered. He wanted to avoid telling him over the phone that it was being used by a Copacabana sleazebag to extort money from drug users, which might inspire him to try to capture the criminal himself, something Espinosa wanted to avoid at all costs. He called in the middle of the morning; Vieira answered panting.

"Espinosa, my man, you've caught me at a delicate moment. I'm trying to tie my shoelaces and I'm not sure whether I should lean over or lift my leg. No matter which way I do it I can't reach my shoes."

"You could hire a shoelace tier, or wear moccasins. You can buy long-handled shoehorns that are perfect for them."

"Damn, Espinosa, are you making fun of my age?"

"Not your age, your belly."

"Shit, I've got nothing to say to that. But you didn't call to talk about my stomach."

"We found your I.D."

"No shit, Espinosa! Finally you bring me some good news."

"Not that good. We found it, but we didn't get it."

"What the fuck do you mean? If you found it, why didn't you get it?"

Espinosa preferred not to explain over the telephone. Since it was almost lunchtime, he suggested they meet at a restaurant near Vieira's house, a modest establishment known for its rack of lamb. When he got there, Vieira was almost done with a bottle of beer and a plate of appetizers. They ordered more beer and the rack of lamb. After a few comments on the restaurant and the grilled lamb, Espinosa began the story of the wallet, omitting a few details but preserving the essentials. Vieira listened in silence, punctuating the narrative with a few obscenities, until Espinosa got to the part about the street kid being burned while he slept.

"Espinosa, I'll take care of it. I'll rip the balls off the son of a bitch."

"You're not going to do anything, Vieira. He's in hiding. If he thinks we're letting down our guard, he might stop by his apartment to get something, but if he thinks we're looking for him he'll vanish forever."

"What do you suggest?"

"We could use your contacts in the Copacabana underworld."

"Espinosa, that guy's new on the scene. Your description doesn't sound like anybody I know. Don't forget that I've been off duty for more than two years, long enough for new people to show up. But I do know what you call the underworld— even though I consider it as much of a world as any other— and there are a few people in it who owe me some favors."

"Vieira, I just don't want you to do anything on your own. Remember that you're mixed up in an investigation in which you're a prime murder suspect and that I'm in charge. I don't want things to get complicated for you . . . or for me."

"All right. You want my help but you don't want me to do anything without your authorization."

"Exactly."

"Okay. Now tell me something. What the fuck does this all have to do with Magali's death?"

"At first glance, the events seem to be independent, unrelated. It's hard to imagine what your dinner at the restaurant, your drunkenness, the loss of your wallet, and Magali's death could have to do with a man who found your wallet after the boy got rid of it, or with the boy who was killed while sleeping. On the other hand, everyone involved has something in common, though they're linked only very tenuously. As long as these links are still so tenuous, you remain the only suspect."

"I'd like to get my I.D. back as soon as possible. I don't like my name mixed up with drugs and extortion. If you don't object, I'll start getting my old contacts involved tonight. You said that the man had women in the square."

"I'm not sure, based on what the boy and the doormen in his building said, but I think that if he's not a pimp he's at least trying to get money off prostitutes."

"I can find out."

"Excellent. Then let's try to find out his name and whether

he has another pad. For now, let's get down to this rack of lamb."

They didn't discuss the case further over lunch. After dessert, during coffee, they came up with a simple plan. Neither of them mentioned Flor. Espinosa left Vieira at his door and took the bus to Magali's apartment. He wanted to check something out before going back to the station. Since he had the key, he went right to the ninth floor, apartment 918. The apartment had still not been emptied; it smelled closed, dead. He went through drawers, boxes, bags, and every inch of the furniture. By the end of the search, he had accumulated almost two dozen keys on the bed, some on key rings, some unattached. Some, obviously old, hadn't been used in a long time; others had clearly been employed recently. He put them all in a plastic bag and went to Flor's apartment. The doorman declared, in the tone of a doorman at a posh building, that Dona Flor was at home but didn't like to be disturbed without a call on the interphone. The police badge resolved this little discrepancy. Once he reached her floor, he had to ring the bell twice, the second time forcefully, before she opened the door. She was wearing a robe that struck a perfect balance between revelation and allusion.

"Officer, what a nice surprise. Please come in. Is this a professional visit?"

"On my part, yes."

"What a shame—I'm free all afternoon."

"But I won't take up more than ten minutes of it."

"Again, what a shame. If that's the way you're going to be, what can I do?"

"I'd just like to clarify one detail. You and Magali were close friends. So close that she left you her man as an inheritance."

"Officer—"

"Don't worry, it's just a clarification and not a value judgment; besides, I'm only repeating your own words. But if you were so close that you had a key to her apartment, I can only guess that she had a key to your apartment."

"Of course. We had the keys to each other's apartment, just in case."

"Right. And I'm sure there was a case."

"Officer, what are you insinuating?"

"I'm not insinuating anything. I'm being as direct as possible. And to prove it, I'd like to try some of the keys I have in my pocket in your door."

Before she could say anything, Espinosa removed the little package of keys from his pocket. Flor waited in silence as he tried the keys one by one. Finally, when none of them worked, she said:

"If you'd just asked me, I could have saved you the effort. She didn't have my key. I took it back the night I found the body."

"Why did you do that?"

"Why? Picture this. Because I didn't want to leave the key to my apartment out there."

"It wasn't out there. It was in your friend's house. Besides which, taking something from a crime scene is an obstruction of justice."

"Listen, Officer. It was the key to my apartment. I didn't hide anything. I came out and told you that she had a copy. I just took my key back."

"And can you show me the copy you brought back?"

"It's somewhere around. I'm not sure where I put it."

"Try to remember. I'll wait."

After searching a minute or two Flor appeared with a key, which she presented with a triumphant air. It opened the door perfectly.

He stayed at the station late, trying to liquidate the mountain of paperwork he had started working through the night before. It seemed to arrive on his desk faster than he could discharge it. It was after seven-thirty when he got home. A message from Kika asked for news of the boy and inquired whether he felt like a pizza and a beer in the Largo do Machado; she asked him to leave her a message either way. Espinosa called and they agreed to meet at nine. The pizzeria, whose awning covered a few dozen tables and spread out across the wide sidewalk, was only about two blocks from where Kika lived. He got there a little before nine. Despite the December heat, a light breeze blew across the square.

Kika, looking especially pretty, walked up the sidewalk, her white T-shirt ending a few inches above and her jeans beginning a few inches below the most enchanting navel Espinosa could recall encountering. He—trying to look more relaxed than usual—wore a short-sleeved sport shirt untucked (the variation allowed him to hide the gun he had attached to his belt). It was their first meeting since the boy disappeared. Though the restaurant had an enclosed, air-conditioned section, they chose the sidewalk. It was clear to Espinosa that she hadn't proposed the meeting to find out about the kid; she could have done *that* on the phone. And her selection of a restaurant near her house, far from the scene of Saturday's events, gave this second meeting a different feel, which was also obvious from her smile, her gaze, the way she moved her hand toward his.

"You don't look like a cop," she said, after studying Espinosa's face.

"Should I take that as a compliment?"

"Sorry. It's just that, like most people, when I think of cops I think of cave dwellers wearing shirts unbuttoned almost to their belt, hairy chests, thick gold chains, big rings on their fingers, bracelets, manicured nails, and a gruff, low-class voice; and when you opened the door on Saturday night I thought you looked like my art history professor."

"And your art history professor doesn't look like a cave-dwelling, hairy-chested, open-shirted . . ."

"Not at all. He's almost as good-looking and charming as you."

It occurred to Espinosa that this was one of the times when a cop should be wearing a bulletproof jacket: a sentence like that, point-blank, was fatal, at least for a nontroglodyte representative of the law. He had to restrain himself from fiddling with the salt shaker and the toothpick dispenser and the bottle of oil and everything else on the table. But women know when they've struck to the marrow.

"I'm the one who should be saying things like that to you."

"And why don't you?"

"You're beautiful, infinitely better looking than my professor of legal philosophy, and you have a navel that proves beyond the shadow of a doubt not only that God exists but that he's a sculptor."

She beamed with happiness; the waiter brought them back to earth.

The conversation veered off into less personal avenues. After comparing Catete and Copacabana, talking about painting and painters, the question surfaced:

"How did someone like you end up in the police?"

It wasn't the first time he'd been asked the question, which always sounded pejorative to him, though he knew that in this case it reflected her positive feelings about him. He knew the unedited version would read something like: "How did an honest, decent, well-educated, literate guy like you end up in an indecent, corrupt, stupid institution like the police force?"

Despite the inherent compliment of the first part, he didn't agree with the second. To his mind, the police force was an institution that acted as a border between social order and crime, just like a psychiatric hospital separated and articulated the difference between sanity and madness. The two worlds were not mutually exclusive but contiguous, or even super-imposed. Madness and crime did not come from a foreign world but from powers within man himself. Both were our intimates. People could try to ignore them, or they could con-front them. As an institution confronting them, the police maintained a dangerous intimacy with crime.

The best response he could muster was: "I went into the police because I wanted to get married."

"What?"

"That's right. I was finishing my law degree and was in love with a fellow student. The closest thing I could get to a job was an unpaid internship at a law firm. Then I saw an announcement that the police force was giving priority to peo-ple with law degrees. I took the test, got in, joined the force, and got married. The marriage ended a few years later, but I stayed in the police. Just like that."

"Do you have any children?"

"I have a son, a teenager, who lives in the United States. I get pictures of him at Christmastime. The first ones came with sweet messages on the back, but the more recent ones only have one sentence, the place, and the date."

"That's too bad."

"Maybe for me. For him, I don't know. Now he's more Amer-ican than Brazilian. And you? Have you ever been married?"

"No. And I don't have any kids. I came close to both, but it wasn't intense enough to go ahead with. Now I'm not sure if marriage and kids are worth the trouble. Does that sound shocking to you?"

"Not in the least."

"Great, because if it had it might have ruined my appetite."

When they left the restaurant, it was almost midnight, and what was left of Espinosa's reason signaled to him that they'd had enough to drink to render problematic any continuation of the evening's program. Not that love and alcohol were incompatible, but for a first encounter—and one that neither hoped would be the last—a modicum of sobriety was needed. They had enough sobriety left to walk arm in arm to her building, but not enough to guard against further acts and words. It was better not to risk it. And once more they said farewell with a kiss—much more amorous than the first—and promised to meet again.

Espinosa thought it was best to leave his car in the Largo do Machado and get a taxi home. On the way, he wondered if the excessive alcohol consumption—not something he (or, he thought, she) was prone to—hadn't been a strategy for avoiding premature complications. It was the most complex, perhaps the only, thought he managed to form before the driver asked which side of Peixoto he wanted. "Drop me at the one closest to my house," he answered. That was when he realized he was truly drunk.

He got to the station a little later than usual. Chaves, the detective in charge of staying in touch with the door-man of the building on the Avenida Copacabana, came to talk to him.

"Espinosa, the guy came by in the morning, grabbed a few things, and left; the night doorman said he didn't let us know because it all happened so fast and he didn't have time to go out and call."

"What was he carrying when he left?"

"A travel bag. He didn't ask the doorman anything and didn't say where he was going."

"What time was this?"

"The doorman says it was between two-thirty and three in the morning. Should we go after him? We could get in touch with the rancher who owns the apartment."

"No. Let's let him think we've forgotten about him. I get the feeling that he doesn't know who he's running from. Look, let's suppose that he kidnapped the boy after chasing him down the Avenida Atlântica. But then let's say that he stopped there, that he wasn't worried about the kid anymore, that he just wanted to give him a scare. In that case, he didn't kidnap or kill the kid. So there wouldn't be any reason for the police to go after him. He knows someone's after him, but he doesn't know who or why."

"And the boy's disappearance?" Chaves asked.

"It could have been voluntary. Remember that the hypothesis of kidnapping depends on the boy's story and the painter's, who only saw the man from across the street, on a sidewalk full of people. Maybe the man laid off the kid at that very moment, and the rest, the kidnapping, is all a fantasy. The relationship between a street kid and a cop is ambivalent. He could have wondered whether he was really being protected. What would happen after the girl and I went home? Were we going to take him with us? The most we could have done was hand him over to a home for abandoned minors, and that was certainly the last thing in the world he'd want. He preferred to run."

"Do you really think that's what happened?"

"I do. No one who has grabbed a child out from under the nose of the police and then killed him would show up to get fresh clothes in his apartment. He's not running from us. Maybe he doesn't even suspect we're after him."

"So who's he running from?"

"I don't know, and I don't think he does either. See if you can find out the full name and address of the owner of apartment 607 from the building management."

The bad taste in his mouth and the package of antacids in his pocket made him remember the car he had left parked near the restaurant the night before. After he went to the Largo do Machado to get the car, he decided to go see Clodoaldo. If he was in fact the one who'd given his name to the kid, he might know where the kid was hiding out. Since the street teacher's place of work wasn't an educational establishment but the streets themselves, it wasn't always easy to find him; the same could be said for looking for a specific street kid. Espinosa knew it was a question of patience. Even though they moved around a lot, street kids weren't exactly nomads. They moved within a restricted area. A Copacabana street kid didn't go downtown or to Leblon; in those places he was a foreigner. They usually stuck to well-demarcated territories, relatively circumscribed, unless there was a problem, which would lead them to seek out their families or institutions like the children's shelter, which lay outside their domain.

Espinosa started the search at two of these shelters, hoping that someone would know where Clodoaldo was. The only lead he got was that he had been hanging out one set day a week on the Avenida Atlântica, around Posto 5, near a discotheque. The kids knew to look for him there on that day, and knew that he would help them. No one was sure exactly which was the designated day of the week, though.

Today was a Wednesday, the middle of the week: a good day for regular periodic meetings, if such considerations applied to street urchins and their teachers. Apparently Clodoaldo spent all day with the kids. For some time the group had met in the Praça do Lido, but for reasons unknown they had moved their meetings to the area around the discotheque.

Coincidence or not, it was the same place where the boy had disappeared.

Before parking the car, Espinosa cruised the streets near the disco where the meetings were supposed to take place, but neither Clodoaldo nor any street kids were to be seen. He drove along the beach to see if they were there, came back, and stopped the car in front of the disco. The attendant, from a distance, had been pointing out a parking place. As he approached the car, Espinosa asked if he'd seen Clodoaldo, the street teacher. No; he hadn't shown up for a few days.

"What day does he usually come?"

"I'm not sure, but I think it's Thursday or Friday. Are you a friend of his?"

"I am. If he comes by, tell him Espinosa wants to talk to him."

"Espinosa?"

"That's right." He gave the attendant a ten so he wouldn't forget his name.

"You don't want me to wax your car, sir?"

"No thanks. It can stay unpresentable."

Espinosa guessed that Clodoaldo must come on Thursday; if it was Friday, the day of the chase, the boy would have gone for him instead of Espinosa. Around a bench in the square, sitting in the sand, under a tree, always in the open air, Clodoaldo and the kids talked about their problems—usually strictly practical ones related to day-to-day survival. Espinosa had heard that they talked about their difficulties with their families, about threats from juvenile delinquents, beggars, private security guards, and cops, and about their dreams. Whoever saw them from a distance would think that the street teacher—a short, muscular man with Indian features and a carrot-colored bowl cut—was a low-class charmer of abandoned children. And they wouldn't be far off. His many years of working on the street had made Clodoaldo respected by boys and girls, by the institutions that supported them, and by the police. The kids affectionately called him "Clodô." But only them, nobody else. When a new detective had once addressed him as such in a street meeting, Clodoaldo, whose voice was surprisingly low for his size, replied, "That name was a gift from the kids. You can't have it." He was capable of the greatest kindness and the greatest violence.

When Espinosa spotted Clodoaldo the next day, the man's orange hair reminded him of a life raft against the blue summer sea. He was seated beneath an almond tree on the strip dividing the two lanes of traffic on the Avenida Atlântica. In his hands he had a big bag of bread, which he was dividing among the ten or so children. He didn't interrupt his speech when the officer approached the group, but extended the bag to offer a warm roll and continued talking about a shelter that they could use. Not until the end of his talk did he make the introduction: "This is Officer Espinosa. He's a cop, but you can trust him like you trust me." Espinosa thanked him and sat on the cement ring surrounding the tree's roots. For almost an hour he listened in silence to the conversation, the topics of which ranged from problems with personal hygiene to the boy who was murdered while he slept. They were afraid it could happen again. At that moment Clodoaldo invited Espinosa to participate in the discussion.

Espinosa explained that he was from the Twelfth Precinct

on the Rua Hilário de Gouveia, and that they could always find him there if they needed him. All they had to do was go to the reception desk and ask for Officer Espinosa. Someone asked if children could come into the station; Espinosa answered that they didn't need to come in, that he would come down to meet them. Then, not without a certain anxiety, he told them, minus a few details, the story of the boy who had supposedly been kidnapped, from the time he was chased by the man up until his disappearance when they were walking to his car last Friday night, close to where they were now sitting.

"There's no proof, or even any hint, that it was the same man who killed your friend. For now, the man has disappeared. He knows that the police want to interrogate him, but he could think it's for some other reason. The boy I mentioned is the only one who can identify him, and the man knows it; if he's the same one who killed your friend on the sidewalk, then the boy's life could be in danger."

"More danger than we live in every day?" The question came from the boy seated next to Clodoaldo; he was a little older and was clearly the leader of the group.

"I think so. Let's say he's in extra danger."

"And what can we do?"

"Help me find the boy and, maybe, help me find the man."

After a few kids offered their views on the subject, Clodoaldo asked for a moment alone with Espinosa. As soon as the kids moved away, the officer asked:

"So? What do you think?"

"I knew the boy who was killed. His name was Washington. That wasn't the work of a group. It was someone acting on his own, but it doesn't sound like the guy you described, a small-time pimp."

"Do you know who he might be?"

"No. Without a picture it's hard to say; it could be a lot of people."

"That's why we have to find the boy."

"Him we can help you find . . . if he's still alive."

"He has to be."

"It's possible. If he was dead we or you would have heard. As for our help, don't count on anything very organized. The kids can help, but not in a very systematic way. If they feel threatened they'll stop immediately. As for me, I'll do whatever I can."

Most of the kids had wandered off. The three who were left were examining a hubcap they'd found near the curb. The sun that came through the leaves of the tree projected hundreds of little circles onto the paving stones. It was one more in a series of splendid summer mornings. It was hard for Espinosa to connect the sight before his eyes with the murder of a boy who had barely entered puberty. He said farewell to Clodoaldo with a handshake and waved to the children.

If the owner was enough of a friend to let the man live in his apartment on the Avenida Copacabana, he was also enough of a friend to hide him for a while on his ranch. That was the main reason they didn't try to call and instead opted to send an agent to the region around Campos. If they needed it, they could get backup from the local police.

Espinosa, for his part, decided to attack another side of the case and brought Flor in to "lend a few clarifications" (as he instructed the bearer of the order to say) about the events leading to her friend's death. Flor answered that she could not come until the next day; it would interfere with today's business. "The police are there to protect honest working people, not to get in their way" was the observation with which she sent away the detective, the same one who had gone to fetch her the first time. "I was waiting for her to say that she would only appear in the presence of her lawyer," he commented.

And that was exactly what happened. The next morning, Flor swooshed in triumphantly accompanied by a lawyer who, in the opinion of those present, wasn't old enough to have a high school diploma. He did. And he wasn't stupid. Espinosa couldn't accomplish what he had hoped to and was forced to dismiss her after a series of questions that led nowhere. She said good-bye, adding that if they wanted to see her, she didn't require an official summons. Espinosa sat wondering where Flor had gotten the lawyer.

He went out to eat something in the neighborhood. Before settling on a place, he walked a good ways, thinking about the little lawyer. The lawyer had prevented Espinosa from capitalizing on the nervousness everyone feels when summoned to a police station. Not that Flor had given any signs, the first time she'd been there, of being prone to nervousness, but the lawyer's presence meant that they wouldn't be able to push her any further today. Espinosa thought about himself at the lawyer's age, trying to enter the force "for more financial security and to be able to get married." The security remained, but the marriage didn't. Espinosa felt like a bandit.

When he snapped out of his reverie, he was on the Avenida Copacabana, almost in front of the Galeria Menescal. His thoughts about the young lawyer were still spinning around his head, along with more practical ones, including the sensation that someone was once again watching him. It was practically the same spot he'd felt it last time. He let his gaze wander distractedly through the arcade, which at that hour was being traversed by hundreds of people moving in both directions; once again he was unable to single anyone out. Instead of taking the Avenida Copacabana route, he returned to the station along Barata Ribeiro, which had fewer pedestrians, stopping in front of a few shop windows, even entering a clothes store, in the hopes of surprising his stalker on the way out. No one. Maybe the young lawyer had messed with his head; even in the best of circumstances, his intimate daydreams could rear up in the light of day in the middle of Copacabana—though he felt more invaded than threatened. He reflected that it would be the height of paradox to be invaded by his own self. No doubt it was all a figment of his hyperactive imagination.

As the afternoon approached the evening, he found himself wanting to walk down the Avenida Atlântica to the place where Kika showed her pictures; he would use the walk as an excuse to have a look around the area, though he wasn't sure what he expected to find, unless the man or the boy was putting in an appearance to fortify his professional esteem. But he didn't follow his whim; he knew that neither the man nor the boy would be there. As for Kika, the best thing was to bear in mind that times had changed and that for a young woman, especially a young woman artist, to go out to dinner with a man meant nothing more than the obvious: that she wanted company. But he let his thoughts take their own course. It occurred to him that this was what was meant by his "contemporaries"—people who weren't contemporaries of the time they lived in. Some were contemporaries of a time that was still to come, and they still had hope; others were contemporaries of a moment that had passed, and such people could do nothing more than live off their memories. Espinosa believed that there was one further complication: his body, his tastes, his clothes, his outlook were perfectly contemporary to the time he was living in, but his system of signs—the code people used to navigate through the world—belonged to a time that had already passed. He felt like a computer from an earlier generation, running on old, outdated software.

As more days passed without any news of the boy, Espinosa became increasingly convinced that he had sought shelter somewhere else, out of the reach of heroes and villains. He knew it wasn't easy to make a corpse disappear, even for professionals, and he was fairly certain that whoever was responsible for the boy's disappearance, if anyone was responsible, was an amateur. Some street children returned periodically to their homes to contribute whatever they'd gathered in the street to their families; the street, for them, wasn't a house but a workplace. That could certainly be the case for this boy.

Stretched out on the sofa in his living room, with the lights off, Espinosa alternately contemplated the blinds and the building on the other side of the square. He was fully aware that the answering machine was blinking behind him; he had avoided listening to his messages. There would surely be one from Kika inviting him to come out to the Avenida Atlântica to keep her company. "Maybe you'll bring me luck," she would say at the end of the phone call, and he would head out to his car like a madman.

Around nine, tired of looking at nothing, he decided to give in to the messages. There were two from Vieira and one from the bank notifying him that his car insurance was expiring the next week. Nothing from Kika. He felt frustrated, angy, and resigned, in that order, after he consulted his saved messages one more time. He mentally reviewed their last meeting and decided yet again that everything had been perfect. All the ingredients for positive future developments had been there, but nothing had happened: no message, no word, no satisfaction. It was what he always said to himself, that his fantasies were the only reality that existed for him; things happened in his head, not in reality. He still didn't understand, though, why he was frustrated and angry. Of the feelings assaulting him at the moment, the one that made him most uncomfortable was the resignation, which among feelings was about as dignified as bad breath on a nun.

It was a few minutes before he focused on the messages from Vieira. The first said that he had gotten some information from the manager of one of the clubs, and that he was waiting for his orders (this part spoken with an ironic tone); the second said that if he waited any longer he would lose his lead and that in the meantime he would conduct some preliminary investigations near his house and the Thirteenth Precinct. Espinosa picked up the phone immediately. Vieira was no longer at home.

It wouldn't take him more than ten minutes to reach the station. It would be overdoing it to call the on-duty officer to ask him to keep Vieira there in the event that he showed up; he was only a retired policeman looking for his stolen I.D. What seemed insufferable was sitting at home staring at the blinds while the world, baked by the summer heat and invigorated by the Christmas spirit, went on outside. He decided to look for his colleague.

Before his retirement, Vieira had been posted for almost three years to the Thirteenth Precinct, only a few blocks from his apartment. The station was in front of the Galeria Alaska, which connected the Avenida Atlântica and the Avenida Copacabana, and which until recently had held the highest concentration of the most varied fauna of the Copacabana underworld. Vieira's intimacy with the area could have made it the starting point for his investigation. A few blocks away, Kika was showing her paintings.

Espinosa stopped by the station first. Only the on-duty officer, out of everyone there, knew who Vieira was, but he hadn't seen him in over a year. Espinosa left the station and went through the Galeria Alaska toward the Avenida Atlântica. It hadn't been so long ago that the cinema, the nightclubs, and the little dives that had made the place famous had metamorphosed into an evangelical church and tasteful boutiques. The people around at night were no longer prostitutes, cruising homosexuals, transvestites, junkies, and dealers, but believers with their Bibles searching for God—the devil had presumably stopped paying. The years of close cohabitation with the police station, however, had given the local businesspeople, the doormen, and the clients an acute ability for spotting a cop anywhere, so that when Espinosa got to the Avenida Atlântica, after passing through the arcade, he was sure that everyone knew that he was a police officer. Not finding Vieira there, he walked down the beach to the place where Kika usually was, taking a sidelong approach; he wanted to see her before she spotted him. He wasn't entirely sure how he would greet her, but the closer he got the more confident he became of the inevitability of the meeting. He could see her figure—tall, slim, gesticulating broadly—half a block away; she had already spotted him before he could choose an approach. A surreptitious arrival was now impossible. She crossed the street toward him, weaving between the cars, and then hugged him affectionately.

Kika was radiant because she had sold a picture, which, she said, covered her Christmas expenses as well as her part of the rent on the house in Catete.

"Let's go celebrate after I finish up here. Maybe with you nearby I'll sell another painting."

She didn't. But they talked for almost two hours about any subject that could be covered in the middle of a little art fair on a busy sidewalk. Their previous conversation, in the Largo do Machado, had taken place in an area of less than a square meter. For Espinosa, a bar table was an almost enclosed space, very intimate, despite the surrounding multitudes. On the beach there were no spatial restrictions like the bar table, so they could allow themselves little movements and twists and turns that both freed them and tied their bodies together. The date concluded almost monastically, on the glassed-in veranda of a restaurant on the avenue. They hadn't wanted the evening to end on a gloomy note, but as they were sitting there in the wee hours, they saw, through the window, Vieira hurrying down the street, only a few meters from them and moving away from the direction of his house. Espinosa threw some money on the table, asked Kika to wait, and stood up to leave the restaurant. A few more seconds were lost when the occupants of the next table rose at the same time, blocking his passage. When he reached the street, he couldn't get Vieira's attention. He ran to the nearest corner but couldn't spot the retired cop on the Avenida Atlântica or on the intersecting street. He climbed on top of a cement bench, but even so he didn't see anyone who looked like Vieira; he ran to the corner of the first street parallel to the beach, but that effort was just as fruitless. Judging from the way Vieira had passed the restaurant, it didn't look like he was heading anywhere in particular; he looked, rather, like he was fleeing or chasing someone. Espinosa went back to the corner on the beach and walked two or three blocks in the direction he'd seen Vieira running. Nothing. It was the same corner where the boy had disappeared. He thought he'd start calling it the Bermuda Triangle. He returned to the restaurant to explain his hasty departure to Kika. She was no longer there. He went home the same way he'd left, on foot and alone.

Before going to sleep, for more than an hour, he called Vieira's house.

PART 3

Espinosa awoke tormented by the image of Vieira running down the sidewalk. He stayed in bed for a while, trying to make sense of the previous evening's events. He made his coffee, stuck a few slices of bread into the toaster, picked up the paper at the door, and debated whether to ring Vieira before or after reading it. Save for exceptional circumstances, he didn't bother people on Saturday or Sunday mornings, but in this case he could justify the call. The toast popped up just as the call went through; he stayed on the line. It rang more than twenty times. It occurred to him that perhaps Vieira had gone on a binge and couldn't hear anything. He also imagined other things. After two hours, he called again, with the same result; he could no longer imagine that his friend had been out on a bender; he started to really worry.

He decided to stop by his colleague's apartment right after lunch, but he hadn't managed to leave before the phone rang. Someone who introduced himself as Joelmar, the policeman stationed in the Hospital Miguel Couto, asked him to come to the men's ward at the request of someone named Vieira, who said he was a police officer. Espinosa left immediately, without even asking how the patient was doing—if he had managed to give Espinosa's name and phone number he could at least talk. Saturday afternoon had just joined the events of Friday night.

"What happened?" The question was directed toward the resident who accompanied him to the ward.

"He was attacked, probably by more than one person . . . such cowards. He's not a young man."

"How is he doing?"

"Pretty beat up, but nothing serious. At his age it's hard to predict how they'll recover from hard blows to the head. In any case, we'll have to run some tests on him in a few weeks."

"Can he be discharged?"

"From a clinical standpoint, he's ready, but you'd have to take responsibility for him.... He's not in a condition to be by himself."

Vieira had lots of cuts and bruises on his face; one eye was so swollen it looked like it wanted to abandon his head entirely. He had a cut lip and some broken dentures, and his nose, along with the open eye, formed one big blob; his body was black-and-blue. He had been admitted to the hospital in the morning, brought by a police car, and they hadn't wanted to release him before making sure that there were no internal fractures. They had also been keeping him because the only number they'd found in his wallet was his own, and no one had picked up.

Just after four in the afternoon, they entered Vieira's apartment. Espinosa helped him stretch out in bed, then placed the analgesics and creams on the bedside table. Before he could ask any questions Vieira started to talk.

"Espinosa, it was the son of a bitch we're looking for.... If not him personally, someone acting for him.... I didn't see anything.... I turned the first corner, and when I turned the second, before I could see anything, they were already on me."

"They? There was more than one?"

"I'm not completely sure; most of the blows were directly to my face.... To protect myself I put my hands over my eyes, I was afraid of going blind.... It could have been just one ... I can't say for sure."

"What were you doing?"

He felt terrible asking such questions at a time like that.

Vieira looked awful; it was hard for him to speak. He had to pause every few words to touch his wounded lip, but Espinosa needed to know what had happened.

"I was waiting for you to call . . . it took you too long. . . . I'd been warned that the fake officer was trying to sell cocaine in the Galeria Alaska. When I got there, he was inside that old cinema that's now an evangelical church. With the help of one of the girls, who's an informer and who'd seen his face, I went in and tried to find him. It was packed. After a few minutes, I noticed some movement in a row near the exit. I sent the girl away and went over to the place; the guy noticed and ran out. I went after him, but no matter how fast I went he still kept a good way ahead. When he got to the sidewalk along the beach he went one block and then turned onto the first street toward the Avenida Copacabana, walking really fast, always looking over his shoulder. I think he was running from me, I'm not sure. He turned one corner, then another, then another, then it happened, I couldn't tell how many they were." He paused to rest and organize his thoughts. After a few seconds, he went on: "The guy really isn't very bright. He takes the powder from the addicts and then immediately sells it for lower than its market value. He doesn't even know who he's selling it to. He won't last long. The only thing I want is to get to him before the traffickers do."

"For now you're not in a state to get anyone. You were lucky that nothing worse happened to you; no matter what, you're going to be out of commission for a few days. I'm going to go buy a few things. Try not to walk if you don't have to; your leg has an ugly wound on it. The guy must have beaten you with an iron bar, as well as with his fists."

"Espinosa."

"What is it?"

"Bring me a mirror. I want to see what my face looks like. . . .

I know it'd be hard to make it any worse, but I want to see how it is."

Espinosa brought him a two-sided mirror he found in the bathroom, the only portable one. Vieira preferred to look in the magnifying side. He was most upset about his broken dentures.

"That's fixable, just like everything else," said Espinosa, trying to cheer him up.

"Espinosa."

"What?"

"I want to call Flor and ask her to come take care of me. The notebook with phone numbers is on top of the table in the living room."

Espinosa left him an hour later, convinced that Vieira felt not self-pity but hatred, which can be as powerful as love. What most intrigued him was the amount of violence employed against someone who wasn't, after all, much of a threat. A small-time lowlife chased by an old man wouldn't have risked attacking him so violently in the middle of the street when he could have simply run faster and hidden. And if he suspected that his pursuer was a policeman, there would have been even more reason to try to escape rather than to assault him. There was a distinct possibility that Vieira had been beaten by mistake.

Espinosa couldn't say what it was about Flor that made him so uncomfortable and so intrigued, in the same proportion and intensity; he couldn't even claim that though she was a hooker she had an infantile ingenuousness, or that she was smart enough to transform her sexual sophistication into innocent artlessness. She wasn't extraordinarily beautiful, but her beauty did turn the heads of men and women, perhaps because it wasn't created only from the usual elements of beauty. In her beauty there was something demonic. The result was more alchemical than aesthetic, and its effect was uncommon. Flor disquieted and attracted him, not only sexually, though sex was the way her fascinating alchemy expressed itself. But Flor presented herself not as an answer to his desires but as a question posed to him, inviting him somewhere he could never really identify, modest but shameless, like a girl in a dirty magazine.

"I'm impressed. Let's see: you worry that something happened to your friend because she doesn't answer your phone calls all afternoon; at night, using a copy of the key to her apartment, you open the door and find your friend—'sister,' as you say—dead, tied to the bed, with a plastic bag around her head, and you calmly remember to get the key to your own apartment, kept in a place you immediately recall, and only then do you leave, scared, and call the doorman and the police."

"Well, that's exactly what happened."

"You didn't take the key back before she was killed, during a fight about who would get to stay with Vieira, for instance?"

"Are you crazy? Don't tell me that even during a conversation on a Sunday, visiting a friend who's been hurt, I'm going to need my lawyer."

"I'm sorry.... You're right. I won't bring it up again ... at least for today."

They were a block away from Vieira's apartment, in a restaurant with food by the kilo, buying their Sunday lunch. The conversation had started in the elevator, a few seconds after they had left Vieira in his bed. Never before had an elevator seemed so small; Espinosa felt that the least movement would make them bump into each other. Flor was wearing a light dress made out of something like silk and held over her shoulders by two slim ribbons; it showed off every curve of her body, completely free beneath the material. Espinosa started to talk out of pure nervousness. The distance to the ground floor seemed interminable. He had brought up the subject because he couldn't manage to think about anything besides the body alluded to by the cut of the dress; once he brought it up he couldn't stop himself. He could let go of it only when Flor reacted. They didn't exchange a single word on the way back. They took up the conversation the second they got back in the elevator.

"I was completely terrified. When I opened the door to the apartment the light was on. . . . She was tied to the bed. . . . The plastic bag . . . it looked like she no longer had a face. . . . I got so scared and I don't know why, but the first thing I thought of was the key."

"Why worry about the key?"

"I was scared."

"Of what?"

"Scared . . . that's all."

The elevator arrived on Vieira's floor.

While Flor helped Vieira eat (he really didn't need help for that), Espinosa opened a beer and sat in an armchair he'd brought in from the living room. Flor was completely focused on her task; the outside world lingered in parentheses.

He could describe what was so attractive about her in detail. What he couldn't say was what it was about her that made him so uncomfortable. Perhaps he should formulate the question another way: why was he so uncomfortable with her attractiveness? The first response that came to mind was: because Flor was a hooker. Or did that make her even more attractive?

He thought that such ideas were leading him down tortuous

paths; those weren't the kinds of questions to resolve rationally. Besides, a splitting headache made reasoning impossible, even in its most basic form. Experience had taught him that the best way to get through moments like this one was to take two aspirin and beat a discreet retreat.

He went home on foot, hoping that the walk would help him concentrate; he had a lot to think over. The second half of the trip took place under a late-afternoon summer rain, which soaked his clothes and shoes. Though it only touched his body he felt that it was also cleansing his soul, and he arrived home renewed, careful to remove his clothes and shoes before stepping off the doormat.

The detective sent to the Campos area came back empty-handed. Not only had nobody at the ranch of Dr. Elói Azevedo—this was the name of the apartment's owner—seen anybody from out of town, but Dr. Elói himself and his wife had been off in São Paulo for almost a month "to put some bridges in his heart," as the ranch's foreman put it.

It had been almost ten days since the boy's disappearance, and still no light had been shed on the matter. With each passing day, the initial events became more thickly and darkly shadowed, blurring the outlines of the facts. The links between the events had become tenuous and the people involved had themselves disappeared from the scene or taken on other roles, diluting a story so unfocused that it could hardly even be called a story. On the one hand, there was Magali's murder, and on the other the boy's disappearance, a disappearance that, from a police standpoint, was not even considered relevant. Espinosa knew that for the police none of the facts was relevant: in their eyes the murders of prostitutes and street children were nonevents. At the most they could inspire some police officer who had a relationship with the victim, but they were incapable of mobilizing even a minimal fraction of the force itself. In the case of the boy, Espinosa was galvanized by the idea that he might still be alive, but after ten days he had hoped to have a little more than banal, inconsistent musings to go on. Over the course of the day, with the release of Magali's apartment and its return to its owner, there was one more surprise added to the clues he already had: the apartment was not in the name of Magali (or Lucimar) but Vieira.

"Damn it, Espinosa, what do you expect? Do you think people rent apartments to whores? Renting in my name was only natural; the owner has almost half of the building and loved the idea of having a cop renting the place."

"Vieira, I'm not judging you. I just don't want any more surprises."

"There aren't any more. I didn't think that the apartment's being in my name was a big deal."

"How's your face?"

"It couldn't be worse than it was. The guy gave me a free face-lift. When the swelling goes down I'll look gorgeous."

Espinosa hung up convinced that there were more surprises in store for him. After all, he liked Vieira: his earthy bluntness, his lack of arrogance, and his ability to get mixed up with evil without being polluted personally, or at least without being polluted mortally. Espinosa considered himself a member of a club that seemed to be shrinking day by day—a club of people who believed that honor was a value worth defending—and within that club, there was an even more rarefied circle for those who believed that honor didn't depend on race, creed, religion, or profession, who believed that even a cop, even a banker or a politician, could be honorable.

The guiding principle of the police force was no different from the one that directed society: if the victim was important, the investigation was immediate and the solution quick; if the victim was unimportant, the investigation took its time on its inexorable course toward the file of unsolved cases, unless the criminal was caught in flagrante delicto. Hookers weren't important. Magali had been important to Vieira, and probably to nobody else. Lucimar may have been important to someone when she was a child, but that person died as soon as Magali was born, or survived only in her dinners with Vieira. The fact was, no one besides Vieira and Flor had missed her, and even they didn't seem too worried about solving the case. And then there was Espinosa, probably the only one who hadn't definitively buried Magali-Lucimar, though he had seen her only once, face twisted in pain, suffocated in a plastic bag. He could have let the case die. But that wasn't his way.

Espinosa thought it was curious how Magali and Lucimar occupied, in Vieira's mind, two separate and independent lives. Even when they'd fucked, he hadn't been with Magali but with Lucimar. His near indifference to the death of his lover could be explained only by this schism: Magali was the one who had been killed. Lucimar had only disappeared, left the scene temporarily, and until she came back Vieira would pass the time with Flor.

It occurred to Espinosa that what he considered Vieira's lack of interest in discovering Magali's murderer could also be interpreted as a realistic acceptance of the facts. A thirst for justice or revenge had probably played a role in his life back when he had hope and plans for the future, but now Vieira's life consisted of moments; justice and revenge required time and energy, both of which were becoming increasingly rare in the life of the ex-policeman. Magali's legacy to Flor, the proof of her supreme love for a woman, could not be written off in the name of a fidelity that he probably had never had even with his own wife; more than an inheritance, Vieira seemed to consider Flor a gift of love and fantasized that Magali had died only so that he could be with Flor. The truth was, however, that nothing could justify a lengthy investigation; a murder had been committed and it had fallen to him, Espinosa, to investigate and find the murderer, no matter what he thought of Vieira's enchantment with Flor. The only clue he had was a collection of fingerprints found on the plastic bag, among them those of Flor and the victim; the rest of the impressions had not been identified. The little can of Mace had yielded no usable prints. As for the motive, whom did Magali's death benefit? The idea that Flor or Vieira had killed Magali to stay together was absurd. He would have to find someone else who had known Magali, and a starting point was the night doorman, who hadn't come to the funeral. Espinosa looked for his name in his notes.

That night, after ten, Espinosa paid a visit to Ismael. He gave him half an hour to get settled into the reception desk, to plug in a little, antiquated black-and-white television he kept under the desk and prepare himself for the shift that would end at six o'clock the next morning. Through the glass door, Ismael's face, illuminated by the bluish light from the television screen, looked like a ghost in the dark hall of the building. Espinosa pressed the doorbell and got his attention. Unable to identify him, even from such a short distance, Ismael got up, visibly irritated. Before the doorman could say anything, Espinosa pressed his badge up against the glass.

"I'm sorry, Officer, I didn't recognize you," Ismael said while looking at the badge and opening the door.

"Good evening, Ismael."

"Good evening, sir."

He seemed to want to receive the officer appropriately, but there wasn't even another chair for Espinosa to take. They remained standing, leaning against the desk, upon which stood a Christmas tree not more than a foot tall, decorated with little silvery threads. The doorman switched off the television and turned on the hall light. For a few seconds, the only noise came from a little fan that was threatening, from on top of the desk, the precarious balance of the little tree.

"How long have you worked here?" Espinosa knew the answer and the doorman knew he knew, but it was a place to start.

"I've worked here almost five years."

"So you must have known Dona Magali pretty well."

"From the beginning. She moved in around the same time I started."

"And how did she act with you?"

"Sir, I'm only not saying she was a saint, God forgive me, because of her profession, but she was a marvelous person. She gave us presents every Christmas; when she got here late at night, she always had a little piece of candy, a chocolate..."

"Besides the occasional tip," Espinosa added.

"Every once in a while she would give a gratuity.... It was a pleasure."

"And because of her occupation, did many people come to see her?"

"Only when it wasn't the other officer's day, and even then it wasn't a lot of people. They had to be recommended."

"And when were those days?"

"Officer Vieira had his own schedule: he came on Wednesday afternoons, Friday nights, and I think she went to his house on Sundays."

"So on Mondays, Tuesdays, Thursdays, and Saturdays she had other men here?"

"Right. But like I said, it was only people who had been referred to her."

"I know. And girlfriends? Didn't any women ever visit?"

"There was Dona Flor. There was also Dona Vanessa, but she lives here in the building."

"What apartment does Dona Vanessa live in?"

"She lives in 803, but she went to visit some relatives for a few days. She was really shaken by Dona Magali's death; she even had to call a doctor. But she should be back soon."

"Do you get along with all the women in the building who share Dona Magali's profession?"

"I'm the night doorman, sir. But they know that I'm very religious and treat me with all due respect, just as I do them."

"And on that Friday night you didn't see her come back?"

"I saw her get out of the car with the other officer and meet Dona Flor in front of the building. They didn't stay long and soon all three of them left. Mr. Vieira was inebriated and couldn't manage to get out of the car; he was halfway in and halfway out. After they left I didn't see any of them again. When Dona Magali came back I was in my room. My stomach wasn't feeling very good that night and I'd had to leave the desk several times."

"That's fine, Ismael. Here's my card with my contact numbers. As soon as Dona Vanessa comes back from her vacation, ask her to call me; you don't need to tell her about our conversation."

A couple entered. She made a slight gesture with her head and arm that could have been a greeting or a signal. The doorman replied with a look as he stuck the card in his pocket. Ismael returned to his chair, and before Espinosa could close the glass door the television was already back on.

The distance to the Peixoto district was short; Espinosa crossed it on foot, contemplating the moral conflicts of a born-again doorman in a building so heavily populated by sinners. In spite of the heavy summer-evening air, announcing an imminent shower, he wasn't in much of a hurry, walking as if he had all the time in the world. Less than two weeks to go before Christmas. The season temporarily transformed the scene: it became cinematic, a kind of romantic noir, and the prostitutes, street kids, and dispossessed of all kinds looked like players in the cast. Not that they were outwardly transformed; they went about their business as usual. The change was extremely subtle; perhaps people saw their own pasts in a new light. For Espinosa, even this rearrangement was not completely conscious or accessible; it was as if the play of light, the shadows of forgotten facts that made up his own past, had shifted, creating relief and nuance where before there had only been flatness. Still, things happened at this time of year that didn't happen in other seasons. On Christmas Eve, the simple sight of an illuminated window cast a kind of spell; the yellowish light of a lampshade seen through the window of an apartment building became a flickering hearth. Around it, a traveler recently returned from distant lands narrated extraordinary exploits to a small group of friends. The hearth came from all those American and European films, where Christmas was always snowy and white, or from the stories of Somerset Maugham, where tales of the South Seas were recounted around an English fireplace. He didn't feel like an idiot ruminating along such lines because he knew he wasn't thinking logically but enjoying a semidelirious daydream (which wasn't to say that he believed logical thinking to be a by-product of reason). The first drops fell on him as soon as he'd crossed the square.

Flor was confused about Espinosa. On the one hand he was Vieira's friend; on the other, he was a policeman in charge of investigating her friend's death. On the two occasions she had been summoned to the station to provide clarifications, it was clear that the motive for the summons was not to strengthen or refresh their friendship. She considered this a shame, since she found the officer very attractive. His own attraction to her had become more obvious: his way of getting closer by distancing himself; the tension in the air whenever they found themselves alone; but above all the sparkle in his eyes, the same sparkle she'd seen in the eyes of the boys in Recife when they deposited on her windowsill crumpled banknotes wet with the sweat of their hands.

These thoughts crossed her mind as she helped Vieira into his bath. She had promised to come by every day, at the beginning of the evening, before the TV news, to help him with his bath and take care of the man she now considered her own. She'd had the idea of putting a little bench inside the shower so that he could bathe while seated; his body ached more than it had the first day. And in order not to get her clothes wet while she was helping him, she had asked his permission to do so in the nude.

The greatest intimacy they had experienced up to that point had been holding hands while walking through the streets of Copacabana. And suddenly this.

"Damn, angel, asking permission to take your clothes off? In front of me? Son of a bitch, I never thought I'd live to see the day."

"You don't want me to? Did I say something I shouldn't have?"

"Damn, Flor, of course not! A beautiful woman like you asking my permission to take her clothes off? Who would have thought? Men ought to get down on their knees to beg you to take your clothes off in front of them!"

"But that's them. You have every right. And you're injured; maybe you wouldn't want it."

"And there are still people who consider *hooker* a bad word."

Before helping Vieira to the bench, Flor tested the water temperature. She twisted the showerhead so the water would fall on his back and not on his scalp, which was bruised in several places. Then she removed her dress—she wasn't wearing a bra—and, after a consulting glance at him, her panties. Flor's youthful splendor contrasted with the tired, wounded body seated on the bench. Leaving the door to the shower open, Flor moved in and out, depending on what part of Vieira's body she needed to lather up. For balance, he leaned on her body, at first timidly and respectfully (he considered it the least he could do for a woman who asked permission to take her clothes off); but as the bath wore on, he began exploring the parts of her body within his reach. She wasn't bothered in the least by his shapeless, flaccid, potbellied body. She encountered plenty of beautiful, athletic bodies in her profession; with the man she had chosen for herself the important thing was the feeling of security and tenderness she felt by his side. Of course, if the two happened to coincide that would be even better, but this wasn't the case with Vieira. Her long-fingered hands soaped up his old body meticulously, careful not to miss any of the healthy parts and careful to avoid all his bruises. Since he was seated and she was standing, every time she bent over to clean his back, the rigid points of her breasts brushed against Vieira's face and lips; his hands moved inside her legs. When she reached his stomach, Flor's movements slowed down, a delay full of caresses. Feeling his erection reach its maximum, Vieira grabbed her waist, pulled her gently down to him, her legs resting on top of his. Mounted on his thighs, though not sitting on them, with her arms pressed against the walls of the shower, Flor delicately lowered herself onto his lap, and without seeking permission, she let him penetrate her as deeply as he could, initiating a slow, smooth movement that only her youth made possible, like a piston picking up speed, never in the least pressing against his legs, until his climax. They remained in this position, the water falling between them, the muscles in Flor's legs trembling from the continuous contraction. When she at last rose, Vieira let himself sit there, enjoying the sensation of the water falling on his back. His mind felt empty; the only thing that counted was his body, which, after relaxing with pleasure, began to ache where he had been beaten. His first thought was that he would be with her until death did them part.

After drying him off and dressing him, Flor gathered up the pillows at the head of the bed so that he could watch the news. Vieira felt pain in several parts of his body, but every corner of his soul rejoiced. The wound on his lips and his broken teeth made it hard for him to ingest solid foods. Flor held the bowl of soup while Vieira, his hand trembling from the previous effort, tried to raise the soup to his mouth without spilling it on his shirt.

"Shit, it seems like I've even got that goddamn Parkinson's."

"What's that?"

"Some fucking disease old people get that makes them all shaky."

"Honey, after what you did there in the bathroom, you can shake all you want. Would you like me to make you some eggnog?"

"Eggnog? Damn it, Flor, an eggnog. . . . I can't tell you how long it's been since I've heard of that. . . . You really are the shit. First you ask me if you can take your clothes off, then you offer me eggnog . . . next thing I know you're going to be calling my dick 'sir.' "

With every remark, Flor frowned coyly. When she said good-bye, before the news came on, she blew him a kiss, saying:

"Sweetheart, if that policeman friend of yours shows up, ask him not to be so pushy."

"Espinosa? What the fuck did he do?"

"Nothing, honey, it's just that he's always summoning me to the station. I don't know what he wants from me.... He even came by my apartment."

"Your apartment? The fuck was he doing there? Did he bother you?"

"No, of course not, he's very polite ... but he sure can be pushy. I just wanted him to lay off a little." And once she was already in the hall, only her head sticking around the door: "Don't call him, babe; cops are like that. Just as well that you're not one of them anymore."

And she closed the door after blowing him a kiss.

"Espinosa! Telephone!"

It was almost lunchtime when Espinosa walked slowly toward the office where he had spent the previous day sorting through paperwork.

"Hello?"

"Espinosa?"

"Yes?"

"It's Clodoaldo. Your kid is still alive. I didn't find out anything about the man. I'm talking from a public phone. Tomorrow I'll be on the Avenida Atlântica again. Bye." Clodoaldo spoke as if dictating the text of a telegram.

Despite the economy of the message, the essential had been conveyed, and the hypothesis that the boy had fled his protection confirmed. Espinosa felt deeply relieved. He left a message for Kika: "The kid's alive. Espinosa." Then he left immediately—for no reason, not even to eat, although it was time; just to free up his mind. He needed to walk a little, even in the beating, noonday December sun. There was a food-by-the-kilo place directly in front of the station, but what he needed at that moment was some space to think. At the old station, he used to sit in the square, right in front of the wharves of the port; now, all he had to do was walk two blocks and he had Copacabana Beach at his disposal, the ocean stretched out as far as the eye could see. He could think better looking out over the sea; he felt his mind relax, and his ideas arrived in digestible form.

As soon as he reached the sidewalk, he turned left and joined the masses of people who were heading to lunch. He felt perfectly happy in a crowd. Unlike most people, he didn't feel suffocated, oppressed, or threatened there; he felt only peace. The noise of the cars, the voices of the pedestrians, the cries of the street vendors, the music from the shops, the quaking of the traffic—all worked as a formless whole, homogeneous and continuous, like the noise of an air conditioner that eliminated external noises without making itself heard. Even visually—when he wanted to see it this way—the fantastic variety of things to see, including people, was stripped of characteristics and acted as an undifferentiated background. For Espinosa, at times like this, the experience of being in the middle of a multitude was not dissimilar from being on a deserted beach.

The contrast between the Avenida Copacabana and the Avenida Atlântica, at that hour, was striking; the first was filled with people hurrying to and from work, the second was overrun by tourists. After going to McDonald's to buy a double hamburger and soft drink, he found a bench in the shade facing away from the buildings, toward the sea. In the immense space made of sky and sea, he let his thoughts run wild, but they didn't go far—they stayed with him, not far from where the boy had vanished. And he was alive. Clodoaldo's telegraphic style didn't allow for details. How had he found out that the boy was alive? From a third party? Had he seen the boy himself? Had he managed to speak to him? Espinosa would have to wait for the next day. While he was thinking and waiting, he fought a desperate battle to get the double-decker sandwich into his mouth without allowing any pink sauce to fall onto his shirt. It was a task that required the experience of a veteran, and he was the right man for the job.

The sea was calm; there were only a few swimmers in the water, a sign that it was cold. No boats on the horizon; the only shapes against the sky were the islands of Farol and Cagarras. He hadn't had any trouble finding the bench beneath the shade of the generous almond tree; at that time of the day, and as hot as it was, anyone who was at the seaside was there for the pleasures of the beach, not to sit on a cement bench on the sidewalk eating a sandwich. But he didn't do it unwillingly. He felt good looking at the green and the blue mixing in the space before his eyes while letting his mind wander. Outings like this one were not precisely "to think"; he knew how much trouble he had keeping his thoughts within minimal levels of rationality. Not that he was, or thought he was, crazy: his colleagues even held him up as a model of a policeman who used his head more than his hands. But what his coworkers didn't know was that his imagination outweighed his logical thinking to such a degree that he sometimes wondered if he'd ever experienced a full sequence of purely logical thoughts. He'd chosen the Avenida Atlântica to think about the case because it was perfect for "concentrating his attention"—a concentration that didn't last for more than a minute. The connection between the boy and Kika met with no resistance, and once he was in possession of the idea of Kika the doors to fantasy were flung wide open. Even before he'd finished his sandwich, he and Kika were already on unspoiled beaches in distant countries. Finishing his lunch, he noticed how far away his thoughts had strayed from any consideration for the kid, and he decided to go back to the station and await the following day, when the solid presence of Clodoaldo would serve as a starting point of reality.

That night, stretched out on his sofa, Espinosa let his mind move from one boy to the other, between the one who had mistakenly been killed and the one who had survived; and he tried to imagine what sort of person would throw gasoline on a sleeping child. He knew of groups that killed beggars, homosexuals, prostitutes, and street children, and he was aware of the surprising number of people burned alive while asleep in the streets of the great cities, but he didn't believe in coincidences like that. That boy had been killed because someone thought he knew something that threatened someone else. He remembered a TV report about people killed while sleeping in the streets; it mentioned ten such attacks per month. The immediate question was: who does things like that? The possible responses were varied: the extreme right, insane pyromaniacs, psychopaths, juvenile delinquents, members of religious cults, racists . . . and the list moved perilously closer to the people one met every day on the street, on the bus, at work, and even in churches, preaching universal love.

In spite of the open windows, he felt beads of sweat forming on his neck. He took off his shirt and got a beer out of the refrigerator. The sofa was hot; he preferred the rocking chair. After a few minutes, the chair's wicker back started to hurt his own; he got up and stood by the balcony at his French

window, looking at the little lights on the hill above the buildings. After a few minutes the beer got hot too. Kika orbited
elliptically; sometimes she was so close he could almost touch
her; at other times she was so far away that he could barely
see her. There was no actual encounter. He drank only half
his beer; he went to the bathroom to wet down his face and
neck, came back to the living room, went into the kitchen,
checked the refrigerator once more, then returned to the balcony. What would happen if Kika came in just then?

Once again, his reflections were interrupted by the phone.
Kika would be suggesting that they move their meeting up,
he thought. It would be Kika saying that she wanted to come
to his apartment, he thought. He was so sure that it took him
a moment to realize that the voice wasn't hers.

"Is this Officer Espinosa?"

"It is."

"This is Vanessa."

"Vanessa?"

"The doorman gave me your card; he said you wanted to
speak with me."

"Oh, yes. Thanks for calling."

"Do you still want to?"

"Want to do what?"

"Talk to me."

"Yes, of course. I'm sorry; I mixed up your voice with someone else's."

"Do you want to talk about Magali?" Her voice was smooth
and secure.

"Yes."

"She was my friend."

"I know. That's why I wanted to speak with you. Can you
meet me tomorrow at noon in the lobby of your building?"

Contrary to the usual rules of procedure, Espinosa preferred to hold his first meetings away from the station, except in the case of interrogations and official depositions. Anyone summoned to the station, no matter how little they had to do with a case, always adopted a defensive posture. Outside of the police ambience, even when they knew they were talking to a policeman, people tended to say things they wouldn't say inside the station. The tactic was best suited to situations like this.

He got to the Avenida Atlântica at exactly ten o'clock. He hadn't set a specific time, but he thought that this way he'd have enough time before meeting Magali's friend. The only available parking place in the three blocks closest to his destination had a sign indicating that it was reserved for the diplomatic representative of a central European country that had recently been divided in two. He took it and waved to the attendant, whom he'd given a good tip, telling him he wouldn't be far. He spotted a few kids on the sidewalk across the street, by the sand, but he didn't see Clodoaldo. Crossing the two lanes, he approached the group. Of the four kids, one recognized him, the same one he himself remembered from the previous week. Clodoaldo hadn't arrived yet. Sometimes he got there later, but he always showed up. Espinosa left to look for a bakery; he remembered the big bag of rolls that Clodoaldo had brought the last time.

At eleven-thirty, the sun had heated the roof of his car so much that he couldn't even rest his hand on it. Espinosa had tried, with no positive results, to get the kids to talk about the death of their colleague. They could talk about day-to-day survival, but when they suspected that the conversation was coming around to themes they found threatening, they clammed up or simply ran toward a car parked at the stoplight to ask the driver for some spare change. He told them he'd come back in the afternoon and left to meet Vanessa, hoping that his meeting with her would be more fruitful.

Vanessa, unlike the angular Flor, was curvy. Not fat, but completely made up of delicate, smooth curves. Her face wasn't particularly beautiful, but her mouth and eyes were extremely alluring. She looked good and healthy. She was twenty-five, at most. This was Espinosa's general impression as he met her in the lobby of the building.

The first exchange was to introduce themselves. When Espinosa mentioned Magali, Vanessa only said, "She was like my big sister." The sentence sounded familiar.

"Have you already eaten?" Espinosa asked.

"Not yet. I don't usually eat much for lunch, maybe just a salad."

"Then I'll take you out for a sandwich or, if you want, a salad at Cervantes, across the street."

The speed with which she looked in the direction of the restaurant, no more than fifty meters from where they were standing, indicated that she must be a regular there.

"I like that place." And they crossed the Rua Barata Ribeiro toward the door of the restaurant.

Until they had sat down and ordered they behaved ceremoniously.

"Vanessa, I don't know if—"

"Maria Regina's my real name. Vanessa's the name I work under."

"And which do you prefer?"

"Depends if you're a client or a friend."

"Can I call you Regina?"

"That's what my friends call me."

"I don't know if you know how your friend was killed."

"I know the details . . . unless there's something you didn't let people know. I know she was found naked, bound to the bed, with a plastic bag tied over her head, and that she died of suffocation."

"There's the detail of the Mace."

"I know about that too. The fact that the murderer put her to sleep in order to kill her doesn't make it any less horrible to me; in fact, it makes the crime all the more awful."

"Do you have any idea who might have done it?"

"No. Nobody I know would have done it. You'd have to be very sick. I'm sure the bastard sat there jacking off while she thrashed around. In my opinion, it had to be some unknown client."

"The doorman didn't see her come back and also didn't see anyone unknown leaving in the morning."

"The night doorman is a great guy, but he spends more time in his room than in the lobby. Anybody who has a key can come in without him noticing."

"Anybody who has a key."

"He could have come in with her. To go out, you don't need a key; the door opens from inside."

"So that's what you think? That the murder was carried out by someone she didn't know?"

"At least that's what I'd like to think. I'm not religious. I believe in people. I couldn't stand to think that a friend or an acquaintance could do something like that."

"When were you with her last?"

"The night before. We went down in the same elevator. She was going to dinner with Vieira."

"Did she look all right?"

"Fine. She loved Friday nights, when she went out to eat with him."

"Do you know Vieira well?"

"I can't say I know him well, but I've known him for a long time, since they started going out."

"And what do you think of him?"

"In spite of his oafish appearance, I think he's one the nicest souls I've ever come across."

"Did you ever go out with them?"

"Only a few times."

"And your friend Flor?"

"She's not my friend. She was Magali's friend, if she was ever really anyone's friend."

"You don't like her?"

"I don't like her and I don't dislike her. She's strange. Nothing ever seems to get through to her, really. Where I'm from we call a person like that a taioba leaf: you dunk it in the water and it comes out dry."

"Where are you from?"

"I'm from Minas."

"Just one more question: where were you on the night of the crime?"

"I was in my apartment asleep, alone. You've got a lot of self-confidence if you think you can ask a question like that and we'll just continue this conversation."

"We can't?"

"When you want to talk again, you can leave another note with the doorman." She got up and left. No hurry. No indignant face.

Espinosa finished his sandwich, thinking that the last question could have been put off or avoided but also thinking that to provoke such an immediate retreat the question must have gone deep into the soul of Regina or Vanessa (maybe they weren't the same). The meeting, and perhaps the friendship, had lasted maybe twenty minutes. And there were still so many things he had wanted to ask. He left the restaurant praying that his car hadn't been towed, hoping he would have more luck with Clodoaldo than with Vanessa.

The car was in the same spot; there was no ticket on the windshield. It took him less than ten minutes to reach Clodoaldo's meeting place, but he didn't even need to turn off the engine; the attendant came up and made a sign with his hand that Clodoaldo still hadn't shown up. The kids were nowhere in sight. He didn't think it was necessary to leave a message. Perhaps today wasn't his lucky day. He went back to the station.

In the evening, instead of going home, he decided to venture out once more to the place where Clodoaldo met the street children. He drove around the nearby blocks and the section of road next to the beach but didn't see them. Maybe they had arranged a new meeting place, but that didn't coincide with what Clodoaldo had said the day before. The lack of children could mean that Clodoaldo hadn't shown, which was unusual. He went around the block and turned onto the Avenida Copacabana.

With the approach of Christmas, the stores were open at night, which meant that traffic in the neighborhood had increased considerably, especially on the big shopping streets. People and cars mixed in a slow, continuous movement. While he was waiting for the light to change, people carrying packages crossed the street in front of him. He thought about buying Kika a present. There hadn't been many Christmases for him with his wife and son; those he had spent with his parents were far enough away that memory and imagination, events and desires had become confused. He remembered more clearly the Christmases he had spent with his grandmother, in the years they'd lived together. She'd made an effort so the day wouldn't be sad. After her death, except for the few years of his marriage, he had never again celebrated Christmas. He lacked faith, and people.

He drove slowly down the Avenida Copacabana until he reached the Peixoto district. Even in the calm of the square he felt an extra buzz. Above the entrance to his building there was a little pine wreath from which three shiny, colored balls hung: the annual manifestation of the building manager's Christmas spirit. He thought of the methodical December withdrawal of a box from the top of someone's closet, untying the string around it, and removing the wreath from inside the box ready to ornament the building.

He opened the door of the apartment as if the ornament were hanging off it. Inside, only the heat of December. There were two messages on the answering machine, both of which could be erased without depriving his life of the slightest significance.

Several images fought for primacy in Espinosa's brain at that instant: that of Kika, who even when pushed aside by other impressions had a way of making her way back to the forefront; that of the boy, who with the passing of time had become less clearly defined (Espinosa noticed that even with concentrated effort his image was becoming more and more blurry); that of Clodoaldo, strong and clear but not persistent; and that of a new figure on the scene: Vanessa. These were not the exclusive, or even the primary, inhabitants of Espinosa's world, but they were the ones who now occupied the stage.

In the shower, he was still trying to figure out why Clodoaldo hadn't come to the scheduled meeting. Street teachers didn't work in offices or have fixed addresses, but that was exactly why they were always so rigorously punctual to their itinerant appointments. They themselves were the office, and their presence created the address. What he thought was strange was that Clodoaldo's absence coincided with the boy's discovery. He tried to convince himself that the two events were unrelated.

When he'd talked with Kika the night before, they had vaguely agreed to meet; now it was after eight and nothing had yet been confirmed. Since she had initiated the last few calls, Espinosa decided it was his turn. He left a message on her voice mail, opened a beer, and was getting settled in his chair when the phone rang. It was Kika. She hadn't gotten the message yet. She was calling to confirm their date.

But at nine-thirty, the designated time, Espinosa was parking the car on the Avenida Atlântica for a very different rendezvous. When he was still at home, the telephone had rung again. He had hesitated between answering and letting the machine pick it up; Kika was waiting for him. He answered it. A recorded message announced a collect call, and then came a weak, hesitant voice that Espinosa recognized immediately.

"Officer?"

"Yes."

"Clodoaldo gave me your number . . ."

"Are you all right?"

"I think . . . I'm fine."

"Where are you?"

"On the beach . . ."

"In the same spot as last time?"

"No. I'm in Leme. In the sand. Next to the rock. . . . Clodoaldo gave me your number."

"Fine. Don't move. I'll be right there."

He didn't pay attention to the noises in the background; the boy could have been calling from one of the public phones installed in the sand, or from the little square in front of Leme Fort; he hadn't even asked if he was alone. After leaving a message for Kika, he headed out the door. On the way, going as fast as traffic would permit, he cursed himself for not asking more questions. The car spent more time stopped than moving; he thought about abandoning it and traveling the rest of the way on foot, but he couldn't just dump the car in the middle of the street. It took him more than twenty minutes to get to Leme. The parking places along the beach were occupied by couples; he deposited the car in the first available spot, next to a bus stop, leaving it unlocked. The boy had said "next to the rock." He headed toward the big stone hill that marked the beginning of Copacabana Beach, sweeping his eyes along the areas of sand illuminated by streetlamps. He had to get close to the stone hill to distinguish the small, fearful figure of the boy seated in the sand. In fact, it was impossible to identify anyone at such a distance at night, but by the figure's size and location it seemed like a good fit. When he was a little more than twenty meters away, he stepped off the sidewalk onto the sand and waved to the boy. The closer he got, the more nervous he became. The child's immobility—his head resting on his chest—seemed strange. When he reached him, he didn't need to touch the vulnerable, fragile body to see that the boy was dead, the back of his head covered with blood. Espinosa was doubly astonished: not only was the boy dead, but he had been killed by a blow to the skull.

The lights on the beach made the scene look artificial, like a film set; the colors, enhanced by the streetlamps, were exaggerated, in contrast to the dark rock; the strong light made the sand seem even whiter, which made the breaking waves look swimming-pool green and the sky and the sea past the breakers look formless and dark. The boy's hands were in his lap, as if the murderer had arranged them there.

Espinosa remained next to the body, leaning against the rock, as stiff as the boy. Someone seeing them from afar would have imagined that a father and son were chatting; they wouldn't have been able to tell that one of them could no longer speak.

When the first policemen arrived, they found Espinosa seated on the sand next to the boy, as if he were looking at the night sky; the boy's head dangled over his chest. The forensic examiners were called, but there was nothing more to be discovered at the scene. For Espinosa there was no doubt that the boy had been killed in the position in which he was found. The murderer—without question an adult—had grabbed the front of his head with one hand and beaten it against the rock, probably more than once.

There was no blood on the sand, and the boy's clothes indicated that there had been no struggle, which in any case would have been noticed by the passersby on the sidewalk; and the beating of a child would certainly have attracted the attention of the lovers seated on the benches along the beach. But not the rapid movement of a head whacked against a rock.

The back of the boy's head had been crushed. The aggressor and the victim must have been seated close to each other, and one moment of trust or distraction would have been enough to have his head jerked back.

Only when the numbers of police cars grew did the pedestrians focus their attention on the body next to the rock. No one had seen anything suspicious, and no one had noticed anyone with the boy.

Espinosa stayed at the scene until the body was removed. Then he examined the surroundings, speaking to the occupants of the cars, interrupting necking couples, interrogating vendors, cleaning ladies, passersby, and curiosity seekers; signaling to the night fishermen with their long poles stuck in the sand; talking again to the night watchman at the fort (a different one this time); and, in an ultimate useless gesture, looking up at the buildings along the Avenida Atlântica, expecting to see some resident signaling to him because he had witnessed from his balcony, with powerful binoculars, a street child being murdered.

It was after one in the morning when Espinosa got in his car and went back home. That wasn't what he wanted to be doing. He wanted to find the other street kids in the hopes of getting some fragment of information from them; more than anything he wanted to find Clodoaldo, whose disappearance seemed as enigmatic as the boy's death; and he still wanted to stop by the shelter—maybe they'd have something to say. But he knew that what he needed to do just then was go home and go to sleep.

He went home, but he couldn't sleep. There were too many questions and no answers. More than anything, he felt immensely confused by what was happening. Three people had died, a fourth had been viciously assaulted, and another had disappeared, without any apparent relation between the events and without an apparent motive for any of the individual attacks. A cloud of absolute mystery hung over Magali's death; Vieira wasn't really a suspect. The murderer of the sleeping boy could be chalked up, with difficulty, to the man with the wallet; yet why would he kill, and so brutally, a street child? Because he'd mixed him up with the other boy who was following him? Why was the other boy so important? And to top it all off, the death of that other boy, a person completely without importance in society, the target of such a cruel attack? These were a few of the questions that were tormenting Espinosa when the first light of dawn crept through the venetian blinds.

PART 4

Vieira was recovering surprisingly well. With his temporary dentures and Flor's care, there were few signs left of the assault he had suffered a week before.

"Fuck it, Espinosa, how is that after thirty years of being a cop something like this happens to me?"

"Do you still feel any pain?"

"Not in my body, only in my soul."

"You can take care of that. You've got an excellent nurse." Espinosa wondered how much truth there was in that observation.

Espinosa knew that Vieira had a hard time reining in his natural tendency toward frankness and indiscretion; his former colleague's newfound conversational restraint struck him as curious. Something was getting under his skin, something that had nothing to do with the attack.

It was ten-thirty in the morning. Vieira was alone; he had just finished showering and dressing when he'd opened the door to Espinosa. After the initial greetings, the old man sat waiting. Even while speaking, he was waiting for what Espinosa had to say; he knew people well enough to be able to distinguish a professional visit from a social call.

Before he brought up the boy's death, Espinosa asked about Vanessa. Vieira didn't immediately make the connection; it took him a few seconds to fit the girl into the series of events.

"I don't know her very well. She went out with us a few times, not many; she seemed like a nice girl and was a good friend of Magali. She lives in the same building. I don't know much else about her. Did something happen to her?"

"No. Is she also friends with Flor?"

"Not as far as I know."

"The four of you never went out?"

"Damn, Espinosa, I'm starting to think you don't believe me. Two weeks ago I barely knew who Flor was; when she called me I had no idea who I was talking to. Same with this Vanessa girl; I have a vague memory of what she looks like, but I'm sure that if I ran into her in the street I wouldn't recognize her. Where the fuck does she suddenly come into this?"

"She didn't just come into this; she's always been there. She was a friend of Magali's and liked her a lot; she's only trying to help."

"And why did she only decide to help now?"

"Because, according to her, she was so shocked by what happened that she went to spend a few days with her family."

"And now that she's over the trauma, she decided to help?"

"More or less. She didn't volunteer. I went to find her. And before you ask me how I found out about her existence, the doorman told me that they were friends. I should add that she didn't like me; she got up and walked out midsentence, while we were eating lunch."

"That's a good sign. While you were waiting for the food to arrive, you probably asked her where she was at the time her friend was murdered."

"Exactly."

"Goddamn it, Espinosa, it might sound like common sense, but hookers have feelings too."

"It was too quick."

"And it wasn't just with her. You've already gone to Flor's apartment looking for a key, and you squeezed her so much at the station that she came back with a lawyer. What are you worried about? Some kind of hooker plot? I confess that, besides me, you don't have any suspects, but that's no reason to go harassing the girls."

Espinosa noticed that he was getting an extra helping of criticism. He knew that it was because of what he'd done to Flor, and he knew that turning Vieira against him was Flor's way of settling the score. It was part of the game.

Vieira's apartment was hot; there was only one air conditioner, in the bedroom, and Espinosa didn't feel like discussing such matters seated on the bed of his only formally identified suspect. He took his coat off and stood as close as possible to the only window in the small living room.

"They killed the boy."

"What?"

"They killed the boy."

"What boy?"

"The one with the wallet . . . they smashed his head against a rock."

"Motherfucker. . . . He was just a child. . . . Why?"

Espinosa told him what he knew and how he had found the boy. Vieira listened in silence, without comment.

"It could be the work of the same guy who attacked me: same style. A guy who punches a white-haired old man could easily smash a child's head against a rock."

"I agree. But what intrigues me is that according to Kika's description, the man who was chasing the boy was slim, well-dressed, and had something in his pocket that she described as a knife or a dagger. Not the kind of guy who would smash someone's head in."

"Why not? He could have hired someone to do it for him."

"I still think it doesn't make sense. Think about it. This first guy has no idea that the boy knows about the wallet. The only thing the kid did was follow him through the streets of Copacabana. For this reason alone, a boy gets burned alive while he's asleep and another has his head smashed in. Those are extreme reactions for such a small inconvenience; that is, if we think the same person killed both of the boys. If not, the situation gets even messier."

For more than an hour, Espinosa and Vieira discussed the various hypotheses about the events since the loss of the wallet. The hypotheses did not lead to possible conclusions; they just raised more unanswerable questions.

Espinosa's main reason for visiting Vieira was to verify a secondary, but by no means unimportant, suspicion: did Flor really want her new lover to become jealous of Espinosa? Clearly she did. But what Espinosa knew and she perhaps didn't was that such strategies were of dubious effectiveness, and not very useful for dealing with Vieira's unruly personality. In any case, he had decided to be extra careful in dealing with Flor. Vieira's policeman's pride had been wounded just as he was feeling most threatened by the onset of old age. Flor was his amulet, protecting him against death; there was no reason to push him too far.

Espinosa's main worry at the moment was Kika. He didn't think the man would attack her just for protecting the boy, but he also realized that such reasoning didn't necessarily apply to someone who crushed children's skulls. He left her a message.

It was past noon when he got in the car and headed for the station. He'd eat something nearby; on the way he thought about the possibility that his case really boiled down to several completely unconnected cases, a notion he'd entertained several times but had never taken seriously. Despite the hour, traffic was light on the short trip to the Rua Hilário de Gouveia. He parked the car in an iffy space near the station, but before he went in he walked another block and returned carrying a small paper bag containing a sandwich, French fries, and a milkshake. The unwise food choice seemed to go well with the day: this Friday was certainly feeling like a Monday.

The preliminary, very tentative results he managed to get over the phone from the forensic experts, as well as from the autopsy, added nothing substantial to the impression he had himself gleaned from the crime scene. He had ordered his team to shake down their informants for details about each of the deaths in the hopes of finding some link between them.

Up until then, the press hadn't connected the deaths. In fact, Espinosa himself could not find any ties, even the most tenuous, that might make sense of it all; the sole common thread was Espinosa. He was afraid that the press would start exploiting the deaths, especially given the media's fascination with serial killers. He thought about concocting a minimally intelligent story in case reporters started asking questions. The call from Kika surprised him in the middle of his first attempt.

"I thought that you'd decided to lay off, or forgotten about me. I must say the second idea scared me more."

"Don't be silly. I need to talk to you, and it's important that it be before you set up your stand tonight."

"Fine. We can meet before I leave for Copacabana."

"Great. I'll get you at six-thirty in front of your building."

The other urgent task was finding Clodoaldo. He made a list of the organizations that helped street children and eliminated the ones he knew Clodoaldo didn't deal with. The list wasn't extensive, and it didn't take long to discover that they knew as much about where Clodoaldo was as he did. He decided to go back to the meeting point on the Avenida Atlântica to try to find out something from the kids. He went back to get the car and headed toward the area around the Galeria Alaska. He found only two kids, who hadn't been there when he'd been introduced to the group, and, on a nearby block, the parking attendant. No one had seen Clodoaldo; he had vanished without a trace.

Espinosa went back to the station, where he disguised his sense of impotence by doling out large numbers of assignments and busily making phone calls. Before finishing his day at the office, the call he had been dreading finally came in: a reporter asking if there was any connection between the deaths of the two street kids. None. And he could answer with a clear conscience; he wasn't lying, because he honestly didn't know of any.

He got out of the car to greet Kika and help her put her pictures in the rear seat of the car, which had to be done quickly because the traffic on the Rua do Catete was intense and parking wasn't allowed.

"You were so mysterious on the phone."

"Mysterious? I hardly said a word."

"Exactly. I mean, not just because of that—you don't talk much anyway—but there was a feeling of mystery on the line."

The car was already on one of the streets leading to Flamengo Beach, which at that hour was packed bumper-to-bumper because of all the cars from downtown heading back to the residential areas.

"Maybe you'll think the question I'm about to ask you is mysterious."

"Didn't I tell you there was mystery in the air? What do you want to know?"

"Would you be able to stop showing your pictures on the Avenida Atlântica for a while?"

"Now?"

"Yes."

"Why?"

"For your own safety."

"But why? What's going on?"

"They killed the boy."

"What?"

"The boy was found dead last night."

"What? Who found him?"

"I did."

"You? Where? Who killed him?"

Espinosa decided to give her a highly abbreviated account, since it was impossible to put a positive spin on the way the boy had been killed. When he tried to skip over that detail, however, Kika interrupted him and demanded full disclosure. By the time the story was over, tears were running down her motionless face. Despite the slow traffic, she didn't say a word until they had reached Copacabana.

"Do you think that whoever killed the boy is going to try to kill me too?"

"I don't think so. But I don't want you taking any chances."

"To get that son of a bitch, it might be worth being the bait."

"Forget it."

"Why?"

"Because the guy already incinerated a sleeping child and smashed in the head of another. Think about it."

"Why do you think he'd want to kill me?"

"Maybe he thinks the boy told you something."

"But what could he have told me?"

"I don't have the slightest idea. And the worst is that I don't think the boy knew either."

"Do you think he was killed by mistake?"

"No. The other one died by mistake. He was deliberately killed by the murderer, who is the only one who knew why he was killing him. He himself didn't know why he was dying."

"I don't understand. I don't even want to understand. I want to get the son of a bitch. I'm not going to hide. The boy hid, and a lot of good it did him."

"Are you sure that's what you want?"

"I'm sure. Besides, it's only a week till Christmas, the time when we sell the most. I'm not rich. I need to pay my bills."

"In that case, I'll stay with you tonight. On other days we'll figure something out."

"I think you're worrying too much. There's no reason for the guy to try anything against me."

"Kika, guys like that don't need a reason."

"If I were a man, would you protect me like this?"

"I don't know if I'd do it like this, but I'd do something."

"What if I refused to be protected?"

"Then you'd make my job a lot harder."

They were still inside the car; a little bit of afternoon light was filtering through the windows, and despite the harsh tone of the dialogue, Kika was looking at Espinosa more affectionately than provocatively. She liked the well-mannered way he approached her, and she liked the way he talked, nearly free of slang and completely devoid of obscenities. She liked the noninvasive way he made his presence felt. Heat was also coming in through the windows.

"What would you say to having a bite to eat before you set up your stand?"

"I couldn't eat after the news you've brought me."

"We wouldn't have to sit down. I could get us some sandwiches."

The first artists were already setting up their stands when Espinosa arrived with the pictures and the metal mount. Kika carried a paper bag with their dinner.

"I need your help for something important," Espinosa said. "I never saw the man who chased the boy. I don't know what he looks like, and if he shows up you have to give me a signal immediately."

Espinosa got the impression that it was only then that Kika realized she was in real danger, that she had to remain alert, that the police officer by her side wasn't (or wasn't only) there to seduce her: people had been killed. The rest of the night passed uneasily, though nothing happened and they were both pleased to be together. Espinosa hovered around Kika like a moth near a flame. Every time a man with straight black hair approached, Espinosa put his hand on his revolver, awaiting some gesture, some head movement, some expression of Kika's, positive or negative. When they got in the car at the end of the night, after storing her apparatus in the garage, Espinosa thought that once again he had taken a big risk in not asking for backup. On the way back to Catete he hardly said a word, aware of every muscle in his body, and even when he got out in front of Kika's building to help her with her pictures, he was still entirely focused on the people moving down the street.

It was Friday night. Just over twenty-four hours earlier he'd found the boy at the rock in Leme. Only a few minutes ago, on the same beach, he had played the role of the girl's protector, a role in which he had failed just days earlier with the boy. On the way home he stopped off for a beer; he would have had something stronger, but he remembered that all he'd eaten that day was two sandwiches. He'd go for a third.

He'd have to wait until Monday for more detailed information about the boy's death, though he wasn't sure exactly what he was hoping to learn. He read only the first section of

the newspaper, but even so couldn't have said what the head-
lines were or identified the most important stories. The voices
of children playing in the street filtered through his open windows, together with the light and the warm morning air. In
shorts, shoeless and shirtless, he was still feeling the December
heat. Body and soul formed a single sticky mess: thinking was
as painful as running or going to the gym; reading was impossible; listening to music, out of the question. He slowly put on
his oldest, lightest tennis shoes, examined his shorts and
decided they were presentable, rummaged through the bottom
of his closet in search of a straw hat he used sometimes when
he walked on the beach, stuck some money in his pocket, and
left, determined to shake off the melancholy that was threatening his weekend.

He walked along Copacabana Beach toward Ipanema
beneath the summer sun; a southwesterly wind blew, keeping
the temperature comfortable. He continued unhurriedly to
the canal of the Jardim de Alá, which separates Ipanema and
Leblon, then doubled back; on his return the sun was at his
back. The stroll took a little more than two hours, including
two stops at kiosks along the beach, where he bought coconut
water and corn on the cob. For some reason, however, that
day's walk didn't lend itself to reflection, as such excercises
usually did.

When he got back home, sweaty and tired, his electronic
guard dog was blinking its red eye at him. The green one let
him know that it hadn't been asleep; he listened to the messages after showering. The first was from Clodoaldo, saying
that he was almost positive he knew who'd killed the boy but
still needed to verify a detail that had something to do with
the man who took the wallet. The message was ambiguous; it
wasn't clear if the man with the wallet was suspected of the
murder or if he could merely throw some light on the crime.

Even though there were no other candidates for the role of murderer, it didn't make sense. Why would the man kill the boy? Even more, given that there was no reason to suppose there were two different killers, why would he kill two boys? What Espinosa couldn't fathom was the purpose of the murders; the first was a case of mistaken identity, but why would anyone want to kill the second boy? He needed to find Clodoaldo, whom he also thought was at risk; maybe his disappearance meant that he had already been attacked. It wouldn't be the first time he'd been in a dangerous situation, and Clodoaldo had vast experience in getting out of such jams. Espinosa was sure, however, of one thing: those deaths had nothing to do with Vieira's lost (and found) wallet. The boy had believed that was why he was being stalked, but it obviously wasn't the real motive. He listened to Clodoaldo's message again in search of some sign of where he was calling from. Nothing. The absence of noises could, at most, indicate that the call was made from a closed phone booth or an apartment. Clodoaldo had never told anyone where he lived.

After Clodoaldo's message came one from Kika. He noticed, not without sadness, that because it followed Clodoaldo's, the message seemed less intense. And yet he couldn't leave her unprotected, especially if she was determined, in spite of his admonishments, to continue doing business on the Avenida Atlântica. He called the newest detective on his team, fresh out of the police academy, who wouldn't be bothered by having to work on a Saturday night. The kid had another advantage: like Espinosa, he was Copacabana born and bred and, like Espinosa, he knew the soul of the area.

Maldonado, the new detective, was short, ugly, and stiff as a fire hydrant. He met Espinosa in front of a chic nightclub on the Avenida Atlântica, and they went off to find Kika. While they were walking, Espinosa brought the kid up-to-date, at least on the details he thought relevant for the task he was about to assign. The detective was worried that no one had a description of the suspect beyond "thirty, straight black hair, medium stature." If he went on that description, he would have to arrest half the men he saw. They arrived before Kika did. Most of the artists were still setting up their booths; many hadn't gotten there yet. They waited for her in front of the garage where she stored her metal stand. Maldonado picked up on Espinosa's worry about the girl's delay and, even though he'd never seen her before, started to look around. When she finally arrived, they clicked immediately: they were the same age and spoke the same dialect, minimizing potential miscommunication. Espinosa, puzzled, watched their immediate understanding unfold. Kika gave a brief description of the man (the same one she'd provided Espinosa), which was enough for Maldonado to get a precise mental portrait. Immediately, despite his stature, he began scanning the horizon.

Espinosa left Kika in the hands of the detective and went to follow a hunch—nothing very strong, but all he had to go on. If Clodoaldo knew who'd killed the boy, he wouldn't sit around waiting for someone to do something; the answering-machine message was a kind of warning or indication that he was about to take the matter into his own hands. There was a serious possibility that the street teacher was hunting the man with the wallet.

The Avenida Atlântica at that hour was even busier than it had been the previous Saturday, and the weather, which had seemed to be shifting earlier in the day, held; the night was dazzling. Espinosa decided to continue on foot. He'd certainly be more mobile that way than moving around in a car in Copacabana Saturday-night traffic. He walked steadily down the blocks that separated him from the Rua Santa Clara; not a great distance, but not exactly nearby, either. He walked

past the restaurant where the wallet episode had taken place
and the spot where the boy had been burned to death, then
turned left and walked one block up to the Avenida Copacabana, where he turned right; from that point on he tried to
be as discreet as possible. A man staying put and staring at a
fixed point would attract more attention than someone moving
with the crowds, which is what Espinosa did in front of the
man's building. First he walked down one sidewalk, then he
crossed the street and walked down the opposite one, paying
close attention to the people entering and leaving the building
as well as to the area around it, since the man himself could
be trying to make sure that no one was watching him. On one
of his passes he noticed a group (or possibly a family) of beggars asking for handouts on the sidewalk across from the building's entrance. The second time he walked by the spot, he
noticed that only the children were left; by the third trip there
was nobody. That was when he realized that the beggar with
his hat pulled down over his head had been Clodoaldo. But
now he was gone.

Espinosa combed the area in search of Clodoaldo; after
walking around the block, scrutinizing every corner, lobby,
garage, and side door, he realized that he couldn't compete
with the street teacher on his own turf. He returned to the
sidewalk in front of the man's building just as the stores were
beginning to shutter down for the evening; this was immediately followed by a decrease in foot traffic. He had decided to
go back to Kika and Maldonado and was taking a last glance
at the lobby of the building when he had his second surprise
of the day. The heavy iron-and-glass door opened to release
Chaves, the detective in charge of tracking the man's comings
and goings. Espinosa stood where he was, taking care not to
be seen; when the detective left, walking down the Avenida
Copacabana, he followed at a prudent distance. Halfway down

the next block the detective got on a bus, leaving time only for his pursuer to note the number of the line. Espinosa walked back to Kika's stand slowly enough to mull over the events he'd just witnessed. Why had Clodoaldo been disguised as a beggar in front of the building? Why had he fled when he saw Espinosa walk by? What had the detective been doing leaving the man's building? Could it be that Clodoaldo had his eye on the detective, rather than the man who'd taken the wallet?

One of the inconveniences of living in a building with no doorman is that newspapers are dumped on the ground floor, forcing the residents to go down to retrieve them themselves and creating opportunities for unwanted meetings. But on that Sunday morning the source of Espinosa's awkwardness was the fact that he had gone to sleep the night before with at least four important questions still unanswered. At least the toaster worked and the coffeemaker cooperated, things he couldn't always take for granted. The toaster often burned the bread and the coffee was too weak, or the coffee was so strong that it stained the cup and the bread emerged from the toaster white. So reaching the balance of a perfectly toasted slice of bread and a tasty cup of coffee would have been nothing to sneeze at—had any of yesterday's questions been resolved.

The weather had changed during the night, and the sky was covered with heavy gray clouds. He was on his second cup of coffee when it started to rain. At first scattered drops, no bigger than the seeds falling from the nearby tree, spattered onto the zinc protecting the air conditioner. Slowly they gathered speed and started to tinge the floor of the little balcony outside the French windows; in a matter of minutes the sky darkened noticeably, and a weighty, momentarily refreshing rain began to fall. Espinosa left the window open, at the risk of getting the living room carpet wet; he sat down in front of the balcony and stared out. He felt like he was watching the world through a veil of water; the nearby building and the distant hill loomed as one indistinct, shallow mass. The rug closest to the window was soaking wet when he uncrossed his legs, which he had rested on the little table in front of the sofa, and got up to close the glass doors; he wanted to keep watching the rain.

At eleven he dialed Vieira's number. A woman's voice answered. In the fraction of a second he needed to recognize the voice of Flor, she identified his and spoke first.

"Officer Espinosa, good morning. How have you been?" Her voice was artificial and forced, as if she were talking not to him but to someone she had with her.

"Not as well as my friend Vieira, but I'm getting by."

"Do you want to talk to him?" Her voice returned to normal.

"If I could."

It took a minute for Vieira to come on.

"Espinosa, buddy! The rain made you nostalgic and you remembered your old friend?"

"Something like that, Vieira. At least the second part is accurate. How are your scars?"

"The ones on my body are fine . . ." There was an interval during which Espinosa guessed that he was touching Flor. "All thanks to Flor. The ones in my heart are almost cured, also thanks to her."

"Maybe this isn't a good time . . ."

"My dear, for you it's always a good time."

"Thanks. I'm just calling to see how you're doing, but it seems you haven't changed a bit."

"That's right, baby. I'm a man blessed by the Almighty. After what I went through . . . and am still going through . . . to get to savor something like this . . ."

Espinosa felt the officer starting to drift off, so he didn't push him any further and hung up. He himself was disturbed; he knew he hadn't called only to find out how Vieira was feeling. He was also interested in finding out if Flor was with him, just as he'd been hoping she'd be the one to pick up the phone. In a corner of his mind, Flor's voice formed part of a whole, together with her body, the smell of her skin, and the grace of her movements. He didn't quite understand why, with Kika so much closer, he was so interested in a woman who belonged to someone else and who hadn't shown any interest in him. Maybe it was because of their very different kinds of beauty: Flor's was a native type, with Asian overtones and the strength of an ancestral Brazilian archetype. But Espinosa suspected that the real source of her provocative powers lay in a perverse glint in her eyes. While he was talking on the phone, he watched the rain, but his attention kept returning to Vieira's little apartment. After he hung up, he focused again on the masses of water framed by the window. He couldn't say how long he sat in that same position, his gaze lost in the brilliant gray of the rain. It was only when it stopped that he got up, as if to do something; he went out to the balcony to make sure the shower had really passed, then turned around and headed for the kitchen, anticipating lunch.

The rain started up again in the early afternoon and, with short intervals, fell for the rest of the day, eliminating the possibility of an exposition on the sidewalk of the Avenida Atlântica and consequently the need to protect Kika. He thought the most honest thing to do that afternoon was to try to break the impasse between the two annotations on the final page of *Lord Jim*—which meant sitting down to read.

Vieira's Sunday was just as rainy, but instead of Conrad he had Flor. At least for part of it. The other part, following Espinosa's phone call, was used to contact colleagues who were still on active duty. Now that he had recovered, it was time to act. Espinosa hadn't allowed him to participate in the investigation into Magali's murder, but he hadn't said anything about conducting a private investigation into the attack on himself. He wanted answers to a series of questions, the first being: who had assaulted him? He also wanted to know if the person responsible knew who he was, if the attack had anything to do with the man who had his wallet, and, finally, who that man was. The best place to start, in his opinion, was with the circle of informers for the Thirteenth Precinct, located right in front of the Galeria Alaska. The beginning of his private investigation led him to make two Sunday visits and a few phone calls; the results of his exertions, he hoped, would become apparent on Monday.

It was night when he got home. He was always sad when Flor wasn't there; he didn't know whether it was because the girl was so attractive or because every day he felt more keenly aware of his own mortality. Seated on the side of his bed, he looked at the reddish bruises on his body, especially on his arms, which he had used to protect himself from the blows, and saw the fragility of his aged body. Though he still had some vigor left, the increasing limits of his age were clear, and that hurt him more than the blows he'd received. He hadn't felt like he needed to stay young for Magali; in some ways his relationship with her was a continuation of his marriage to Maria Zilda. With Flor it was different. Her youth, even when she tried to play it down, marked a dramatic difference between them. Magali had made herself look older to go out with him to restaurants; Flor wasn't his day-to-day accessory but a concrete fulfillment of his fantasies. Flor didn't live in his world; she lived in his dreams.

He had undressed to his underwear and, still sitting on the side of his bed, was trying to remove his socks; his belly was like a float around his waist, preventing him from bending over. The simplest everyday task left him out of breath. He squeezed his hands, trying to strengthen the muscles in his arms, and noticed that they still responded. But if he kept squeezing them they threatened to start aching; fortunately his legs were still fine. He examined every part of his body in this way, thinking about Flor—and when he thought about Flor he put a different part of his body to the test.

The night before, he'd suggested to Flor that they move in together, with the understanding that she would stop working as a prostitute. Her response made him swell with pride. She would love to, she said, but they ought to wait a little longer. It was still early to make such a radical decision; maybe he'd be excited by her youth at first but would come to regret his suggestion eventually. For her part, she'd move in the next day, but for his own good they had better give it some time. There was a long pause while they stretched out on the bed, looking at the ceiling.

"Damn it, sweetheart. I don't have enough time left to think about it. I'm already living on borrowed time."

"Don't talk like that, focusing on the negative. We always have to think positively. It's just like energy. There's positive and negative."

"Okay, love. But I'm running on fumes. If you don't fill me up I'm going to run out of gas."

He firmly believed that the afternoon's intense activity was a direct response to that of the night before. And yet he felt Flor's absence keenly. Sunday-afternoon television bordered on the repugnant; at night it was merely insufferable. He found the least awful movie, opened a beer, and let himself relax, still thinking about Flor.

On the way to the station, one image kept popping into Espinosa's brain: the detective leaving the building on Saturday night. He didn't know what to conclude, even though he'd thought about it a lot. The man had been in the precinct for less than a month, arriving the night before Magali's murder, and the assignment to keep an eye on the building, like his trip to Campos to talk to the owner of the apartment, was a way to keep him busy until they had a better sense for what kind of man he was.

"He left on business? On whose orders? To go where?"

"Neither you nor the chief was here. He said he'd be back before noon. Hadn't you asked him to keep in touch with the doorman of that building on the Avenida Copacabana?"

"That's right."

"So he must be there."

Whenever Espinosa was suspicious of a colleague he felt conflicted, but it was difficult to view the detective's presence in the building at ten o'clock on Saturday night as proof of professional zeal. He'd told the kid to keep an eye on the building—not even to watch the building, actually, just to stop by a couple of times a day to see if the man had shown up. He didn't like the expression he had seen on the detective's face. He looked more like someone who had just wrapped up a deal than a cop investigating a murder suspect.

Until lunchtime, he was given over to bureaucratic tasks. At exactly noon, Chaves climbed the stairs leading to the second story and greeted Espinosa with a big, bright smile.

"How are things in the man's building?" Espinosa asked

the question disagreeably, barely raising his eyes from the file he was examining.

"Nothing new, sir, except . . ."

"Except?"

"Nothing, sir, it's nonsense."

"Nothing is nonsense when people are being murdered all around us."

"Well, it could just be my imagination, but I get the feeling I'm being followed."

"What do you mean?"

"It's nothing objective, and it's not always, but I have the feeling someone's following me."

"Really?"

"That's all. Just an impression."

"When did you start having this impression?"

"In the last few days, especially after the boy's death. Maybe, after feeling that he was being watched, the man set up a watchman."

"Could be. When were you there last?"

"This morning. The doorman confirmed that he hadn't been there."

"And before today, when were you there last?"

"Sunday night and Saturday night. I go by twice a day, but never at the same time, in case the employees are in touch with the man."

Espinosa sat wondering if he'd been unfair to the kid, or if the kid was smarter than he looked. He could have seen Espinosa as he was leaving the building—or noticed the almost brand-new sneakers on the beggar across the street, the one with the ridiculous wool hat pulled down to his ears on a hot summer night. He'd had all of Sunday to come up with a convincing story. That wasn't hard, since he'd been assigned to keep an eye on the very same building he'd been seen leaving.

"Is there a problem?" Chaves asked. "Do you want me to put the squeeze on the doormen? I think we're acting pretty delicately. The guy could be paying them off and threatening them. They're not going to cooperate."

"Don't do anything for now."

"Sir, if I may say so, I don't think we're going to get anything the way we're behaving."

"And what do you suggest?"

"I think we should call the doormen to the station to put a little pressure on them. Nothing violent. Just a little squeeze."

"And then the guy's going to find out that we're after him. . . . Don't forget that he doesn't know what we know . . . or what we suspect."

"So why is he hiding?"

"And who says he's hiding from us?"

Espinosa remained seated, with the kid standing in front of him: jeans, tennis shoes, cotton jacket, and a mesh shirt, looking just like any other recent graduate of the police academy. There was no sign that he had more money than usual. No reason to pressure him; the only result would be to put him on the defensive.

He was hungry, but he didn't feel like going out. At times like these, he usually resorted to the by-the-kilo place across the street, a better choice than most of the other cheap restaurants in the area. From his office window he could see the movement in the restaurant; he noticed that it wasn't so busy and had decided to head over there when he saw a familiar figure crossing the street toward the station. It was Vieira. He was walking slowly, limping slightly, and, despite the flowery shirt he wore loosely over cotton trousers, he was showing his age. Espinosa went down immediately to save him from having to climb the stairs.

"Espinosa, baby! I was afraid you'd already gone to lunch."

"I wouldn't call what I was about to do going to lunch."

"Let's go to the Polaca, for old times' sake."

"It's not Polaca, it's the Polonesa. Polacas are a thing of the past."

"Damn, isn't that right? There was a Polish girl like you wouldn't believe on the Rua Viveiro de Castro. Boy, I was a little kid, as healthy as a prizewinning bull, and I had a tab with the Polish girl just like people have accounts at the corner store. Her name was Gertrude, but I called her Gerda."

The restaurant was almost next door to the station; he spoke these last words as they were entering and being greeted by the waiter. They were still getting settled in when Vieira said:

"Espinosa, the son of a bitch who assaulted me has nothing to do with the guy with the wallet."

"What are you saying?"

"Just what you heard. The information that led me to the guy in the Galeria Alaska was wrong. Those people are heavy into drugs and don't give a fuck about a wallet; they would have dumped that shit if they'd found it. They have a well-organized cocaine-delivery system, and some of our people are on their payroll. Big shots and small change. They attacked me because they thought I was trying to get in on their turf."

"How did you find this out?"

"I promised not to tell ... the person who told me is on their list. . . . We used to be friends. He owed me one, and today he paid it back."

"This just complicates things even more. Or adds an element that's only been in the background. The guy who found your wallet used it to shake down junkies, but he's no dealer. At least there's no relation between him and these guys you're talking about. And so if your thinking is right, these guys have no knowledge of the murdered boys. As violent as they may be, they weren't responsible for those deaths."

"Espinosa, you can't keep me out of this. Everything you're investigating has to do with me: Magali's murder, my I.D., the assault. As happy as I am with Flor, I still want to get the son of a bitch who killed Magali."

"Speaking of which, have you managed to remember any fragments of that night?"

"Nothing. And I don't think I'm going to. I know you're skeptical about amnesia, but believe me, Espinosa, no one wishes it hadn't happened more than me. The only thing worse than my anguish about not being able to say a word about the night Magali was murdered is the nightmare that I could have done it myself. The psychologist who examined me said that pieces of what I forgot could resurface in dreams or even as fragments of scenes, quick flashes, during the day, when I least expect it. But nothing like that has happened."

The rest of the lunch was a debate about the benefits of joining forces. They said good-bye at two-forty without having reached an agreement. Espinosa later regretted not paying attention to the food, especially the apple pie.

In the detectives' office, he found a note. Vanessa had left a phone number and a message that she'd be free the rest of the night. Espinosa called.

"Sorry, I think I overreacted the other day. Do you still want to talk?"

"Certainly. I can come over right away."

"All right, but instead of talking outside you'd better come up. My apartment is 803."

Unlike Flor, Vanessa received Espinosa wearing normal

clothes, as if she were about to go shopping. Both of them knew that this wasn't usual police procedure; people were supposed to testify at the station, not in witnesses' apartments, especially not in a studio apartment taken up almost entirely by an ample double bed. But Espinosa still thought that a friendly approach was more likely to pay off. Vanessa was a lot more comfortable, and her distrust had apparently yielded to cooperation.

"My attitude the other day didn't help you find my friend's murderer. I was annoyed that you didn't trust me."

"It's not that I didn't trust you. I just asked you what you were doing at the time the crime was committed."

"And isn't that not trusting me?"

"Not necessarily."

"Fine. What do you want to know?"

"Whatever you have to tell me. Remember that this is a conversation, not a deposition."

"Officer, it's hard to talk with a policeman like I'm talking to a friend. You didn't come find me just to make friends."

"It was to ask for your help."

"I only had two friends. Magali was one of them."

"Is Flor the other?"

"I told you before: Flor isn't my friend, if that's what you want to know. Magali was friends with both of us, but we're not friends with each other. We're acquaintances and live nearby. With Magali it was different. She was a little like my older, more experienced sister. She gave me advice and helped me through tough times. She did the same with Flor."

"And where did Magali go when times where tough for her?"

"She had Vieira."

"How was their relationship?"

"Great. He acts a little boorish, but he's a good person. He was always very kind to Magali. On the few occasions they fought, he exploded, screamed, cursed God and the world, but after two minutes he'd completely forgotten about it."

"Did he ever threaten to kill her at times like that?"

"Every time. But he threatened Magali the same way he threatened his neighbors, his doorman, me, anyone who was around. Of course, he never laid a hand on either of us except in love."

"Who do you think might have killed Magali?"

"Like I said last time, any client could have done it, or one of those people who kill prostitutes, taxi drivers, beggars, solitary old ladies..."

"Besides those, who else do you think could have done it?"

"That's the worst thing. Besides them I can't imagine anybody else. Moreover, I can't imagine who would have done it like that. That's what scares me and makes me think it must have been a lunatic, because there's no defense against someone like that, who shows up all nice, sweet, generous, and when you're least expecting it you're tied to the bed being cut up, choked, suffocated. What we do to protect ourselves is not open the door to anybody who hasn't called for an appointment. That way we know they're coming and notify the doorman. That doesn't protect us from violence, but it lowers the risk."

"Do all of you have phones?"

"Almost everyone. To keep the costs down, one of us rents the line and, after the phone is installed, extends it to two other people and splits the bill. I divide my phone with two other girls. Magali's phone is the same as Flor's. It's like a shared line."

"Do you have any method for answering, since you live in different apartments?"

"Sort of. Nothing too fixed. The way we do it is that everyone answers on the third ring. The first one who speaks asks the caller who they want to talk to. Depending on what they say, the other two hang up. It's worked up till now."

"So you mean that in Magali's case, Flor could know about all her calls, and vice versa?"

"I think so. But Friday was Magali's night out with Vieira, and Flor knew that."

"Could anyone come in and go up at night without the doorman's noticing?"

"Certainly. The doorman lives with his wife and daughter in a room at the back of the building. He's always leaving to take care of something at home. The building has more than a hundred apartments. A lot of people come and go; anyone could slip in with a resident. It's the same thing if you ring the bell for the doorman—all you have to do is give someone's name and he lets you in. He rarely bothers to call on the intercom, and even if he did a lot of them don't work anyway."

They were seated at a small table with two chairs beside a window that looked out at a hill behind the building. While he was listening to Vanessa, alias Regina, Espinosa played with a small vase with two plastic daisies in it, the only object on the table besides the plastic tablecloth.

"Oh my God. I didn't even offer you a coffee!"

"Thanks. You've already given me a lot today."

Espinosa sat awhile looking at the girl, trying to imagine her as a teenager, leaving her hometown in Minas because of some mistake she'd made; once that first mistake was out of the way, why not make some more, somewhere more lucrative? He said his farewells to Vanessa-Regina with the promise that he'd come back for coffee another time.

His working day was almost over. All he needed was some news from Clodoaldo to round out his satisfying afternoon, but the day ended, back at the station, without a word. Nor did

Kika call. The news that wrapped up his day arrived by fax from São Paulo: the police had, at Espinosa's request, inquired at all the hospitals in that city that performed heart surgery. There were no patients by the name of Elói Azevedo.

The light was blinking on his answering machine. The phone must have rung during the night or early in the morning, but sleep was more powerful than the ringing, and he hadn't heard it. It was Clodoaldo. He had called at five in the morning to make an appointment for nine o'clock in the square in front of Espinosa's building. It was eight now. Espinosa plugged in the coffeemaker, stuck some bread in the toaster, and went downstairs to the lobby to get his paper.

When he went back downstairs at nine, Clodoaldo was nowhere to be found. He crossed the square diagonally, walking slowly, checking out the benches, almost all occupied by mothers and nannies. Someone came up from behind and touched his shoulder.

"Hey, buddy."

"Clodoaldo, I didn't think I'd ever see you again."

"It almost happened."

"What?"

"I don't know everything, only bits and pieces. Maybe only small ones."

"Let's go find an empty bench."

"I'd rather go somewhere else."

"Are you being followed?"

"I don't know. Maybe. For the last few days all I've done is follow people. Let's go somewhere where we can see who's coming."

Espinosa knew how adverse Clodoaldo was to any kind of personal exposure, but he could tell that there was something else bothering him now. They went back to Espinosa's building and got in his car. They drove aimlessly for a while, long enough to throw off any potential stalker, and parked on the Avenida Atlântica, not far from the place where Clodoaldo met the kids. The morning was cloudy and the beach was deserted. They picked a bench next to the sand, where they could easily be seen but where they could also spot anyone approaching. They sat next to each other, but each turned in a different direction: Espinosa looked out at the sea, while Clodoaldo faced the street. Neither had opened their mouths; the first to speak was Clodoaldo.

"I'm sorry about what happened to the boy. He refused to accept police protection, including from you. He thought he was betraying something, but he didn't know what. I suggested that he go spend some time at his mother's house in the Baixada Fluminense. But he didn't manage to stay put three days. He'd gotten it in his head that his mission was to follow the man with the wallet. He didn't think logically, he just followed his whims. The fact is, something about that man had gotten under his skin. Naturally, the guy noticed and turned the tables. Not that he was worried about a street kid following him. He was worried about who was paying the kid to do it. I noticed that the boy wasn't the only one following the man, but that someone else was after him. It wasn't too hard to find out that it was someone from the police. The boy also noticed that someone else was interested in the man. That's when he came and found me, all nervous, and told me that someone had tried to get him. He wasn't exactly sure who, just that it was someone really big, not the same one as before. I ordered him to hide again and only to come back out when things had calmed down. I myself kept watching the man and made a surprising discovery: besides me and the policeman, there was a big, strong guy, according to one of the doormen, who also wanted to know where the man was. I don't think those door-men had ever been under so much pressure.

"Three days later, the boy resurfaced, even more frightened than before. I gave him your number and told him to call you the minute anyone bothered him again. The next day I found out about his death. I would have dropped the whole thing, following people and keeping watch. But I couldn't get past the sight of that cop walking into the man's building, looking so right at home, and always leaving looking so happy with himself. Damn, we both know that following someone is one of the most annoying things in the world. So why was that kid always looking so thrilled? To make things even more complicated, on one of the nights I was watching him, I bumped into you on the lookout too, and suddenly I didn't know who was spying on who, and why. And the final twist came when I noticed that I was being followed as well, and not by the cop, who didn't look very experienced to me—but by someone who knew how to tail like a professional, so much that I never managed to make an I.D. And I'm pretty sure the guy doesn't want to meet me to make friends. So there we are."

If he hadn't had such a peaceful expression on his face and spoken so clearly, Clodoaldo's serious voice would have lent the narrative a sinister tone. But once he finished his story, he looked at Espinosa with the tranquillity of someone at mass.

"Clodoaldo, what do all these stakeouts and stalkings have to do with the boy's murder? Why was he killed?"

"If I knew, I would've already told you."

"He didn't say anything to you?"

"As much as he told you."

"Everything indicates that the man who was after him wasn't the same one he was fleeing on the beach, when he sought protection."

"For me there's only one thing that doesn't make sense. I know street kids well. For the rest of society, they're not even people. They're like almost-people, and nobody worries about them, except maybe a couple of nice ladies who give them bread and milk. So why, for no other reason, do two men go after a kid like that and end up killing him?"

"Because the boy knew something."

"But what?"

"In my opinion, the boy himself didn't realize he'd discovered something. The way he was killed suggests that someone was trying to get something out of him, or eliminate a witness."

They sat quietly for a while, each contemplating a different part of the tableau. On the side Clodoaldo was facing, between the sidewalk and the street, there was the bike path, where someone could approach quickly without being noticed in time. Clodoaldo was fully aware that the idea was paranoid, since nobody could know they were there, but in his experience there was no such thing as paranoia. Then Espinosa turned his body around on the cement bench; they both sat with their backs to the sea. Clodoaldo picked up the conversation again.

"Today I'm going back to my post to try to identify the guy who's following me."

"Take care. If you need help, call me; if I'm not in, leave a message."

They stood up, shaking the sand from their pants. They crossed the two lanes of the Avenida Atlântica and stopped next to the parked car.

"Do you want me to drop you off somewhere?" Espinosa asked.

"No thanks, I'm already home."

Espinosa and Clodoaldo both agreed that there was no plausible motive for the murders. Neither the world of crime as a whole nor a solitary criminal was so threatened that anyone needed to react by attacking senior citizens and killing children. But the truth was that people were being killed, street kids. Some people might not consider them human beings, but that didn't mean they went around lighting them on fire while they slept or breaking their heads against rocks.

Espinosa didn't head straight to work; he dropped his car off in Peixoto first. He parked in front of his building (one of the privileges of the area), glanced around his apartment, and, as he did every day, walked the three blocks that separated him from his workplace. During the walk, he wrestled with the news that there was no Elói Azevedo in any hospital equipped to carry out cardiac surgery in São Paulo. Either Dr. Elói had lied to the foreman, or the foreman had lied to Chaves, or Chaves had lied to Espinosa.

Chaves was out on the beat. Espinosa, sticking to his decision not to show any special interest in the kid, said nothing about him. Which didn't stop him from requesting information on Chaves from his former precinct. Of all the people who could be lying, Chaves was the closest both physically and professionally to Espinosa.

Espinosa's decision not to make hurried decisions that might only complicate things further made him turn his attention back to Magali's murder, which, almost a month after it had been committed, was still in mothballs, pushed out of the foreground by the death of the first boy and the attack on Vieira. As for the murder of the first boy, Espinosa had no doubt that it was a case of mistaken identity. The whole picture worried him. However, on that morning, for some reason, something else bothered him, something he couldn't put his finger on.

He thought about Kika. But she wasn't really a concern; she was more of a happy, promising fantasy. He thought about Flor and Vanessa. They, too, were more fantasies than worries. He finally decided that he was looking for even more problems than he already had. But the decision didn't change the tension he felt.

He was about to return his attention to the neglected paperwork when an image flashed through his brain like a lightning bolt. The first time it appeared so quickly that he retained only the intensity of the experience, unable to identify it. The second time the image was crystal clear: the window of his apartment. That morning, when he'd parked his car in front of his building, after his meeting with Clodoaldo, he had glanced quickly at his apartment before heading to the station. The window was open; he had left it closed. And it wasn't the cleaning lady's day.

PART 5

Several parts of his body were still aching, and they hurt even more when he bumped into a piece of furniture or when Flor overdid it with her loving caresses. He was worried about his head. Who the fuck beats an old man in the head? It could cause a brain hemorrhage! And the guy who beat him wasn't fucking around, either. Lucky that...

"Are you talking to yourself, baby?"

"Huh?"

"I asked if you were talking to yourself."

"Of course not. Aren't you here with me?"

"I am, but you're in the bedroom and I'm in the bathroom."

"But still you heard me."

"What were you talking about?"

"I was asking who the fuck hits an old man in the head. It could cause a hemorrhage."

"You're not an old man and you're not going to get a hemorrhage. Speaking of which, your friend the cop has been leaving us alone lately."

"Speaking of what? About being old or getting a hemorrhage?"

"About... on that subject. He does like to ruffle feathers."

"He's only doing his job, Flor."

"Well, fine. Still, he could lay off a little."

"If he laid off any more he'd be tucking me in at night."

"I don't know about you, but he'd certainly like to do that for me."

"Why? Did he try something with you?"

"No. He just has that look about him. Women can always tell with men."

Flor had bought Vieira a new belt. He was trying to stick it through the loops at the back of his pants. This was one of the operations that made his collarbone hurt.

"Flor, have you realized that everything in this story has happened to the wrong people?"

"Who was wrong?" she asked coming into the room wrapped up in a towel while she dried her hair with another one.

"All the people were wrong. The kid who was burned to death was killed by mistake. I'm almost sure that I was attacked by mistake. Now all that's missing is to find out that Magali was killed by mistake."

"Which wouldn't bring her back."

"No."

"So why think about it?" She continued drying her hair but tossed the other towel onto the foot of the bed, standing there entirely nude. Vieira forgot what it was he'd been talking about.

He had never doubted Espinosa's friendship, at least up till now. What he didn't know was whom the cop actually suspected. Was it just standard procedure, or did Espinosa have doubts as to whether he had done it? And what was this about his checking out Flor? Didn't he have his own girl, damn it?

"What girl, baby? Who are you talking about?"

"Nothing, dear. I'm just thinking out loud."

Flor put on her panties and snapped on her bra. Vieira reflected on how similar these movements were to the ones he made to put on his belt, but she was infinitely more graceful and light and could pull them off without any effort. He wanted to use the rest of the afternoon to go to the Thirteenth

Precinct to see if anything new had come up. Flor had finished dressing and was ready to go out.

"Are you sure you have to work today?" Vieira asked.

"Of course, sweetheart. It's how I earn my bread."

"Damn it, Flor, why do you need to earn your bread? You don't need that shit anymore."

"Of course I do, love. It's the only thing I've got."

"Fucking hell, Flor! Didn't I tell you to come live with me?"

"But I have my own apartment."

"And they can kick you out and you can't do anything about it."

"So what do you want me to do?"

"Marry me."

"You're overexcited. You like me as a woman, but getting married is something else."

"Fuck, women are complicated."

If they started talking now, he would get there too late, and he didn't know the people on the next shift. They left at the same time and rode down in the elevator in silence, though Flor lovingly adjusted his collar and fixed his hair.

"Tomorrow we'll talk about this seriously," Vieira declared on the street.

Flor was still holding the money he'd given her to pay for the taxi. She liked taxis. She felt important. She always looked for the very newest ones, with four doors and air-conditioning, those that looked most like the ones she saw in movies. She sat in the back seat, on the side opposite the driver. She knew that whenever they could they checked out her legs. She only granted them a quick glance before concealing her legs behind the front passenger seat. The driver would have to content himself with looking at her face; if she was wearing something sleeveless, he might get a glimpse of her arms, maybe her cleavage. While the poor man was checking her out, she looked out the window, feigning fascination with the people walking down the sidewalk. One of her dreams was to have a chauffeured car. A real lady had her own driver. She would prefer him to have graying hair. A black guy with graying hair. She'd seen that in a TV movie. He would say, when he dropped her off somewhere, "Would madam like me to wait?" or "What time would madam like me to pick her up?" She could even hear his voice.

"Where on Barata Ribeiro do you want to get off, ma'am?"

"At the beginning . . . right at the beginning."

When she went shopping, the driver would get out and open the door for her. "Should I wait, madam?" "Thank you, George"—George, not Jorge—"but I'm going to walk a little to take some exercise."

"Is this all right for you here?"

"Thank you. . . . Fine."

She responded mechanically to the doorman's greeting and mechanically took the electric bill he held out for her, and in the elevator she was still pondering, for the umpteenth time, how she could manage it. Nothing would ever come of the old fart plantation owner; she'd fuck Junior and would still be fucking Junior's own son, without getting her hands on anything more stable. The guy was terrified of his wife. Vieira was great, but he wasn't adequately financed: he only had an apartment and a car that had been painted more times than her nails. Her one hope was to snare someone while her body was at its pinnacle; her purchasing power would decline with her beauty. The competition in Rio was fierce. Every summer there was a new crop on the market; plus, she still had to compete with rich people's daughters. And just a few days ago she'd heard two girls who couldn't have been more than fifteen splitting the proceeds of a trick at the mall. But they were just brats; they weren't competition. The truth was, since her days in Recife she'd always known how to run her business. She couldn't let down her guard now, however, right when her beauty was peaking.

"How are you, officer? Wounds healing nicely?"

"On my body, almost all of them."

"I've got good news. I think we got your man. At least one of them. Want to have a look?"

"Of course. How'd they get the son of a bitch?"

"By chance. He tried to attack a cop during a getaway. From your description, and since he was so violent, we thought it might be the same guy. We've got him here."

One thing that had never changed since he'd entered the force was the condition of the cells. The apparent chaos disguised a rigorous internal order: domination and servitude on opposite sides. Reigning over this order, and independent of it, was a special brand of nastiness. The man was standing at the back of the cell, a space so cramped that he wouldn't have been able to sit down if he'd wanted to (and if he'd been allowed to). The warden ordered him to come up to the front, which he did amid complaints, curses, and shoving. He looked at Vieira as if he'd never seen him. Vieira couldn't identify him definitively. He was the same height, and the hands and arms looked familiar, but he couldn't swear it was the same guy. Maybe neither of them could recognize the other. It had been dark, and it had all happened so fast. The difference was that Vieira was the victim and was on one side of the bars, while the other man was in that cell and would probably spend some time there, unless someone arranged a little "confusion" to finish him off.

"Thanks, big guy. I'm sorry that I can't identify him positively, but I'm not absolutely sure it was him."

"Maybe he'll say something. In any case, he attacked a cop, so we'll leave him in there to cool down for a few days."

Five-thirty in the afternoon. The station was three blocks from his building. He'd stop by the supermarket; he needed to pick up a few things. Magali used to go every week for him. On the way back, the street headed uphill slightly, but enough to leave him out of breath, especially because he was carrying a bag. He shifted it from hand to hand. He arrived home sweaty, his arms aching, his legs tired. He chalked it up to the heat and the attack. He'd be fine in a minute.

He couldn't understand why Flor was being so cautious. There was no doubt that she liked him: she had declared herself Magali's estate and him the only beneficiary. He himself had given her proof of his love, even asking her to marry him. What was she waiting for? What the fuck was she talking about, rushing things? Every day that went by was a day spent without dedicating themselves entirely to each other; a day not lived to the fullest; a day when some asshole could make a date with her—and that she still had to arrange around her "job." What the fuck was she talking about? He could support her perfectly, and she would become Mrs. Vieira Crisóstomo, just like the departed Maria Zilda.

The elevator stopped on his floor. He got out, practically dragging the shopping bag, opened the door to his apartment, then rested awhile against the door, looking at the L-shaped living room, still decorated with the furniture Maria Zilda had picked out. A lone window pierced the shorter leg of the L, while the bigger part received only a reflected, fragile light that made it look permanently abandoned. The bedroom was illuminated by a wide window that faced directly onto the street. He liked the apartment. It was small but comfortable—and above all it was his. He pictured Flor waiting for him as Mrs. Vieira Crisóstomo. He'd never proposed such a thing to

Magali, nor had she asked him to; they had a tacit agreement that she would be his companion for nights on the town and dinners but would never become his wife. He remembered coming home with her in the wee hours and her putting him in bed and taking off his clothes. The memory gave way to a still-fresh image of Flor completely naked, standing at the foot of the bed, drying her hair after her shower. Three women, two of whom were dead; and a worrying memory lapse. What would he do if suddenly he remembered that night in its entirety and discovered that he was a murderer? He tried to push the idea away, labeling it as absurd. It didn't make sense. The fact that Magali's legs were tied with his own belt was proof that it wasn't him: he wouldn't be stupid enough to sign a crime like that. He realized the door was still open and closed it. Maybe he wouldn't remember anything because there wasn't anything to remember.

Ever since she was a girl, she'd been accustomed to being admired and desired; her professional success was a direct result of her untarnished beauty and sensuality. She wouldn't know how to live without this constant confirmation of her value as a woman, and what Vieira was proposing was precisely to trade those daily affirmations for the peace of a home. The thing she believed in least was a home; even less, in the peace of a home. The so-called attractions of home didn't attract her. Kids? She didn't have any and didn't want any. Servants to command? Ridiculous in an apartment that size. Money? Vieira's pension. On the other hand, there was security. Though she'd be restricted, she'd also have a life safeguarded against daily fluctuations. Besides, as Vieira's eventual widow, she'd get her own pension and the apartment. Vieira was her retirement, without her having to put in the long years of work for it: it would be effective immediately. The uncomfortable detail was that she would be a "retiree" before hitting thirty. A formidable piece of war matériel scrapped by a greedy general.

With every day that passed, she found it harder to tolerate her miserable apartment, with its single window opening not onto the street but onto hundreds of other similar windows. Hookers' apartments were all the same; even hookers themselves ended up the same. She had begun to notice it when she'd realized that Magali's apartment smelled exactly like hers. It was true that she'd moved up considerably in the world from the little shanty with its dirt floor she'd inhabited in Recife, but she was still a long way from her dream of a penthouse.

The heat was insufferable, and the rain that at the end of the afternoon had seemed on its way hadn't managed to fall. With the ceiling fan on, stretched out in bed wearing only her panties, Flor looked at her feet, which rested at the end of the bed; she savored the contrast of her dark skin with her pale, unpainted toenails. A quick evaluation confirmed what she repeated to herself several times a day: her body showed no sign of its countless encounters. She thought the same of her soul, which she wasn't sure was as beautiful as her body, but she couldn't complain: she'd fought the battles of ten years of life in Rio de Janeiro and emerged victorious. What she had to decide was whether to compete in the bush leagues or get ready for the World Series.

In the last few years, she'd nearly stopped receiving clients at home, with the exception of her benefactor and Junior (who still couldn't distinguish a woman from an ice-cream cone); her specialty was businessmen from other states visiting Rio for work. Her business sense had worked wonders for her with the managers of two hotels in Copacabana. When Vieira offered to marry her, with monogamy a condition of marriage, he didn't realize he was proposing shutting her out of a scam more lucrative than the pension of a retired police officer.

She tried, with her nails, to remove something tiny in the skin of her thigh. It was invisible to the eye but sensitive to the touch. In her line of work, both senses were equally important. And that night she had a date: a friendly, generous client from the interior of São Paulo. She sat in bed looking at the plastic bags that, together with a few stacked-up boxes, were piled in a corner of the room. Magali's things, sent by Vieira; they had emptied her apartment, but Flor didn't know what to do with all that stuff. The furniture, which in fact amounted to only one piece, had been sold to the first person who'd made an offer. Flor thought it would be a noble gesture to give her friend's things to the kind of charity bazaar that crops up at Christmastime in empty commercial spaces.

Some time ago, she'd reached a decision she characterized as stylistic. It had to do with her professional life. She knew that she could divide men into two large groups: those who want a prostitute who looks the stereotypical part—a low-cut, tight black dress, high heels, heavily made-up face, painted fingernails and toenails, and a few other details—and those who weren't looking for a prostitute but a model middle-class girl they couldn't get on their own and were willing to rent for the night. Flor had chosen the second category for strictly commercial reasons. That's what made her different from Magali, and that was why Vieira was proposing to her without ever having made a similar proposal to his former lover. Vieira didn't feel even a little uncomfortable being seen in a restaurant with a prostitute, but he wouldn't want her to be mistaken for his wife. Wife and hooker were two different species, incompatible beneath the same roof.

She, Flor, belonged to a third species. She wasn't a hooker

and she wasn't a wife: she was in transition. That's why she needed to maintain her style, satisfying Vieira's desire, and sense of morality, while still fueling the fantasies of business-men who called their homes in some other state on Friday night to tell their wives that the deal still hadn't closed. Men like that didn't want to be spotted by people they knew having a drink with a whore, but they would be proud to be seen with a pretty business or law student. If that student happened to be Flor, the man wouldn't mind if his fellow out-of-towner spread the news back home, even at the risk of word getting back to his wife.

Flor had learned all these things with time. With time and with men. She didn't want to have to throw them all away to satisfy Vieira. Of course, even if she were married, men would still ogle and desire her; that didn't worry her. But another thing she'd learned with time and with men was that being ogled and desired was not a purely passive condition. She had to do more than simply allow herself to be seen. A combination of passivity and activity—the exact proportion was hard to describe—took her to the next level: not only being captured by the male gaze, but capturing it herself. The balance wasn't easy; it was attained only by training and constant practice. Such practice could disappear with marriage. That was the part that would vanish in the transition from woman to wife. Flor had already lost a lot of things in her life. She didn't want to lose that.

From far off, crossing the square, Espinosa focused on the living room window. He could make out the colonial green of the venetian blinds, but he couldn't tell if they were com-pletely closed. When he arrived in front of the building he confirmed that they were closed. Unsatisfied, he took the stairs two at a time, opened the door, not bothering to close it, and ran to the French windows, which looked onto the square. They were closed and locked, just as he'd left them. He automatically glanced at the answering machine: neither light was blinking. He examined the rest of the apartment and found nothing out of place (well, lots of things were out of place, but not out of the places he'd left them). In his bedroom, he opened the drawer of his bedside table to see if the extra gun he kept at home was there. It wasn't. When he went back into the living room, wondering where else he could have left the weapon, he ran into a man pointing it at his chest. He was standing next to the door, tall and strong enough not to need any gun at all, though he seemed perfectly comfortable with it in his hand.

"Who are you? What are you doing here?"

"I've got the gun. You shut up."

The voice, unexpectedly high for a man of his size, was ice-cold. The fact that he was unconcerned about hiding his face was disconcerting: either he wasn't worried about being recognized afterward or he was sure that no one would be left to recognize him. The man was less than three meters from Espinosa, and the firmness with which he held the revolver suggested beyond a shadow of a doubt that if he wanted to he'd hit his target. He closed the door to the hallway, crossed the living room in two strides, and stuck the gun under Espinosa's chin while removing, with his free hand, the gun Espinosa carried in a holster on his belt. He stuck it in his pocket and pushed Espinosa toward the bathroom.

The man removed a roll of nylon cord from the inside pocket of his jacket, ordered Espinosa to lie on the bathroom floor, tied his hands and feet behind his back, and, without cutting the cord, wrapped the rest of it around his body, from his neck to his ankles; finally, he gagged him with duct tape.

He made sure it was good and tight, testing the resistance of the knots, and, once he was satisfied with the job, started dragging Espinosa like a heavy sack, depositing him inside the shower before closing the curtain. That calmed Espinosa a little; if he was taking those measures it was because he didn't mean to kill him, at least not immediately. Then Espinosa heard the noise of the bathroom door being closed and the stereo in the living room turned on, the same CD Espinosa had left in there, but the volume louder than usual.

The cord held his arms and legs tightly, but the most irritating thing was the tape over his mouth. He normally breathed a little through both his nose and his mouth; with his mouth covered he was worried about suffocating. The CD ended and started up again. He couldn't make out any other sound in the apartment. When the CD was about halfway through for the second time, Espinosa started to try to squirm out of the shower. He managed, but only with great effort. Now he was stuck between the sink and the toilet. As he was lying on his side, he could move only by pushing his knee against something and twisting his torso. The space he was caught in made such a movement nearly impossible. When he managed to reach the door, he put his ear to it to try to hear something besides the music. He figured he'd been tied up for more than an hour. He pulled himself up to a kneeling position by the door and on the third try managed to budge the knob with his jaw. The door opened toward the inside, so as he was opening it he had to move away and lower himself down the wall, prying it open first with his forehead and then with his whole body.

His first view of the living room revealed that he was alone. He started to drag himself toward the kitchen to try to reach a knife. With his mouth taped shut, he couldn't conceive of a way to open the silverware drawer; he tried to remember if he had left a knife on top of the counter (inside the sink wouldn't do him any good). After moving around a few pieces of furniture and stopping a few times to rest and catch his breath, he managed to cross the threshold of the kitchen and make it to the counter. He got back on his knees and examined the counter. It was perfectly clean. The handles on the drawers were little metal balls; there wasn't the slightest chance that he could open them. Even on his knees, he could do no more than slide his back along the counter, and the tips of his fingers still wouldn't reach the handles. He looked around for something that could cut the duct tape. The most useful thing he saw was a box of matches. He quickly abandoned the idea of using these, not wanting to set fire to his shirt and himself. He tried to remove the tape from his mouth by scraping it against the counter and then against the bottom of the oven. He cut his face, but the tape held firm.

He dragged himself back to the living room and managed to jerk the stereo plug out of the wall. He crossed the living room again and stuck his ear against the door to try to hear if there was anyone on the stairs or in the hallway. Each movement took him longer than the previous and left him more exhausted. After resting for a few minutes, he began beating his body against the door, in the hopes that somebody would hear it. The cast-iron door from the building to the street was heavy, and every time someone closed it he could hear the noise. He took each slam as his cue to beat at the apartment door. He repeated the procedure countless times, until he grew convinced that it would work only when someone was on his floor, where there was only one other apartment. While waiting for his neighbor to arrive, and between bangs on the downstairs door, he knocked the phone onto the floor and tried to dial. But since his hands were tied behind his back, he couldn't hear anything, even when, after great effort and numerous attempts, he managed to dial the three-digit number for the police. He could hear someone's voice, but he couldn't make any audible, much less comprehensible, sound. Since he wasn't in an American movie, the attempt ended with a click on the other end of the line. It occurred to him that if he could open the French windows in the living room he could make it onto the balcony; someone would surely notice him and come to his rescue. But the window stayed shut. Any more radical efforts would put his life in danger, and he was determined to save it.

He leaned his body against the door, keeping his ear to the ground in order to hear any noises from inside the building, and felt the slow passage of time. After his attempt to get help over the phone, he had managed to replace the receiver. The phone rang three times at intervals of approximately one hour. He heard Kika's voice all three times. He occasionally had to turn his body to change sides; the forced position of his arms and legs made his whole body ache. He tried to breathe slowly and steadily; the last thing he wanted with his mouth taped shut was a respiratory attack brought on by sheer nervousness.

He thought about the man. A professional from out of town, paid for his services? That could be the only explanation for his carelessness about revealing his identity. If not, he would have killed his victim once the job was done. Espinosa was sure he wasn't an opportunist; he was too calm and efficient to be anything other than a pro. And he was as strong as a gorilla. He thought about the attack on Vieira. He thought about the death of the boy. He thought about Kika. He thought about Clodoaldo. What was the man looking for? Apparently, he hadn't disturbed anything in the apartment. Everything was as usual, and there were no open drawers or closets. If the man had been looking for something in the apartment, it had to be too big to fit into drawers and closets. Unless he was looking not for a thing but a person, which would explain why he had waited for Espinosa to return, supposing that Espinosa and the other person would come back together. If that was the case, why hadn't he asked him any questions? Maybe because he didn't want to give away the identity of the object of his search. As Espinosa was wondering about these different possibilities, he shifted his body painfully, pausing whenever he heard sounds outside the door.

When his next-door neighbor finally rang the bell in response to the strange noises at the door, he was met only with more scratching and guttural noises and called the police, who in less than fifteen minutes broke down the door and rescued Officer Espinosa of the Twelfth Precinct. He would have preferred to be freed by colleagues from his own station, but he couldn't be choosy.

His saviors were still there when the two detectives from his team arrived. They waited for everyone to leave, including the residents of the building who had been attracted by the commotion and the noise of the door being broken down. Espinosa thanked his neighbor from the bottom of his heart and closed the door as best he could.

"Damn, Espinosa, what happened? What happened to your face?"

"Nothing. I did it myself when I was trying to take off the duct tape."

"What duct tape?"

"The guy tied me up with cord and duct tape."

"What guy? What was he doing inside your apartment?"

"That's what I'd love to know. Can I offer you some coffee while I tell you what happened?"

Espinosa went to the kitchen, happy to be able to do it on his two feet rather than by dragging his body. He put some coffee in the machine. While all three of them had a cup, Espinosa related the story from the moment in the station when he'd realized that the apartment window was open.

"I have no doubt that he waited for me to leave in the morning to come into the apartment. What I don't know is what he expected to find here. And I don't know how he managed to get in. Neither the door downstairs nor this door showed any signs of being forced."

His two colleagues asked for permission to examine the apartment. The phone rang. It was Kika. Espinosa told her what happened and said he'd have to double up her security for a few days.

"How many days?"

"I don't know. Until the weekend. Maybe more, maybe less."

"Am I going to be able to show my pictures on the Avenida Atlântica?"

"The ideal would be to avoid unnecessary risks."

"What if I think it's necessary?"

"Then I would have to agree."

The two detectives found nothing that indicated the man's presence in the apartment, except the remaining duct tape and nylon cord. They said their farewells, postponing the investigation till the morning, by which time they would have written up a report.

While he was showering, Espinosa thought about what had happened, adding nothing to the reflections from the hours when he was bound and gagged and waiting for help.

The yellowish light from the old lamp shade brightened the room as he stretched out on the sofa, and every part of his body began to ache. He felt a different pain in his legs and arms than in his shoulders and neck. Even though he'd let hot water fall on his neck for more than half an hour, it still felt like a plank. The windows were wide open, and the clarity of the night allowed him to pick out the silhouettes of the distant hills. He rubbed a cold beer can across his forehead—a gesture he'd seen in countless films, but which in his case only gave him a wet forehead. He didn't drink the whole beer; it had warmed up while he was gazing out the window.

The guy was looking for someone he'd thought would be with Espinosa. That was the only explanation for his behavior. The most far-fetched hypothesis was Kika; the most plausible was Clodoaldo. He'd probably been on the lookout since that morning. He'd seen Espinosa leave and seen Clodoaldo with him, but he hadn't seen where Clodoaldo had come from. He must have imagined that Clodoaldo had been with Espinosa to begin with. He'd seen the two leave together in the car and had taken advantage of their absence to get into the apartment and wait, knowing that the policeman didn't drive to the station. He surely wasn't interested in Espinosa. It'd be easy to get to him (as in fact he'd proven). He was after somebody slippery, somebody who had information precious enough to justify invading a policeman's apartment and tying him up at gunpoint. Espinosa found himself wondering whether the two detectives had examined the apartment in order to find some clue left by the interloper—or in order to remove any traces of his presence.

Clodoaldo had been watching the building on the Avenida Copacabana for several days and was following someone, in addition to, as he said, being followed himself. He was aware of how much danger the dead boy had been in, so much so that he had given him Espinosa's phone number. Maybe the kid had passed along some information; the man had killed the boy and now was after Clodoaldo.

It was too early to go to sleep. He hadn't had lunch or dinner, and since he didn't feel like warming up something from the freezer, he went out to eat. On the street, though the stores were already closed, lots of people were carrying bags laden with gifts. Only five days until Christmas.

The body was down at the Forensic Institute and hadn't been claimed. The news reached Espinosa through Vieira.

"Espinosa, they found the son of a bitch—dead."

"Which one?"

"The one with my wallet. My I.D. was on him, so they called me . . . wanting to know if I was the dead guy. Shit, Espinosa, the police are subtle."

"How did they know it was him?"

"They didn't. They just found my I.D. on him."

The story wasn't quite so simple. Over the course of the day, Espinosa learned that the body of a white man between thirty and thirty-five had been found a few days earlier in some bushes near the Lagoon of Marapendi in Barra da Tijuca. The victim had been tortured before being shot to death. Near the body they had found a billfold, with no money and nothing to identify the dead man. After two weeks, the Sixteenth Precinct, in Barra da Tijuca, had received a plastic I.D. holder discovered on a dirt road near where the body had been found. It was Officer Vieira's. They remembered the unidentified body picked up two weeks before and concluded that it could be Vieira.

Though there was no one to identify the body, Espinosa had no doubt that it was the same man the boy said he'd followed through the streets of Copacabana. This confirmed his suspicion that he wasn't the one who had killed the boy: he had already been dead for more than a week when the boy's head was dashed against the rock in Leme. He thought of the man in his apartment.

The autopsy report made it clear that the man had been tortured so much that he would have confessed to anything, things he knew and things he didn't. Espinosa wondered what they wanted to learn from him and what he had said. It started to make sense, the deaths of the boys and the hunt for Clodoaldo. Not having anything to offer his torturers, the man had passed the buck. The first boy had been murdered because the killer was in a hurry to eliminate the witness; getting the wrong kid didn't really matter, from an operational perspective. It was a simple accident; the only downside was that now he'd have to kill the right one: something else to do. The murderer went after the right boy, found him, and smashed his head in. A cheap, primitive way to kill. He must have thought that bullets were only for grown-ups. Espinosa's biggest worry was how many other names the wallet snatcher would have given up in his desperation to please his torturers. He himself could be among them, and so could Kika.

From the station, he called and left a message for her. Detective Maldonado was assigned to protect her at night, while she was showing her pictures on the sidewalk of the Avenida Atlântica. Espinosa was a little skeptical about the effectiveness of such protection; a man who could get into a police officer's apartment and tie him up would not be much put out by a young and inexperienced detective. But for now that was all he had.

Vieira hadn't completely recovered from the attack and still couldn't drive. Espinosa took him to Barra da Tijuca to pick up his I.D. Since it was a magnificent sunny morning, he took the Avenida Niemeyer. The view that the seaside highway provided of the intense green ocean and the almost purple blue of the sky more than compensated for any annoyance he may have felt at having to drive Vieira. Despite his wounded mouth, Vieira managed to yap during the whole drive, jumping from one subject to another, punctuating every transition with a commentary on the landscape, but without making a single reference to Flor.

On the brown envelope they were handed in the lobby of the Barra station, several phone numbers had been jotted down; all were crossed off except the last one, Vieira's, which had been circled.

"I think it's the first time a dead man has ever come by to pick up his I.D.," said Vieira, joking with the officer on duty.

"Sorry about the call, Officer, but we had to verify it."

"Of course, buddy. I'm happy not to be that body in the morgue."

They talked for more than an hour, discussing new cases and reminiscing about old exploits.

On the way back, in possession of his identification, Vieira was just as chatty, though a little more confident. That's when he mentioned Flor.

"What do you think about Flor?"

For Espinosa, the question sounded ambiguous. Not that Vieira was being sneaky: that wasn't his style. But what did he want his opinion about? About Flor the woman, or the Flor mixed up in the investigation?

"I think she's a beautiful woman."

"Damn, Espinosa, waking up in the morning with that woman by my side is like winning the lottery every day."

"The problem is the price of the ticket."

"What the fuck ... the fuck do you mean by that?"

"I mean that as long as Magali's death hasn't been put to rest, your lovely inheritance is tainted by a murder case in which you are the only suspect, which, in the eyes of other people, may spoil your relationship with Flor."

"Espinosa, other people can fuck themselves with their opinions."

" 'Other people,' Vieira, is a nice way of saying the law. Don't forget that in the eyes of the law you and Flor are the only suspects."

"I can't believe that you, my friend, are telling me this."

"I'm telling you precisely *because* I'm your friend."

Even though he was driving, Espinosa could still see Vieira shrivel up and grow older. The scars from his wounds grew clearer, and the almost imperceptible tremor in the hand resting on his leg caught Espinosa's peripheral vision.

"Why did you go to her apartment?"

"Because, in case you're forgetting, I'm investigating Magali's death."

"So why didn't you call her down to the station?"

"I did. And she showed up both times. Once with her lawyer." It was a way to get the story on the lawyer.

"Lawyer? What fucking lawyer?"

"I don't remember his name, but he was a young, pretty efficient guy." Espinosa was sorry about adding the "young"; it wasn't necessary now that he already knew what he wanted to find out: that the lawyer hadn't been Vieira's work.

"But what fucking lawyer are you talking about? Flor doesn't have a lawyer. I'm her lawyer. What's the little shit's name?"

"I don't remember. I know he was really young, but that in spite of that defended his client brilliantly."

"And why didn't you tell me about it?"

"Because I thought you knew. Don't worry about it. It was only a routine procedure."

"Was going to her apartment also just a routine procedure?" Viera asked harshly.

"Certainly. I needed to find out if any of the keys in

Magali's apartment matched Flor's door and vice versa, and I had to do it on site."

He had opted for the tunnel on the way back instead of taking the Avenida Niemeyer. The conversation continued inside the tunnel, their faces weakly lit by the lights embedded in the walls.

"Listen, Vieira. I'm not against you, and I'm not competing with you for Flor's affections, which are entirely focused on you."

"Fine . . . don't worry about it. . . . The attack's made me a little paranoid. I don't want you to think I'm happy as a clam with a new woman. I liked Magali a lot; she was my partner and knew me better than even Maria Zilda. She took care of me, and I took care of her. She protected me when I had too much to drink, and I protected her when she felt threatened. In spite of Flor's beauty and youth, I miss Magali. . . . I think about her every day."

When the car left the tunnel, they were blinded by the midday sun. They didn't say a word until arriving at Vieira's building.

Espinosa spent part of the afternoon in the morgue at the Forensic Institute. The description Kika and the boy had given perfectly matched the body pulled out from a drawer. It was his first sighting of the man he'd spent almost a month trying to find, and the vision was far from pleasant. If anyone cared to, the face could be recognized, but the rest of the body had been pretty badly used. The torturers hadn't been concerned with hiding the dead man's identity; it even seemed they'd made a point of leaving the face and hands intact enough to make the body identifiable, a sort of message "to whom it may concern." Espinosa was certain that only in the last moments before his death had the man realized what he was dying for . . . if he had still been in a state to realize anything.

It was the fourth cadaver in the series that had begun with Magali, and Espinosa had the mournful feeling that it wouldn't be the last.

At the station, no response from Kika to his message. Maldonado had gone out early, concerned about protecting Kika on her way to the Avenida Atlântica. At five-thirty, he called Espinosa from the street.

"Officer, the girl's not home, no one was around to give me any information, and her downstairs neighbor didn't see when she left. I've been here since five; she could have gone straight to the Avenida Atlântica without stopping off at home."

"Meet me on the Avenida Atlântica."

There wasn't a service car available, and he didn't have time to borrow one; he got a taxi on the corner. It was still light outside and the traffic coming from downtown was heavy, but there weren't many people on the sidewalk and none of the salespeople had yet arrived. There was no sign of Kika. Espinosa looked in the garage where she stored her metal stand, glanced into the nearby bars and checked the benches and coconut stalls by the beach, but the people around were completely different from the ones who showed up after seven. The heavy traffic meant that he had to wait quite a while for Maldonado.

"Stay here," he told the younger cop when he arrived. "I'm going to my apartment to see if she's left a message on my machine. If you need to call, use the pay phone across the street. I'll be back as soon as I can."

"It's still early, Officer. She could be on her way."

"But from where? She always comes from her house. She wouldn't have been walking around all day carrying the paintings she shows at night. It's strange that she didn't stop off at home." He said the last sentence while hailing a taxi.

He opened the door to his apartment with his eye set on the answering machine; it blinked, indicating more than one message. None was from Kika. He called her answering service again, leaving an urgent message. He got his car and headed for the Rua do Catete. Most of the traffic was traveling in the other direction, but it was still slow going. He parked in front of the house at six-ten, even though a sign indicated that curb-side parking was allowed only after eight. The window of Kika's apartment was open, and there was a light on on the third floor. He had to ring the bell a few times before someone buzzed him up. Espinosa ran up the three flights of stairs; when the girl opened the apartment door he was gasping.

"Espinosa . . . Officer Espinosa . . . friend of Kika's."

"Calm down. I know who you are. Take a deep breath. What happened?"

"Is Kika here?"

"No. She should be on the Avenida Atlântica."

"I've just come from there. Do you know if she came by here?"

"I don't know. I only got here about fifteen minutes ago."

"And the other friend of yours?"

"She's on duty tonight."

"Can you look in Kika's room to see if her pictures are there?"

"Sure. Did something happen to her?"

"No. I hope not."

The girl didn't invite Espinosa in. He thought it might have been because of the tiny proportions of the hot pants she was wearing, or perhaps because of the mess prevailing in the house, which he could see from the doorway. She left the door open while doing what he asked. She returned immediately, shaking her head.

"They're all there. The ones she shows are wrapped up.

What are you worried about? Is there something you're not telling me?"

"No, nothing. It must be my imagination. I don't think anything happened. It's just that things have happened in the last few days. Any idea where she might have gone?"

"The week before Christmas she wouldn't go anywhere but the Avenida Atlântica. She's got high hopes of selling at least three more paintings."

"If she comes back, tell her to call my house immediately."

He returned to the Avenida Atlântica convinced that she wouldn't show up that night. The first vendors were setting up, and Maldonado was standing by the door to the garage where Kika kept her stand. When Espinosa got there, he was talking with the building's doorman.

"Nothing, Officer. She hasn't been here."

"She didn't go home to get her pictures, either, or leave me a message."

"What do you think?"

"I don't know. I don't have any idea. The only thing that reassures me is that the guy who attacked me didn't mention her name. Though, in fact, he didn't mention anyone's name. She must have gone to an opening, a party, or run into an old flame, or gone to visit some relative . . ."

"Definitely."

"There's something else. The man who attacked me didn't waste his energy. He didn't take advantage of my being tied up to assault me or do anything unnecessary; he was extremely economical with his actions."

"Why are you telling me this?"

"Because if he didn't see Kika with the kid—and she was only with him once—there's no reason to try anything on her."

"Definitely."

"You already said that."

"It's all I've got for now, Officer."

"All right, Maldonado, sorry. Let's try to find the girl."

It was eight; there was still time for Kika to arrive, but neither of the policemen believed that would happen. Espinosa left a note with the garage doorman, expressly ordering him to give the note to the girl with the pictures and not to leave her side until putting her in the first taxi that appeared. They decided that the only possibility was her apartment. Before heading there, however, they stopped by Espinosa's to see if there were any messages.

The machine was blinking. The message was from Kika. "Shit, you never pick up. . . . I'm home. . . . I'm scared."

It took them only about ten minutes to reach the house in Catete. Her friend opened the door, making sure that it was them and no one else. Both of the girls were frightened. The reality of all the recent deaths and their implicit threat had suddenly sunk into Kika's mind. She was seated on her bed, dressed, shoes on, anxiety written on her face, as if she was prepared for immediate danger. When she saw the two detectives, she smiled, relieved, but didn't get up from the bed.

"What happened?" Espinosa asked as soon as he walked into the room.

"When I came home to get the pictures, my downstairs neighbor told me that a big, tall man had come looking for me, talking in a commanding voice. From his description, it was nobody I knew. I immediately remembered the message that you left about the guy who broke into your apartment. I also remembered the kid. I called the station, but you'd already left; I called your house, but the machine picked up. I was scared to go back home. If he had been looking for me, he surely would have come back. So I started walking through the streets, killing time until you got home; when I realized that you still weren't there, I went to a movie theater and waited there. I changed places several times, but nobody was behind me; when the lights came back on, I exited with everybody else, left a message for you, and came back home. Do you think it was the same guy who broke into your apartment?"

Her description left no room for doubt. It was the same man. Espinosa didn't want her to panic, but he also didn't want to downplay the situation and allow her to let down her guard.

"I'm not sure. But just in case, let's pretend it was. Until we get the guy, you're not going anywhere without protection. If it's the same guy, we're dealing with a pro. We can't make it any easier for him."

"What great timing."

"We're going to try to make sure that you have a safe Christmas."

The fact was, Espinosa had no idea how to do that. He decided to spend the night at her house. He told the girls that he would sleep on the sofa in the living room and dismissed Maldonado until the next morning.

The three of them sat talking until almost midnight. After Kika and her friend went to their rooms, Espinosa settled down on the sofa, his pistol next to his body. On a little round table in front of him, there was a fake Christmas tree, ornamented with two strings of blinking colored lights. As soon as the lights were out and silence fell in the apartment, he realized that he wouldn't have been able to sleep even if he'd wanted to. He thought of it as "silence" only because no one was talking; there were plenty of strange noises: creaking boards, slamming doors, different sounds coming from the ceiling; and the traffic on the Rua do Catete didn't ease up even in the wee hours. For someone used to Peixoto, the apartment seemed like a room of special sound effects. Sleep was impossible. Whenever he managed to nod off, he always awoke with a jerk, fumbling on the sofa for his gun.

When the third roommate arrived in the morning, she came face-to-face with a pistol lying on the sofa next to a man's overcoat. Espinosa was in the kitchen trying to hook up the coffeemaker. He had a little bit of trouble explaining what he was doing there, but since the girl had already heard about him and was coming off her night shift (just like Espinosa himself) and they were both so drowsy, they saved the explanations for later.

When Maldonado got there at eight in the morning, the three girls were asleep. Espinosa decided to stay in the apartment until the first of the girls woke up; after that, he and Maldonado would change places, alternating between the apartment and the sidewalk near the building's entrance, where they could react quickly. The only access to the second and third floors was via the wooden staircase that led directly to the door on the street; it groaned terribly beneath the slightest weight, like an alarm.

For Vieira, reclaiming his I.D. was like reclaiming his identity as a police officer. Nobody is an ex–police officer, he thought. A police officer is like a general or a president: even after they leave office, people still call them General or President—sometimes even General-President. The comparison did not imply in any way that he was equating those offices; it was simply an acknowledgment that certain jobs bestowed a permanent title. The first precaution he vowed to take the morning after he recovered his wallet was to have a color copy made of the card; he would leave the original at home. Neither the original officer nor the original wallet would be out on the streets.

He finished reading his newspaper but stayed in bed waiting for Flor; though he no longer needed her to help with his medicine, she still came by every morning to tend his wounds. She had her own key and entered without having to ring the bell. The neighbors wondered if she was the officer's new wife. She looked more like his daughter. Not because they looked alike—she was too cute—but because of her age. Flor feigned ignorance of their curiosity, slipping the key in the door and walking inside with confidence. In order to reach the same status that Magali had had, all she was missing was a joint checking account, but that was just a matter of time.

The goal of the compresses and the creams was to diminish the horrible reddish-yellowish color of his bruises, but for Vieira, Flor's administration was much more loving than nursing, an activity that she extended far beyond the call of duty. His genitals had not been wounded by the attacker's blows, but very often a little oil or a compress would be applied to activate his blood flow. It was rather common for the nursing to stretch out for more than an hour.

"Let's have lunch together," Vieira proposed.

"Sure, love."

"This afternoon, I've been thinking about going to buy your Christmas present."

"Wow!"

"Do you want to come with me to choose it?"

"No, baby, that would ruin the surprise."

"But you'd be sure I wouldn't buy the wrong thing."

"There's no such thing! It'd be a present from you, and that's what matters."

"So you don't want to come with me?"

"It's not that, sweetheart, it's that a Christmas present has to be a surprise. You have to find it at the foot of the bed when you wake up."

"That's for people who still believe in Santa Claus. We're grown-ups, we can go have lunch and choose your present."

"I can't today, sweetheart."

"Goddamn it, don't tell me you have to work this afternoon."

"It's just that Junior's coming by today."

"Who?"

"Junior. It's his first time. His dad made the date."

"Junior? Who the fuck is Junior? Is Junior a name, or what? Junior, to me, is someone who has the same name as his father."

"That's exactly it. He has the same name as his father, except he has 'Junior' at the end of it."

"Whose junior is this Junior, damn it?"

"His father's! Who else's?"

"And who the fuck is the father?"

"The guy who brought me from Recife to Rio. He's helped me a lot. He's the one who rented my apartment for me. I promised him that Junior's first time would be with me."

"Motherfucker! You've been promised to him? Who's getting off here, you or him?"

"You're overreacting, darling. He's just a kid."

"And he's going to stay that way, damn it—at least as long as his father has to grab his dick and stick it in a woman's cunt."

Vieira was storming through the apartment. The clothes he had planned to wear were thrown on the ground; his screams gave way to coughing, and his anger made his bruises even redder.

"You're all wound up."

"Wound up? Wound up, me? Wound up? You've never seen me wound up. This is just the beginning."

"And what's the end like, huh? Do you end by killing women?"

Vieira stopped short. He looked at Flor as if she were a stranger. He kept quiet long enough for his blood to resume its normal flow. With difficulty, he picked up the things that he had thrown on the floor. He took his shirt and started getting dressed.

"Sorry . . . I didn't mean . . ."

Flor approached him with outstretched arms.

Vieira continued to button his shirt slowly; he tucked it into his pants—the belt was the one that Flor had bought him to replace the one that had been found tied around Magali's legs—then picked up his wallet and keys from the dresser and started moving toward the door.

"Darling, I'm sorry, I didn't mean that you were the one who killed . . ."

Vieira didn't say anything. He didn't even look at her. He walked toward the door, checked to make sure that he had his keys, and left.

He went down the Rua Francisco Sá, turned left onto the Avenida Copacabana, and walked several blocks. He needed to do something, and since he didn't know what to do he kept walking. After strolling for a while, he remembered the plan to make a copy of his I.D. card. Even though, after Flor's behavior, it no longer mattered to him. He didn't want to think about Flor's words; if he did, he would have to do some-thing, and he didn't want to do anything, so he didn't think about it. It occurred to him that he no longer walked the way he used to: his strides long, his chest puffed out, his head erect, his expression set, even when he wasn't looking for anything or anyone in particular. He had walked only about five hundred meters now and could already feel the muscles in his legs tiring. He'd passed more than one print shop, but none of them made color copies. If it wasn't color, the word POLICE, in red, wouldn't stand out the way it needed to. In one of the places, they informed him that there was a stationery shop that made color copies two blocks farther along.

"Front and back?" the guy in the stationery shop asked. It was a rhetorical question, so much so that he didn't even wait for the confirmation.

Vieira didn't answer. He stood staring at the photocopier, one machine looking at another. Once the lamination was complete, he paid without even glancing at the finished product. He put the original document in his back pocket together with the copy and kept walking. He thought about Flor again only when his muscles started to hurt. More specifically, he thought about what Flor had said. In normal circumstances, he wouldn't have worried about it, or he would've screamed loud enough to burst her eardrums. But he was paralyzed by the possibility that what she'd said was true, and the fact that it had been Flor who'd said it, and in such an aggressive way. He liked Flor as much as he had liked Magali. They were both so different from Maria Zilda. He walked slowly. He attributed his fatigue not to the distance he had covered but to the weight of the ideas in his head.

He entered his apartment hoping to see Flor. Until he opened the door, he didn't know what he would do or say if he found her there. He couldn't stay angry for long; he just needed a catharsis. He wasn't a resentful person, even though Flor's accusatory phrase had struck him deeper than most. His own reaction had been unusual; he didn't usually answer with silence. He couldn't even call it a reaction: it was more of a nonreaction. He had been paralyzed and had chosen to run away, something he had never done before.

Flor was no longer there.

Kika emerged from her room wearing an oversized T-shirt that nearly reached her knees, with only a pair of panties underneath. She was surprised to see Maldonado on the same sofa where she'd left Espinosa the night before. Even though she liked the detective, she had to control her expression in order not to reveal her disappointment. But she was relieved not to encounter a stranger.

"Morning, Kika. Sorry about barging in like this."

"Good morning, Maldonado, I wasn't expecting—"

"Espinosa went home to sleep a little; from the way he looked when I got here this morning, he hadn't slept a wink. Are you feeling any better?"

"I am. Maybe I was overreacting, maybe it wasn't the same guy, maybe—"

"In situations like this, a maybe means a possibility, and you can't take chances with a possibility like that."

"But . . . how long is this going to last?"

"This what? The threat or the protection?"

"I don't know. . . . It's an exceptional situation. Why don't we have a cup of coffee to clear our minds . . . my mind, I mean."

"Mine too. I'd love some coffee."

Kika was taller than Maldonado, and together they looked like a Hollywood comedy team. But there was no amusement in their faces this morning. He was one of the few—maybe the only—officer in the precinct Espinosa trusted to guard Kika, and he was aware of this.

They drank their coffee in silence. Her cerebral activity was far below the level she would call "life." It was even below what she would describe as "animal life," miles away from "human life." She was somewhere between a passive vegetable and a chameleon warming itself in the sun. Maldonado patiently awaited a signal from her that her day had begun. Kika finished her first cup of coffee, refilled both their cups without a word, and extended her legs under the table, forcing Maldonado to withdraw his. It was quiet not because they weren't talking but because at that hour they just didn't have any words. She rubbed her face several times with her hands, looking up at the ceiling; she stretched her arms in front of and above her head; she stared at the detective, leaving him with no doubt that she was really looking right through him. Then she opened her eyes normally, focusing them on objects that actually existed. At that moment, for her, the day began. Maldonado was spellbound.

"There's no reason for me to remain inside the apartment. You girls won't be able to move around. Why don't I stay on the sidewalk, near the doorway, so that I can watch anybody going into the building. If I need anything I'll ring the bell."

"Whatever you think is best. If you want to stay inside here, it's no problem."

While he was on the sidewalk guarding the entrance, every single man headed in the direction of the doorway seemed to match the description Espinosa had provided. Maldonado could protect the girls only if he managed to protect himself. The man who had attacked Espinosa was competent enough to know how to spot a plainclothes policeman and take him out. So he had to be careful not to be taken by surprise; if he were neutralized, Kika would be easy prey.

With only three days to go until Christmas, so many people were walking down the Rua do Catete that it was almost impossible to move. Maldonado therefore had to pay extra attention, and he knew that the crowds would complicate any quick intervention. The mere idea of a shootout in that multitude sent a chill down his spine. If in fact the man was smooth enough to find him immediately, there was no reason to hide anything; instead of standing on the sidewalk in front of the building, he could sit on the bottom steps of the staircase. He'd be an easier target, but he could also react without endangering other people. His decision to sit on the staircase was made easier because it had started to rain: on the sidewalk, he'd be soaked in a matter of minutes.

The ground floor of the house was occupied by a stationer's shop; the door giving onto the staircase and the upper floors was on the left side of the building, and the staircase was entirely separated from the store by a wall. The only way anyone could reach the upper floors without taking these stairs was through the store and up the back of the building, which was extremely difficult, though not impossible. Maldonado alerted the owner and the clerk to the possibility. If anyone tried anything like that, they would come next door to warn him.

Around lunchtime, Kika came down with a sandwich wrapped in waxed paper and a can of diet soda.

"I hope you like cold sandwiches and diet guaraná."

The stairs were wide enough that they could sit next to each other. Kika also had a sandwich. She was wearing a T-shirt similar to the one she'd been wearing earlier, except that this one was completely stained by ink of every possible color, along with similarly speckled shorts and sandals. Maldonado worried that she was exposed, but he was also fascinated by the figure seated at his side.

Espinosa woke with a start, an idea shooting through his brain so fast that it almost burst out of his skull. The man who'd broken into his apartment and tied him up was a cop or was working for the police. The absence of unnecessary aggression, the coldness and efficiency with which he'd acted, the daring involved in invading and subjugating a police officer, not to mention the theft of the guns—one of which was a police-issue .38—everything added up and pointed to the police itself. He was unworried about being identified because there was no risk of being called to account. But then Espinosa decided that the idea was absurd. There was no motive for attacking him. He didn't belong to any clique that could make him a target of another. Or maybe that itself was the reason. In the force, people who didn't belong to any clique, who weren't mixed up with any of them, were independent, which was much more dangerous than belonging to the worst of the groups. But he'd been in the police force for more than fifteen years: why would they only start worrying about him now? Because of his relation to Vieira?

He got up. He slowly returned to reality. He remembered Kika, the man with the gun in his hand, Maldonado, and that it was time for him to replace the younger cop. He hadn't slept much more than four hours, which, together with the short naps at Kika's apartment, was about enough for him. While he was putting shaving cream on his face he plugged in the coffee-maker in the kitchen, then went back to the bathroom to finish shaving. He didn't understand why he was in such a rush; if he got back to the Rua do Catete by around two, that would be perfectly reasonable, and Maldonado could have lunch at a normal time. But he was in a rush. Maybe because of the hurried rhythm of the last few days, or maybe because he didn't want to leave Kika under Maldonado's care for too long.

On his way to Catete, he thought about what he was doing. Nobody back at the station knew that he was protecting Kika; if something went wrong, it would be entirely his responsibility. He stopped the car two blocks from Kika's building, on a side street off the Rua do Catete, and proceeded the rest of the way on foot, as if he himself were the stalker trying to make his way into the building. As soon as he could see the facade of the building, he started to look for Maldonado—who should have been near the entrance. The street was wet from the rain that had fallen a couple of hours earlier, but there were still a lot of pedestrians on the sidewalk. The door was now clearly visible, and as he approached, Espinosa sought the detective in vain. He was preparing to ring the doorbell when he heard a voice in his ear.

"Looking for someone, Officer?"

Espinosa had to admit that the kid was more efficient than he supposed. And he had to abandon some of the fantasies he'd been feeding for the past few days, which he did with the utmost happiness.

"Maldonado, I confess: you got me. Seems it's been getting easier and easier to do that these past few weeks. How are things going?"

"No sign of the man. The girls are calm. Right now Kika's home, painting, and the med student is asleep. The third one went to work. The only possible access is through the front door; the neighboring buildings have no communication with ours. Someone really nimble could try to climb up the back wall, but they'd have to go through the store on the ground floor, and I already talked to the owner and the other guy working there."

"Very good, Maldonado. I'll stay on guard until eight tonight. I left a message at the station, telling them that we're both on a stakeout outside the city, so don't show up over there."

Then he went upstairs to tell Kika about the changing of the guard.

It rained all afternoon, forcing Espinosa to divide his watch between Kika's living room and the stairway. Kika wanted to know if she could go to the Avenida Atlântica. The decision was made by the weather—it was still raining in the evening. In spite of the rain, daylight saving time meant that it was still light at seven-thirty, when Maldonado came back to replace Espinosa. He would stay for two hours, time enough for Espinosa to return home, and when he came back they would discuss a strategy for the night and the next day.

It was eight-fifteen when he opened the door to his apartment. The red light on the answering machine was blinking. He pressed the button to listen while he walked across the room to open the blinds. The first message was from Clodoaldo, who left only his name. The second was from him as well, in his signature style: "Espinosa, I have to talk to you urgently. Clodoaldo." There had been a third call from someone who hadn't left a message. The last message was from the station. Clodoaldo had been found dead.

PART 6

Clodoaldo had been murdered with a shot to his temple, point-blank, and the gun beside the body would have suggested suicide to someone unaware of recent events. The idea wouldn't even have occurred to anyone who knew the street teacher. He himself had been a street kid, had survived every kind of threat, and would never have killed himself. The thought certainly didn't cross Espinosa's mind. He had gotten the news in more than one installment. The first piece came by phone, without many details; the second he received personally, from the officer on duty at the station, with a single detail: the gun found beside his body, an official police-issue .38, was the one stolen from his apartment. The body had been found on the back seat of a taxi parked in a quiet street in Copacabana minutes after the driver had filed a complaint at the station, claiming that he had been forced to abandon the car by a man with a revolver. On the seat, next to Clodoaldo's body, was the stolen .38.

Espinosa couldn't believe that the criminal had gone to his apartment and attacked him merely to steal the revolver he was planning to use to kill his friend, then left the piece as a calling card. He felt a shiver in his spine when he remembered that the man still had his other weapon and could use it to leave another signature. And he was certain that last night's silent message was the murderer's announcement of Clodoaldo's death.

At the Forensic Institute, Espinosa was the sole claimant on the body. As far as Espinosa knew, the street teacher had no relatives, but Espinosa planned, just in case, to ask around at the homeless shelters. Only then would he make arrangements for the body. The clerk on duty, whom Espinosa knew, tried to comfort him while he removed the body from its drawer—death had been instantaneous, the officer's friend hadn't suffered. The clerk also said other things that Espinosa didn't manage to hear while looking at the jaundiced, cold body before his eyes. Clodoaldo had died immediately, there had been no pain, but that was not what mattered most: Espinosa was hurting not because of the absence of pain but because of the absence of life. Clodoaldo had known pain since the moment he was born.

While he was taking care of the paperwork in the Forensic Institute, he thought of his many meetings with Clodoaldo, of the occasions when they'd teamed up to combat the urban predators who preyed on street kids; he thought of the mutual respect and admiration they'd built up over the years when they both worked downtown; he thought about how to deliver the news to the boys and girls on the Avenida Atlântica. He realized that the man had gone to Kika's neighbor's apartment to throw him off the scent and keep him away from Clodoaldo.

On the sidewalk, in front of the Forensic Institute, he could barely hear the boy who was waving at him. "Taxi, sir?" After asking a couple of times, he gave up. Espinosa left on foot, looking for his car, which he'd parked on a side street, but was unable to focus on the search. What most intrigued him about the many events that had followed Magali's death was that nothing made sense. Nothing had anything to do with anything else. The nonsense had culminated with the break-in at his apartment and the theft of the weapon later used to murder Clodoaldo. Why go to so much trouble? The only objective could be to deliver a message, a kind of advance warning. But was it the advance warning of his own death or someone else's? Besides Clodoaldo, who else, of the people he knew, could be next—and why? The sight of the white arches, lit up against the sky, of the old aqueduct at Lapa brought him back to his senses. He must have long since passed his car; he would have to go back a few blocks; but it was hard to take his attention off the view in his head. A little more alert, he retraced his steps. He didn't have to walk far to spot the car. Maldonado was seated on the hood.

"You walked right by me, just a few feet away. I figured you needed to think. I didn't want to interrupt. I'm so sorry about what happened to Clodoaldo. Since you hadn't shown up, I called your house, but no one answered. I called the station, and they gave me the news."

Espinosa asked his colleague to drive. They got in the car and didn't say a word until they arrived in Copacabana. Back home, alone, leaning over the little balcony that looked onto the square, he felt tears welling up.

It had been less than three hours since he had heard the message on the answering machine. He hadn't had dinner, and he wasn't at all sleepy. From his balcony, he could see the windows of nearby buildings, lit up by colorful Christmas trees. For those people, crimes were news in the papers, and loved ones died from natural causes; Christmas, for them, was the commemoration of a birth, not an occasion for macabre recollections.

A taxi stopped in front of his building. A woman got out. Looking from above, without much light, he couldn't make out her face, but he could see that she had a nice figure. The intercom rang. When Espinosa opened the door of his apartment, Flor seemed slightly winded, just enough for him to notice the movement of her chest under the neckline of her dress.

"Surprised?"

"A little."

"May I come in?"

"Sure. Come in."

Flor was wearing the same dress that had so disturbed Espinosa on the Sunday when they went out to get lunch for Vieira. And he knew that she knew that it had disturbed him. She came into the apartment with possessive ease. She looked around, judging the resident by his residence, gestured toward the balcony, moved her head slightly, as if to show her approval, and turned to face Espinosa, who had remained standing in the middle of the room.

"You must think it's strange for me to show up like this, especially after the earlier unpleasantness."

"I think I went too far."

"It's fine. For me, it's over."

"How's Vieira?"

"We got in a fight."

"A fight?"

"Yeah. It was all my fault. I said something I shouldn't have. We fought over nothing. I said that he was angry. He said that I didn't know what he was like when he was really angry. I asked if he killed women when he was angry. I shouldn't have said it. He left without saying a word."

"And why did you say it? Do you think he killed Magali? Were you afraid he'd kill you?"

"No. I don't know. He was really wound up. I was a little scared, but I don't think that he could kill someone."

"What about Magali?"

"No. I think I overdid it."

They were still standing in the middle of the living room. While she was talking, Flor was moving around, touching objects without picking them up. Smoothly, looking at him, turning her body slowly while she talked, she moved as if weightless.

"Can't we sit down?"

"Sorry. Have a seat, of course."

Flor sat on the sofa and Espinosa in the armchair, even though he read her choice of the sofa as a veiled invitation to sit next to her. She still hadn't indicated the reason for her visit, and Espinosa wasn't inclined to guess.

"You must be wondering what I came for."

"True. And I don't think it's just to tell me that you had a fight with Vieira."

"Of course not."

"So?"

"I've come to seduce you."

"Now you've really surprised me."

"And what do you think of the idea?"

"I think that you—"

The sentence was cut off by the doorbell. It wasn't the intercom, but the doorbell to the apartment itself. He got up, still reeling under the impact of Flor's declaration, crossed the living room, and opened the door. It was Kika. Before anyone could say anything, Flor stood up. Kika looked at her and at Espinosa.

"I'm sorry, I came without calling. I didn't know you had company." She turned around and ran down the stairs. Espinosa stood with the door open until he heard the door to the entrance slam.

"I must be interfering with something, but it seems that both of us arrived without warning. I just happened to get here first."

"You're not interfering with anything."

"Then let's get back to where we were before the doorbell rang."

"Flor, it's not a good day. I just came from the Forensic Institute, where I identified the body of a friend who was murdered this afternoon. Besides, your fight with Vieira is only temporary. I wouldn't want him to think that I called you here."

"I didn't know about your friend. . . . I'm sorry. Good-bye."

She got up and sashayed out, the same way she'd come in. Espinosa didn't like the visit, Flor's barging in, the ambiguity she'd used to describe the fight with Vieira, her running into Kika. She had indeed come to seduce him, he reflected. What he didn't understand was why. It was late; it had been an intense day.

He got up early. His first thought was of Clodoaldo. He felt hungover when, in fact, he'd had only two beers the night before, to take the edge off. He was still on his first cup of coffee when Vieira called.

"Sorry it's so early, but I have to talk to you."

"Did something happen?" Espinosa immediately thought of Clodoaldo's murder, but didn't say anything to Vieira.

"Nothing. Nothing yet. But I think something's about to. Some son of a bitch has been calling me to ask if I'm ready for another meeting in the street. I also think I'm being followed. I'm not sure; it could just be paranoia. But I've never been very paranoid. What worries me most is that my revolver disappeared."

"When was that?"

"That what?"

"The disappearance of your revolver."

"I don't know. I only noticed it was missing this morning. Ever since these fuckers started following me, I decided I wouldn't go out unarmed. When I went to get the gun today, it was gone. I already looked through the whole apartment. I always kept it in the same place, I never moved it, and it's not in the drawer where it always was. There's only the space where it was. Someone came in here and took my fucking gun."

Vieira didn't know that Espinosa's apartment had been broken into or that his guns had been stolen; and Espinosa still hadn't had his second cup of coffee or eaten the extra slice of toast. He also didn't want to tell Vieira about Clodoaldo over the phone. They decided to meet at the station. Before leaving, he left a message for Kika.

The night before, Espinosa had sent the main newspapers the news of the teacher's death, along with some details about his work with street kids, hoping that the obituary would attract the attention of some possible relative.

He walked to the station with long strides, without looking at shop windows, people, or cars, and without letting himself be distracted by anything. He didn't expect the autopsy to turn up any more clues to the identity of the murderer. He was still working on his report of the previous day's events when Vieira arrived. Even before saying hello to anyone, Vieira realized that something was wrong. As soon as he heard that Clodoaldo was the victim, he took a seat in the nearest chair and sat staring at the floor, murmuring words no one could make out but that anyone who knew him could guess.

When Espinosa finished the story, Vieira grabbed his arm and dragged him out of the office.

"Let's go down to the corner for a coffee." And as soon as they were on the sidewalk, he squeezed the arm he was still holding and said: "Fuck, Espinosa. The bastard is either from the police or was hired by the police. There's no way around it. If you want to find the motherfucker, you'd better start at home."

"I'd already thought of that, but what makes you so sure?"

"Because I'm sure, damn it. Think about it, Espinosa: who, besides the police, would go into your apartment, steal your official service weapon, and leave it next to the body? Fuck, the guy's as cold as ice. He's already killed four people, and it doesn't look like he's ready to stop. Nobody pulls shit like that without guarantees. Even if he's a hired professional, he's got to be counting on police protection if something goes wrong."

"But why would they be doing it with me, specifically?"

"That's what I can't figure out, baby. Unless you've gotten yourself into trouble . . . Sorry, buddy. Forget what I just said, that was stupid."

"It's not that stupid, and you might be on to something. I doubt that someone so well organized could be mixing me up with someone else, but maybe he or whoever's behind him is misinterpreting something I actually did do. Think with me. Bad cops have tried to coopt me over the years. When they realized they weren't getting anywhere, they gave up and left me alone. I think something like that happened to you. Maybe people like us are more threatening than declared enemies."

"But why only now?"

"Because we haven't given them a chance until now. The chance came, even though we didn't mean to give it to them."

"When, for fuck's sake?"

"When you lost your wallet."

"What does that—"

"Let me finish. When the kid realized he'd gotten his hands on a police I.D., he got scared and dumped it. The guy who found it was a lowlife who'd always been in trouble with the law. Once he'd gotten his hands on the I.D., he decided to make some money without much risk, or at least that's what he thought, and tried out a gay disco where he knew there were drugs. He got a lot of powder, which he started selling cheaper than the street price. So on the second or third try the big dealers find out. But find out what? That some Officer Vieira's responsible. They start following the guy and find out that there's always a kid tracking him, and sometimes a guy with red hair, and sometimes even a guy from the Twelfth Precinct, from my team. Just afterward, they see you leave the Thirteenth Precinct and follow one of their distributors into the Galeria Alaska. They must have thought that it was a new group trying to get into the drug business without going through the traffickers, simply taking drugs off junkies and reselling them at reasonable prices. They get the guy with the wallet, torture him to get him to turn in the rest of the group, but it turns out there's no group. In a desperate attempt to escape death, he remembers Clodoaldo and the kid, simply because they're the only people he's got—he'd noticed them a few times looking suspicious—and fingers them. They kill him, then they kill the first kid by mistake, then the second kid; and when they go to kill Clodoaldo, since they knew he was my friend, they use my own gun to make it look like I'd killed him myself. They didn't have the balls to kill two police officers. In your case, they beat you up as a warning. As for me, I don't know what's going to happen. I just know that if they stole the weapon to warn us what they'd do, they still have my other gun. And now you tell me that they've stolen yours as well. They can still sign two checks."

"Very good."

"There's one other thing that's been worrying me. If the murderer really does like to sign his crimes, he couldn't have left a clearer signature than your belt around Magali's legs."

"You don't think they could be unrelated incidents? That Magali's death might have nothing to do with the other murders?"

"I did until I noticed the murderer's habit of leaving his

personal mark at the scene of the crime. The belt is such an extraordinary coincidence that I doubt it's truly a coincidence."

They didn't go to the corner to have a coffee; they had walked beyond it and had almost made a complete pass around the block. If they turned, they'd be back in front of the station, so they decided to keep walking straight, toward the beach. Vieira was still holding on to Espinosa's arm, partly for support but also because he was always affectionate with his friends. They stopped in a café on the last block before the beach. Espinosa was no longer worried about possible stalkers, since after the break-in at his apartment the criminal had no reason to beat around the bush: they knew who he was, where he worked, where he lived, where he hung out, and who his friends were; they could follow him as much as they wanted, but it wouldn't make any difference. Even so, he kept his eyes peeled.

"Espinosa."

"What?"

"Do you really think someone in the police thinks that we're involved in drugs?"

"They might not think it themselves, but might want other people to think so."

"What do you think is going to happen?"

"The stolen guns could mean two things: that they want to kill us, each with the other's gun; or that they want to kill, with our guns, people connected to us. No one would break into our apartments just for the pleasure of collecting guns from cops."

They had left the café and were on the Avenida Atlântica, turning the corner to head back to the station.

"Listen. If some group in the police force suspects that we're working together in some drug deal, they'd certainly see the visits we pay each other, the walks, like this one, that we take together: it could all add up to prove that we're hiding something. Everything we've done in the last few days would confirm their suspicions."

"What are we going to do?" Vieira asked.

"I don't think they're going to keep the pressure on us for very long. It's risky; the guy could get caught. I think they're trying to keep the attacks and the murders close together, in order to make us feel besieged. Up till now they've killed two street kids, a trivial lowlife, and a street teacher, also trivial in his own way. Even without crediting them with Magali's murder, they've killed people the police consider peripheral. They might even think they're doing a little social cleansing. As for us two, they've only showed that they could have killed us but didn't, because we're both police officers. It wouldn't look good to be killing colleagues. I have the feeling that before they try anything on us, they're going to take a stab at people connected to us. That makes Kika and Flor the favored targets, and if the mind planning this is as fascist as I suspect, Flor will be the next victim."

Clodoaldo's body would stay at the Forensic Institute, waiting for someone to claim it, for three more days. If nobody appeared, Espinosa would take charge of the burial. He hoped to get the murderer before those three days were up.

Kika called around lunchtime, as she'd promised. She didn't want to have lunch, but she accepted his invitation for "a salad" in the restaurant at the Museum of the Republic, almost directly in front of her building. They both wanted to talk about the meeting with Flor the night before; they both felt guilty for something they couldn't quite pinpoint. They met at the door of Kika's building twenty minutes after the phone call. They crossed the street, and half a block later they found themselves in front of the former Catete Palace.

"Sorry about interrupting your meeting last night."

"It wasn't a meeting; she showed up like you, without calling, just before you rang the bell. Both of you surprised each other, and I must say that I was even more surprised."

"Is she your girlfriend?"

"No. She's the girlfriend of a friend of mine."

"Isn't it strange that your friend's girlfriend should be with you in your apartment late at night?"

"Strange things have happened in the last few days. It's not just friends' girlfriends who have been coming into my apartment."

"Espinosa, what's happening? None of this has to do with the kid, does it?"

"No. The kid, totally unawares, was just a part of what's been going on."

"And what's going on?"

"I'm not entirely sure. And I don't think anybody is."

"Who's doing it?"

"I don't know that either. The guy who's killing the people is just a hired gun; Vieira and I've been trying to find out who he is through informers. As soon as we get a break we'll go after him."

"The guy who's been killing people? What people? Who else has he killed, besides the kid?"

"Clodoaldo. Yesterday. Right before you came to my apartment. I'd just gotten back from the Forensic Institute."

"I'm sorry. I didn't know."

They were in the museum's restaurant, a kind of veranda at the level of the treetops, above the gardens of Catete Palace. Kika put her hands on top of Espinosa's. Sadness replaced worry. Once, when they were out together, Espinosa had told her about Clodoaldo. She knew of their friendship and mutual admiration.

"The girl who was in your apartment, was that his girl-friend?"

"No. She's Vieira's girlfriend; she doesn't even know Clodoaldo."

"And are you worried about her?"

"I am."

"Is she in danger?"

"I think so."

"What about me?"

"A little, also."

"A little? What's a little?"

"I don't think your life is in danger, but I think they might threaten you."

"But why? What have I done?"

"You haven't done anything. They're trying to get to me."

"And what did you do?"

"It's not about what I've done, but what they think I've done."

"And what do they think you've done?"

"They think that I'm trying to get a piece of the drug market."

"Holy shit! And who are they? Traffickers?"

"No."

Kika shot him a blank look.

"The police."

"The police?"

"Yeah. The police. Not all of it. A part of it."

"Let me see if I understand. Some group of the police force itself is threatening you because they think you're trying to get into the drug market. Based on this suspicion, they've already killed four people and attacked two, just to dissuade you. The next candidates are me and your friend's girlfriend? Is that it?"

"That's what I think."

"And do you also think that I'm in real danger?" Kika was talking through her teeth, but even so people at the neighboring tables were looking at her.

"I think there is in fact some danger, even though I also think that in your case they'll behave a little differently."

"Could you be a little clearer, please?"

"It's like this. Until now, they've only killed what they consider to be the trash of society. They think they're acting along the lines of the Department of Urban Sanitation. As for eliminating actual human beings, they don't think it's a very important detail, something they're rarely called to account for, except when there's some scandal and the press and public opinion weigh in. Street kids, beggars, transvestites don't count as part of humanity. They look as much like people as a trash can looks like a plate of food served in a restaurant. You're college educated, middle class, professional; you belong to the kind of people they're supposed to protect, not eliminate, so I don't think they'll try anything too radical; but that doesn't mean they won't try to scare you."

"And these public sanitation employees are the same ones who sell powder to adults and children, people who belong to the same society they think they're cleaning up?"

"Precisely because they think that way."

"I still don't get why they think you're trying to get into their business."

"Because of a series of coincidences that began with the loss of a wallet, which was found by the kid who asked you for help. You know the story involving him; what you don't know is the other part, about Vieira and me."

Espinosa briefly related the events that, to his mind, formed a series but not necessarily a story, adding that he didn't think that the series of deaths had ended with Clodoaldo's murder.

"Unless the perpetrators are convinced that we've gotten out of the business, though it's even harder to convince them that we were never in it in the first place."

The conversation and meeting itself created an absurd scene that Espinosa tried to tie together with a thread he couldn't quite find. It was two days before Christmas, he was with a gorgeous woman in a place that looked like a set from a romantic movie, and yet he couldn't figure out the plot line. He was a cop harassed by the police; the girl wasn't his girlfriend, only a victim of the same persecution; the set could quickly change from romantic movie to detective story.

They decided that for at least the next two days he and Maldonado would keep guarding her, and that she wouldn't go anywhere at all without warning them first. The rest of the lunch was tense, with silences broken by short phrases and muttered curses from Kika, who ate her own salad and Espinosa's meal as well.

They left the restaurant unhurriedly. The difference in temperature between the terrace beneath the trees and the Rua do Catete, packed full of people, was enough to make Espinosa's forehead break out in sweat, even though it was only a short walk to Kika's building from the restaurant. Maldonado was waiting for them at the door. Before going up with the detective, Kika kissed Espinosa quickly, partly on his cheek, partly on the side of his mouth.

"Sorry about yesterday."

From the same public phone Kika usually used, Espinosa called Vieira. He wanted to know if he'd called Flor or taken any protective measures for her; he himself didn't want to do anything without telling his friend.

"We had a quick conversation to work out a misunderstanding and decided to go out tonight."

"Vieira, something tells me that the guy is going to try something today, or tomorrow at the latest; don't make it any easier for him. I know it's risky, but the only way to get to him quickly is to let him get to us first, unless we come across some information. But remember, that doesn't mean we can let him get to anybody else. Just to us."

"Damn it, buddy, you think I'm an amateur?"

"I know you're not, but I'm sure he isn't either. He's got your gun, and I forgot to ask you this morning if you've got another one."

"I borrowed one that's even better than my own."

"Great. I mean, well, use it only in extreme cases."

"Fuck, Espinosa, we are the extreme cases. Anything that wasn't extreme he's already eliminated. The guy who got me the gun agreed to check with his contacts to find out who the son of a bitch is. He said he'd check back with me as soon as he had a lead."

The moment Espinosa hung up, Vieira tried calling Flor. Nobody answered. He tried a few more times in the next half hour, and the result was the same. I bet that little shit, Junior, still hasn't managed to aim at the bucket, he thought. Or maybe the dad decided to give a demonstration to the retard? Flor must be feeling like a real institution. Since nineteen whatever, from father to son. She could order a plaque for the door of her apartment.

He opened his dresser drawer, the same one from which his first weapon had been stolen, and removed the automatic he'd borrowed from the station near his house—surely a gun taken off some sleazebag—along with the ammunition that came with it. He threw everything onto the bed and started counting the bullets. He stopped halfway. Bullshit. He'd never been in a shootout where he'd needed more ammo than a gun could hold. By the time the bullets ran out, somebody would be dead.

He was still sitting on the side of the bed. He loaded the clip, put a bullet in the barrel, and flicked on the safety; then he gathered the remaining bullets. As he was putting them back in the drawer, one of them fell on the floor, rolling underneath the dresser. The job of fishing it out forced him onto his hands and knees; he had to stretch his body twice, getting down and standing up again, which not only took him quite a while but left him breathless for a few minutes afterward. He was shirtless, wearing shorts and no shoes. The effort had produced sweat deep in the folds of his belly. He wondered how he could maintain the pretense that he was protecting someone from a professional assassin when the simple effort of picking up a bullet from the carpet practically finished him off. His body still bore traces of the attack; his mouth was trying to adjust to his new dentures; and his soul was trying to adjust to more recent apparitions. He doubted seriously whether he could defend himself and Flor.

He didn't know what to do while he was waiting. He didn't even know what he was waiting for: if it was Flor, who would never again be simply soft and sweet; or if it was the man, breaking down the door and shooting before he could even reach the gun beside him in his bed. His aesthetic sense was not his most highly developed, but even he didn't think that it was proper to fight wearing only a pair of Bermuda shorts; he imagined his picture in the papers, looking just like one of the lowlifes, who never seemed to be wearing a shirt when they got killed. He was also uncomfortable because his feet were slightly puffy, probably because of the heat. He dismissed the idea of putting on a shirt and shoes, turned on the air conditioner in his room, looked for a movie on TV, and sat down to wait.

Flor headed toward the door against her better instincts; she didn't like to answer the doorbell without knowing who it was first. The intercom hadn't buzzed; new doorman, she thought. These people aren't used to modern technology. She opened the door.

"Officer, what a pleasant surprise. Could it be that my attempt to seduce you worked after all?"

"You're seductive. You don't need to seduce anyone. But that's not why I'm here."

"Really?"

"Yes. May I come in?"

"Of course. Excuse me. Come in."

As always in her presence, Espinosa's sense of discomfort only grew.

"Today it's your turn to ask what I'm doing here."

"Unfortunately, it's never for the reason I want. But now that you ask, Officer, what are you doing here?"

"I came to find out what you were doing last night in my apartment."

"But I already spelled it out for you: I went to try to seduce you."

"That's what you said. And what didn't you say?"

"What are you trying to find out? It's not the first time you've come into my apartment to ask accusatory questions."

"I've never accused you of anything, and I've never come into your apartment without your consent or without being invited in."

"What do you want to know?"

"I want to know what you were hoping to accomplish in my apartment last night."

"Besides getting in the way of your plans with that girl?"

"Besides getting in the way of my plans with that girl."

"Why are you hung up on this?"

"Because we both know that you didn't come over to seduce me. Or rather, you did, but that wasn't the main reason. Just like we both know that you didn't seek out Vieira because Magali asked you to. She never asked you a thing like that. And it wasn't that you were her legacy to Vieira; Vieira's the one who's been inherited by you, your guarantee of a possible future."

"Officer, if I invited you in, now I'm inviting you to leave."

"Fine. But remember that you still haven't answered my question."

Vieira woke when the telephone rang, not immediately sure whether the phone was part of the movie he was watching. He stared at the television while realizing that the phone was still ringing. He answered.

"Hi, sweetheart. It took you a while to answer."

"Flor."

"Vieira, I'm scared."

"What happened? Did they do something?" Vieira's hand patted the bed in search of the weapon as he snapped to full wakefulness.

"Nothing new. It was your friend Espinosa who came over here again. He scares me. He shows up without warning, undresses me with his eyes, and asks questions that make me uncomfortable, questions about Magali."

"But what? He just called me to say that we needed to protect you. He was worried about you."

"Maybe that's really why he called, or maybe he was calling to make sure you were home and that he could come over here without the risk of running into you?"

"Flor, Espinosa's my friend. He's a serious guy."

"Serious friends also have dicks, and it wouldn't take much to get his hard."

"Did he try something? Proposition you?"

"No. He was only asking me questions to scare me. But you'll see, I bet that's what he wants, to scare me so he can come save the day."

"I don't think that's it, Flor. I've known Espinosa for a long time, and he's always been trustworthy."

"Darling, when there's a woman or money involved, no man is completely trustworthy."

"Flor, get in a cab and come over here."

"Now?"

"Yes."

"Because of what I said?"

"Espinosa's not the one who worries me. There's a guy who's making threats. They might try something on you, just to shake you up. I don't want anything to happen."

After he hung up, Vieira sat wondering whether the threats Espinosa had invoked were real. After all, when there was a woman involved, no man was completely trustworthy.

From Flor's building to the Rua Hilário de Gouveia was less than ten short blocks. In spite of the heat and the time of day, Espinosa preferred to walk. As anticipated, he was already sweating when he reached the entrance to the station, and he still had to walk up a flight of stairs. No sooner had he set eyes on the second floor than a detective announced that Vieira had been calling nonstop for the past half hour. Before any-thing else, though, Espinosa found an air-conditioned room and waited a few minutes, until he had dried off a bit. Appar-ently, Vieira had called every ten minutes. He hadn't left any messages, only demanding urgently to speak with Espinosa. When Espinosa called, Vieira answered on the first ring.

"Espinosa, I think we've found the guy."

"How? Who is it? Where?"

"Wait. Call me from a public phone."

Espinosa took the stairs much more quickly than usual and found a public phone that wasn't directly in front of the sta-tion. Once again, Vieira answered instantaneously.

"The guy didn't let us have the tip for cheap. We had to release his boyfriend, who was being held at the station. Listen closely before you go running off after the son of a bitch. He's staying in a hotel in Catete, near the palace. The informant didn't know the name, but he said it was two blocks from the Museum of the Republic, which gives us four likely addresses, two on the Rua do Catete and two on a side street. I know what you're thinking—that the bastard's only a few feet away from your friend that girl the painter and we've got to act fast. The guy isn't a cop, but he was hired by a group of cops that includes two sergeants, which means that we can't count on anyone besides your friend Maldonado, who I really hope is on our side, 'cause if he's not we're fucked. Flor's here with me and is going to stay locked in here; I've told her not to open the door to anyone while we're looking for the guy. I'm going to get a taxi. I'll pick you up in ten minutes on the corner of the Avenida Copacabana."

Espinosa had left his suit coat to dry in front of the air conditioner; his pistol was in a desk drawer. He went back upstairs, got the gun and an extra cartridge clip, put on his jacket, and announced that he was going down to the Forensic Institute to meet one of Clodoaldo's relatives. Before ten minutes were up, he was on the corner Vieira had indicated; in five more, a taxi drove up, blinking its lights at him.

They went straight to Kika's apartment to make sure she was all right and to draw up a plan with Maldonado. They found the kid sitting on the staircase landing between the first and second stories of the building. From where he was sitting, he could see anyone coming up the stairs and could also keep an eye on the girls' door. He looked suspicious when he saw Espinosa approaching with someone he didn't know. The paper bag covering his right hand was pointed straight at Vieira's chest. Espinosa introduced them to each other and the hand emerged from the paper bag grasping an automatic pistol, which he shifted to his other hand while he greeted the retired officer.

They went up to Kika's apartment. She opened the door wearing her painting clothes; her T-shirt looked like an abstract canvas. The courtesies were quick, as was the decision to leave one of them to guard Kika while the other two went to investigate the likeliest hotels. For Vieira, there was no question that the kid would keep an eye on the girl; for Maldonado, who didn't like to be treated like a kid, it seemed risky to let an old man run after a murderer; Espinosa preferred to leave Kika with the kid rather than with the old man. The conversation, between just the three of them, took place in the living room. The closed blinds filtered the intense light of an early-summer afternoon through the room. They decided to leave Kika with Maldonado while the two officers visited the hotels.

They started with the one closest to Kika's apartment. It was a pretty colonial building, recently renovated, and, while not luxurious, was certainly attractive. The manager guaranteed that none of her guests met Espinosa's description. Espinosa's emphasis on the importance of the information she was giving didn't alter her certainty. The hotel didn't have many rooms; many were occupied by permanent guests, and she remembered the short-term occupants perfectly. The next hotel was just down the block, less than a hundred meters away. It was much more modest, unattractively designed for less refined tastes. The manager fit the establishment: he wasn't very clean or welcoming and was made visibly uncomfortable by the presence of the police. He spread a pile of registration forms over the counter. They appeared to have been filled out when the hotel was first opened; he seemed to hope that that would fulfill his duties toward the law. When Espinosa asked for some more recent paperwork, he mumbled something unintelligible and started rummaging through the papers on the counter. The scene would probably have gone on for some time if Vieira hadn't thought to speed things up by pulling the guy across the counter, scattering the papers on the ground, and sticking the barrel of his revolver under his cheek.

"I'm gonna count to ten, to give you time to think, and if I've gotten to ten and you haven't told us everything we want to know, this motherfucking gun's gonna accidentally go off inside your mouth, ripping out your brain on its way out, which would be a terrible loss. One, two, three . . ."

They left absolutely convinced that the guy they were looking for wasn't there, though they did learn the names of all the lowlifes who occasionally took shelter in that cave. As they walked out the door, Vieira noticed his colleague's disapproving stare.

"Sorry, buddy, but we're in a hurry."

"I can tell."

The next hotel took a lot more time to get through. It was much bigger than the previous two, boasting a few stars on the plaque by the door, comfortable and distinguished. The registry was up-to-date, but there were a lot of single male guests, any number of whom could have matched Espinosa's description. After asking a few maids, doormen, and waiters, he was pretty sure that there were no one-hundred-percent matches. Of the few who had something in common with the description, two were now in their rooms. Only after protesting did the manager allow them to fake a room service order so that Espinosa could see them. Both were annoyed to be awakened from their naps. The two who weren't in had stayed in the hotel before; Espinosa and Vieira agreed that they weren't suspects.

The fourth hotel was smaller and less formal, and most of the guests were Spanish speakers, which made them easier to dismiss as suspects. Even so, they wasted another hour confirming that the man wasn't now and had never been a guest there. They decided to try one more hotel, on the corner of Flamengo Beach. Its location didn't match the informant's description, but it was the only one left in the area.

As they were walking back to Kika's building, silent, tired, and disappointed, they both reached the same conclusion at the same time. The man had never been in a hotel in the vicinity. While Espinosa ran up the stairs to tell Maldonado, Vieira called his apartment. No one answered.

He had instructed Flor not to leave under any circumstances whatsoever; he had even told her not to answer if someone rang the doorbell, or if the phone rang—the guy could be calling to see if anyone was home. She wasn't answering.

He met Espinosa coming down the stairs with Maldonado behind him, asking questions.

"Well?" asked Espinosa.

"I don't know what's going on at home; I told Flor not even to answer the phone, so there's no point in calling. I'm going there now. Someone has to keep watch over the painter girl . . . and God help the rest of us."

"Do you want to tell me what's going on?" Maldonado no longer knew what he was protecting or against whom.

"It's simple." Vieira was the one who answered. "The fucking informant was planted by the police. I did think he got back to us pretty fast; we contacted him one day and two days later he was already back with all the information we needed. He sent us over here, while the guy we're looking for is taking his time getting ready somewhere else. They've been playing with us the whole time, while they kill people they consider dispensable."

"Why go to so much trouble?"

"Because they want to show us how powerful they are, because they want to scare us, because they think we're trying to take away their business."

Flor didn't like being alone in Vieira's apartment; she felt the eyes of Maria Zilda and Magali watching her. Nothing in that apartment was familiar to her; even the TV dated back to the dead wife. She bet he hadn't even changed the toilet seat; she probably had to sit where the old bitch had stuck her ass. Fantasies and imaginary dialogues occupied her waiting time. She didn't have the slightest curiosity about looking through the closets, the drawers, the shelves, the kitchen: nothing interested her. To her mind, the past was a bunch of debris awaiting removal.

Vieira had been gone for more than an hour when the doorbell rang. She remembered what Vieira had said. She went to the door and looked through the peephole. There was a man in a suit looking at her. She shrank back, holding her breath, looking for another door, which didn't exist. She thought about going to the window and screaming for help. She started to move away when she heard a voice.

"Dona Flor, I'm Detective Marcos. Sergeant Vieira sent me to protect you."

Flor went back to the door and, moving slowly, looked through the peephole once again. The man was there. He looked normal enough, was decently dressed, and wasn't trying to force his way in. He was waiting for her to make up her mind.

"Show me your badge," she said, her mouth stuck to the door, as if to lend her words the necessary touch of drama.

The man took a wallet from his pocket and held it up to the peephole. Flor saw something shiny that looked like a police I.D., but even so she hesitated to open the door.

"Dona Flor, I know that Officer Vieira told you not to open the door to anyone until he got back, but he didn't know he was going to run into me."

"He never mentioned any Marcos to me."

"I'm not a friend of his, I'm a friend of Officer Espinosa's."

Flor thought the two references were good enough. She undid the latch, turned the lock, and removed the chain, pulling open the door. The man greeted her, asked if he could come in, and waited patiently for her to lock the door again. After they'd examined each other for a few seconds—during which time Flor decided that she'd made the right decision—the man took one of the chairs from the dinner table, placed it with its back to the window and its face to the door, then sat down himself to make sure it was where he wanted it. He got up, slid one of his hands inside his jacket, and stuck the other into the outside pocket. The first returned with a revolver, the second with a roll of nylon rope. With the gun pointed to Flor's head, he said in a clear, sharp voice:

"Sit down, please."

Flor shrank back and looked toward the door.

"Don't try any nonsense. If you try to scream, I guarantee that I'll blow your brains out before the sound leaves your mouth. Sit down and place your arms behind the back of the chair."

The man secured her wrists with the nylon rope and taped her mouth shut with duct tape. He tied her legs to the chair. The only thing that remained relatively free was her neck, allowing Flor to nod and shake her head. His work done, the man walked toward the door, where he stood for a few seconds observing the scene.

"If you try to jerk the chair onto the ground, you'll stand a good chance of breaking your neck. I suggest you don't experiment."

He turned around, unlocked the door, looked into the hallway in both directions, and, slamming the door, left. Only after she heard the noise of the elevator door could Flor convince herself that she wasn't dead. Her eyes filled with tears, but she tried desperately to restrain herself from crying; if her nose got clogged up, she wouldn't have any way to breathe. With the effort and the panic, she wet her pants. She tried to cheer up: at least she was alive. Vieira would come back and free her. She thought about dragging the chair over to the window to put herself in sight of the people in the building across the street, but the man had tied her feet high enough off the ground that she didn't have any support and would fall over. The urine leaked through her clothes and the wicker seat of the chair and formed a puddle on the floor. She thought that if it had been feces instead of urine she might have vomited, in which case she'd be dead. Every thought deepened her panic.

When Vieira found her, an hour and a half later, she had almost fainted.

"Espinosa, I'm going to kill the son of a bitch! I will kill him myself! I'm going to rip off——"

"Hold on. What happened?"

"What happened is I'm going to rip the balls off the son of a bitch."

After a few attempts, interrupting himself with exclamations, Vieira managed to provide a rough outline. His anger far surpassed what he had felt when he himself had been attacked. He was drooling with rage and spitting into the telephone. His sentences were punctuated with obscenities and couldn't convey the indignation that had overtaken him.

"Espinosa, the faggot came into my apartment, tied my woman to a chair, and vanished without a word, just leaving the scene set up to show what he could do——"

"Did he hurt Flor? Did he do anything to her?"

"Nothing more than gag her and tie her up to a chair like a mummy. The guy is fucking with us. He tied you up inside your own home, and now he's tied up Flor inside my apartment. Damn, Espinosa, we're sure looking like idiots."

"How's Flor?"

"She's terrified. She said she wouldn't stay here for another minute and went back to her house. She left here completely humiliated. And that's how I feel too. The son of a bitch is humiliating us, Espinosa."

"Try to calm down. Go to Flor's apartment and see how she's doing. I'm just getting out of the shower and have to go replace

Maldonado. Kika's the only one he hasn't touched yet. I'll talk to you again later."

On his way to Catete, Espinosa thought about what had happened. The episode with Flor could mean a qualitative change in the threats, or even an end to the attacks. The fact that they hadn't killed Flor was only a demonstration of power, a last warning to Vieira.

Or perhaps they really were playing, like an animal plays with his prey before devouring it.

"Espinosa, Kika's saying that today is the day before Christmas Eve and she's going to the Avenida Atlântica to sell her paintings, that she's not going to be stopped by a maniac, and a bunch of other things."

"Don't worry; I'll talk to her. If she can't be talked out of it, I'll go with her."

They were having the conversation at the door, outside the apartment, before buzzing Kika's doorbell. When she answered, Kika looked at Espinosa quizzically, guessing at what the two had been talking about outside and awaiting a decision.

"All right. I'll go with you."

Kika jumped toward him and gave him two kisses.

"This is the problem with having no rank," said Maldonado. "The prize always goes to the boss. But remember that at Christmas the little ones get the presents."

Kika leaned over to make up the difference in height and gave him two kisses.

It was ten to seven when Espinosa and Kika sat at the table in the living room, the same table where he, Maldonado, and Vieira had sat earlier that afternoon to plot their hotel search. He hadn't rested for a minute all day. He couldn't remember if he'd had lunch. Parts of the day seemed to belong to the day before. They both sat with their bodies bent over, whether from fatigue or worry they couldn't say, and their arms stretched out across the table.

The apartment's layout was curious. Two of the bedrooms bordered the living room. The double doors leading to them were two and a half meters tall, topped by half-moon-shaped panels of stained glass. The yellowish late-afternoon light filtered through the oblique, multicolored glass, a play of light and shadow that underscored the irregularities in the floorboards. If it hadn't been for the noise of the street, they might have imagined themselves transported to another era.

Their hands on the table were a hair's breath from each other's. They'd been sitting there for some time; neither of them knew exactly how long. In the reflected light, the minuscule grains of dust on top of the table and the tiny golden hairs on Kika's arms acquired a microscopic and magical intensity. The only movement in the room was their breathing, though Kika's was more noticeable because it lifted her breasts beneath her sleeveless T-shirt. As the minutes passed, it became slower and the noise of the street seemed to recede to a distant murmur; their gazes locked. Espinosa's thumb touched Kika's little finger, as if by accident, and in the same movement his thumb ran up the finger to her nail, slid over the top, slipped up to the place where it met the next finger, and then passed over each finger meticulously until his thumb was on top of hers. Then their palms clasped. Time slowed down—a minute might have passed, or an hour. With their elbows resting on the table, their forearms lifted, hands still interlocked; their faces were less than a hand's width apart. Espinosa felt Kika's soft warm breath on his eyes, his cheeks, his lips. A sound, at first undefined, began to insinuate itself into Espinosa's conscience just as he was overcome by her scent. The sound began to take shape, though it was still unclear, mixing with her breath, the smell of her hair and her skin; sound and scent fighting for preeminence in his mind. Their lips were on the verge of touching when the heels on the stairs joined the noise of the key in the lock. The door opened. It was one of Kika's roommates.

"Are you praying?"

"I can't believe that your ex-wife or Magali were ever humiliated in the way I was. And to think you sent me to your apartment because I'd be safer there! Fuck it, I promise that I'd be safer walking the streets at night than in your apartment. Never since I've been on this earth has anybody done to me what that guy did, and inside the house of a police officer. Just think what would happen to me if I went to live there like you wanted—they'll end up tearing my guts out."

"You don't need to talk like that. Don't use dirty language: it's ugly on a girl. And just to make sure you understand, that fucker also got into Espinosa's house, left him tied up in the bathroom, and took his guns. So don't think you're the only victim or that he's interested in ripping your guts out: if he wanted to do anything more than tie you up, he would have done it. Don't start heaping blame on me, as if it were my fault."

"It's not? Weren't you the one who lost your wallet? Weren't you the one who decided to follow the drug dealer?"

"What the fuck, Magali, in my—"

"See? You're already confusing my name."

"Goddamn it, what the fuck is going on here? Are you taking this out on me? I need some time off. It happens to everyone."

"Except with me. I've never gotten your name wrong. And I'm the one who needs some time off. Never in my life have I been tied up like that. I don't want to experience it again, and from what I can understand, the guy can do anything he wants; nobody can get him."

Vieira didn't answer. He was pacing around Flor's apartment with tired steps, even though he was confined to the short distance between the bed where they were sitting, the window, and the door. Ten paces were enough to cover the small triangle. Hands behind his back, head leaning on his chest, moving his lips as if reading to himself, Vieira paced back and forth.

"Cut it out, Vieira. You're making me nervous."

He walked around three more times without a word. On the fourth, as he was walking past the door, he left.

There were only two days until Christmas, and residents and tourists were out in force. Creeping traffic, jam-packed bars and restaurants, street vendors everywhere: even the most deeply buried urban fauna surfaced in the weeks of Christmas and New Year's. When they came to the place where Kika usually displayed her work, the other vendors had to squeeze together to allow Kika her spot on the sidewalk.

Espinosa still hadn't recovered entirely from the scene Kika's friend had interrupted. He helped her set up her metal stand and hang the pictures. From the moment they'd left Catete and headed toward Copacabana, they hadn't spoken more than they'd absolutely had to and had avoided each other's eyes. He couldn't ever remember seeing the sidewalks so busy. The attacker wouldn't have the slightest trouble getting close to them, if that was what he wanted. Since all Espinosa's attention was focused on Kika and her immediate surroundings, he himself was extremely vulnerable to attack. He didn't want to think about the Magali case just then; he didn't want to get distracted. He scanned the area, combing the crowds with his eyes, but he couldn't shake the picture of Magali tied to the bed and of Clodoaldo in a drawer at the morgue. The same could happen to Kika. He moved so close to her that no one could come between them.

Under the circumstances, he was slightly reassured that the man hadn't done more than tie Flor up. He'd already had his little fun that day; maybe he'd decide to take the weekend off. Espinosa feared that he was paying so much attention to the faces around him that he'd erase his mental image of the man's face. He wanted to remember every detail of that face, the clipped way he spoke, the way he moved, the glint in his eye, even the way he clenched his jaw when he walked; he remembered it all as in a high-resolution photograph. But the night ended without any incidents. The only memorable event was the sale of one more painting, the smallest one Kika had brought. The transaction left her bursting with happiness.

"After we store the rest of the stuff we'll go celebrate," Espinosa proposed. "This time nobody will interrupt us."

Kika was glowing. The sale of two pictures this week would see her through not only Christmas but the following month as well. She didn't look too concerned by the latest events, or at least didn't seem to believe that she would be targeted as Espinosa and Flor had been. As for the people who had died, in her eyes it was as if they belonged to a different story.

After they'd stored the metal stand in the garage, they walked to the restaurant where they'd been sitting when Vieira was attacked. Even at that hour—it was after midnight—almost all of the tables were full, but they managed to get one right by the window, almost directly beside the one they'd had the last time. Seated facing each other, it seemed they'd taken up where the scene earlier that evening had left off. The most striking physical difference was that between the deep calm of the old house on the Rua do Catete and the chattering crowds of a beachside restaurant on a Friday night in December. There was no way to return to exactly where they'd been when Kika's friend had walked in; the moment and the environment were too different.

"Are you still worried about me?"

"Yes, in both senses of the question."

"What are those?"

"First, about your safety. I still think you're running some risk, even if only because you're the only one who hasn't been attacked. This could mean two things: either our man's decided not to bother you, or you're the final card he has to play. And until I find out which one it is, I'm not going to leave you alone."

"That's a risk I'm willing to run."

The dinner passed peacefully; Vieira didn't come running down the sidewalk, and the man didn't put in any dramatic appearances. It was a quarter to two when Espinosa parked his car in front of the old house on the Rua do Catete. Since the next day was Saturday, he could leave the car parked right there.

"Do you really think you have to spend another night awake in the living room?"

"If I went home, I wouldn't sleep anyway."

They walked up the old staircase. Its countless creaks and groans provided a more than adequate warning against intruders—though it couldn't tell the good from the bad.

The other two girls were already asleep in their rooms. Espinosa avoided the table. He turned on a little lamp on a side table in the corner, took off his coat, and sat on the sofa with his pistol at his side.

Espinosa awoke with the first light of day. Traffic was still light on the Rua do Catete. Only the little bars were open, serving buttered rolls to their regular clients. He waited another hour, hoping one of the girls would wake up, but they didn't. He left, locking the door from the outside and sliding the key back under it. He was well aware that his night vigils were more to reassure them than to offer any real protection. The man surely wouldn't try anything if he knew that Espinosa was inside the apartment. He was there for their peace of mind, not because the man couldn't get in if he wanted to.

He reached home before eight, after a coffee in a bar in Catete. The first mothers and nannies were arriving in the square, pushing their strollers. Espinosa's exhausted eyes couldn't immediately identify the feminine figure walking in his direction.

"Good morning, Officer."

"Flor, what are you doing here at this hour?"

"I waited for you yesterday until after midnight, and then I came back as soon as the sun came up."

"What happened? Where's Vieira?"

"I don't know. He came to my apartment early yesterday evening, we got in a fight over the man who tied me up, Vieira left without saying anything, he didn't go home, and he hasn't shown up since then."

Espinosa had just locked his car and was walking toward the lobby of his building. He'd slept three hours at most, often awakened by the noises of the old house. All he wanted to do now was take a shower and lie down for a couple of hours. Flor seemed to notice the fatigue behind Espinosa's eyes.

"Can I come up? I've been waiting in this square for more

than two hours, and I'm scared of being by myself in my apartment."

"I need to rest. I haven't slept all night."

"I'll be quiet, waiting. Don't worry. I didn't come hoping to seduce you, like the other day."

"Flor, your power to seduce is independent of your intentions. But let's go up. I can hardly get out a full sentence."

"Just say the verb."

"For now it's *sleep*."

They walked upstairs in silence. Flor went ahead of Espinosa, who, despite his exhaustion, still found the energy to admire the body moving in front of him. As she'd done the first time, she looked around the apartment as if inspecting a new conquest.

"You can stop being scared now. The man did what he wanted to do, which was to humiliate Vieira. He won't try anything more on you."

"Espinosa, even if there's no reason to be scared, I'm still scared, and I'm the one who was humiliated. I was bound and gagged, with no idea what that guy was going to do to me. When he left, I didn't know if he was going to come back to kill me. I sat there for hours with my mouth shut with duct tape, scared to death that I would cry or vomit and die of suffocation. Nothing you can say can convince me to stop being scared."

"Sorry. Sit down and try to relax. If you want some coffee, the machine's in the kitchen. I'm going to take a shower."

Espinosa got into the shower and let the hot water run down his neck for a while; only when he felt his muscles relaxing a little did he turn the temperature down. He took longer than usual, not only to relax himself but to give Flor time to calm herself. On the way from the bathroom to the bedroom he found Flor buck naked, holding a condom in her hand.

"I found this on your bedside table, and since you've got to get dressed, I thought we'd start with this."

There was no way back. He knew what would happen: she had worked to make it happen, and she couldn't have chosen a better time. Espinosa, towel in hand, still drying off, was paralyzed by the vision of the willowy brown body: lush hair, narrow hips stretching in one line down to long legs and up to generous breasts. Flor removed the towel from his hands, then slid her body down Espinosa's until she was on her knees, rubbing his dick across her cheeks, her mouth, her eyes, her hair, her nose, before putting on the condom. She stood back up, brushing her breasts along Espinosa's chest, until they were once again face-to-face. They moved slowly, bodies pressed together, to the side of the bed. Sliding his hands along Flor's thighs, he lifted her up and crossed her legs around his waist; the muscles in his legs trembled almost imperceptibly. Then he moved his body lightly until he found the spot he was looking for and slid into her smoothly. Only then, slowly, did they fall onto the bed.

He stared at his watch for a while, waiting for it to come into focus. It read ten-fifteen. He stretched his arm across to the other side, tapping the bed in search of Flor. It was empty. He called her name, but his voice came out hoarse and almost inaudible; he cleared his throat and tried again. The apartment was completely silent. He abruptly imagined that he was dreaming; he still felt the fatigue of the day before, the excess tension. The towel on the floor wasn't enough evidence to make the scene completely believable. But it was difficult to deny the smell of Flor's body on his own.

He'd slept for an hour, but deeply. Flor's departure made

him uneasy—it seemed at odds with the breathless exclamations of the morning—and he was uneasy about Vieira's disappearance. He rose, legs and head still a little wobbly, and got back under the shower, which helped him sort out his thoughts. He drank his coffee and ate some toast; still in his underwear, he opened the living room blinds to see what the weather was like. That was when he noticed the answering machine. It had probably been blinking since the day before, as he hadn't heard the phone ring this morning. There were four messages, one from Flor and three from Vieira. Flor's asked him to call her as soon as he got in. Vieira's were charged with emotion. "Espinosa, I'm gonna get the son of a bitch. I feel awful; I've got to find the guy no matter what." The two others were variations on the same theme. "I'm humiliated. I was kicked out, Flor attacked me because of what happened, and she's right: the guy could have wiped his ass with my shirt." The last one was the most worrisome: "I've got a way to find out who the guy is. I'll give you news soon."

Espinosa called Vieira's apartment; no answer. He called Flor; no answer. He called the Thirteenth Precinct, where Vieira had gotten the name of the informant who'd indicated the hotels in Catete. Vieira had indeed stopped by there the night before, but they didn't know if he'd left by himself or with someone, and they didn't know where he'd been heading. At ten forty-five Maldonado called, wanting to know if Espinosa needed his help. Espinosa said he did and gave him some instructions. At noon on the dot Vieira called.

"Espinosa, thank God I've found you. Wait for me, I'll be there in fifteen minutes." His voice was nervous, and he sounded out of breath.

Espinosa sat speculating about what would have happened if Vieira had decided to stop by earlier that morning. He'd been spared that, but he couldn't help wondering how the tryst would affect their future relationship. Flor would be sure to mention the episode to Vieira; he didn't dismiss the possibility that she'd cooked up the whole thing just to be able to hold it against him later.

Vieira arrived visibly agitated and physically exhausted, unshaven, his clothes rumpled. The stairs had left him so winded that he couldn't speak. Espinosa helped him to a chair, offering a glass of water and urging him to wait a minute before he started talking, but Vieira couldn't contain himself. He gulped down the water his friend offered.

"I know who the guy is and where to find him." The sentence came out so quickly that he had to repeat it to make Espinosa understand.

"What did you find out?"

"Listen to this. He was hired by a group from inside the police itself, a group that didn't want to do its own dirty work. The job was to get the man, who they realized wasn't an officer at all; to get the kid, who they thought was a runner; and Clodoaldo. They thought it was a group working under our protection. They got the sleazeball with my wallet and worked him over. Except the guy didn't have anything to say. They thought he was hiding something, so they squeezed him until he turned in the people who were after him, meaning the kid, Clodoaldo, and me—except he didn't have anything to say about me. They must have pushed him too hard, and he died. All they knew about you is that they'd seen us together. All they wanted was for us to get off their turf. They ordered the kid killed, the guy with the wallet, and Clodoaldo; and they fucked with you and Flor. I don't know what else they planned to do."

"How'd you find out all of this?"

"Don't ask me how. I'm not in the police anymore, and I don't have to obey the fucking rules. The sons of bitches humiliated me and put me out of commission. What did you expect? That I'd take it like a good boy?"

"Fine. No further questions. You said you know where the guy is."

"Here's what happened. He's hiding not only from the people he's attacking but also from the people who hired him. He moves every two days. I got the address of the place where he was. I went there this morning. He'd just left the hotel. I went over every inch of the place and didn't find a thing. He's careful, but he made a mistake. He made some calls from the phone in the lobby to avoid leaving behind a list of numbers. But it so happened that between the time he left and when I got there, there weren't many calls made from that phone. They were all to residential numbers except for two, each to two different hotels. I called the second one and they confirmed that he was staying there. He used the same name he'd used at the hotel he'd left. He must have fake papers."

"If he's moved to another hotel, it's because he's going to stay at least until tomorrow."

"Maybe the son of a bitch is sentimental and wants to spend Christmas at home."

"We could get Maldonado."

"I'd rather we didn't. Think about it, Espinosa—the fucker's always been one step ahead of us. He's competent, but he's got to be getting information from the police itself. If not that, then our phones are tapped. That's why I didn't say anything over the phone. We'd better act without talking to anyone."

"Where is he?"

"The last place you'd think to look for a hired gun. On the Avenida Atlântica, in the Le Meridien hotel."

"He can't be paying for it himself."

"Do you have a plan? Or should we just ring the doorbell and shoot the son of a bitch in the face?"

"Which is a plan."

"Fuck, Espinosa, I'm serious. The guy could get away."

"If he's thinking of escaping, he wouldn't have moved to another hotel. I think he's going to try something tonight."

"Why do you think that?"

"The guy likes to make an impression. Everything he's done so far has had a cinematic touch: killing Clodoaldo inside a taxi, with my gun; tying Flor to a chair strategically placed right in front of the door, for maximum impact when you walked in. Even the kid, sitting in the sand and with his back to the rock, could have been a scene from the movies. He likes what he does and thinks he's got style."

"Goddamn it, the guy's a murderer and you're talking to me about how he's got style?"

"Calm down. You found out who the guy is and where. Now we just have to choose the best moment to get him, and I have a suspicion of what he's planning. I'll say it again: he likes to put together scenes, and there's nothing more Hollywood than Christmas. And today's Christmas Eve. I think he's going to try something tonight."

"And what do you think it could be?"

"Could be any one of several things. All involving people connected to us, or us ourselves."

"What do you suggest?"

"I suggest that you use my bathroom, take a shower, shave, choose a clean shirt from my wardrobe. Once you've done that, we'll go to the Meridien."

It was two-twenty in the afternoon, but the sky had grown dark with rain clouds when they arrived at the hotel. The valet parking attendant looked at Espinosa's car as if it were a garbage truck but still deigned to put his hand on the handle

and open the door. Instead of going to reception, they sought
out the head of security. They knew from experience that hotel
managers and cops didn't get on very well.

The man who was introduced to them could just as well
have been a bookkeeper or the coatroom supervisor; few would
have guessed that he was, in fact, the chief of security. Espinosa showed his badge, which the man examined without
touching it; then he looked at Vieira as if to ask if he too were
a cop. In a short time and with few words it became clear that
he wasn't the bookkeeper. Espinosa summed up the story not
entirely truthfully, failing to mention his suspicion that
another murder would be committed that very night. He
didn't want to make the guests and management unduly
uncomfortable.

"What can I do for you, sir?"

"I'd like to know if he is in fact staying in the hotel, and
if he is, which room he's in. I promise you we won't do anything without talking to you first."

The security chief was not only satisfied with the way the
officer presented the situation; he was visibly thrilled to have
been consulted in the first place. He went to reception and,
after checking the computer, returned with the manager, who
had the information they sought.

"The man you're looking for checked in this morning. He
arrived before noon, and since he didn't want to pay the full rate
for a one-hour difference, he registered, paid for one night, and
asked us to hang on to his suitcase while he went to lunch and
did a little shopping. The hotel has a Christmas dinner, so we
asked if he wanted to make a reservation, and he said yes, for
two. He should be back any minute now, and since he still
doesn't know what room he's staying in, he'll have to stop off at
reception. If you gentlemen would like to make yourselves comfortable, we'll let you know as soon as he arrives."

Espinosa knew that the manager would want them to make themselves comfortable somewhere out of range of even the most curious guest. Since he didn't plan to hang out in the employees' rest room, he asked where the manager would suggest.

"The reception's right above the ground floor, just in front of the escalator. On the floor directly above that there's a lounge where you won't be seen by anyone entering the hotel. You can also intercept the elevators arriving from the ground floor and the reception area. I'll leave a walkie-talkie with you; someone at reception will let you know as soon as the man picks up the key."

It was three in the afternoon when, seated in a comfortable leather chair, Espinosa tested the walkie-talkie. During the next hour Vieira dozed off for a few long minutes, snapping to attention every time the walkie-talkie crackled. Espinosa contacted the guard at reception: "Nothing to report, Officer." Even if the man came in through another door, he'd have to pass through reception to find out what room he was in and to get the key. At four in the afternoon, he still hadn't arrived. Something was wrong.

"Vieira, you said that the guy made two phone calls to hotels. What was the other one?"

"I don't remember. What's the difference? Didn't he come here?"

"Did he?"

"Of course, damn it. He checked in here, didn't he?"

"He checked in, but that doesn't mean he's staying here."

"Motherfucker!"

"Exactly. You didn't check out the other call because you were sure that the last one was where he'd decided to go. You called here, found out that somebody with that name had checked in here, and didn't think anything more about it. All that's here is a suitcase. Which is probably full of old news-papers."

"Motherfucker!"

"You already said that."

"The other hotel was … it was … the Miramar!"

From reception, they called the Miramar Palace, also located on the Avenida Atlântica, but all the way at the other end of the beach. They gave the same name the man had used.

"I'm sorry, sir, but there's no one here by that name."

"Please, check again. It's extremely important. Look under his first name and last."

"Nothing, sir. There's no one registered under that name."

Vieira, who was right next to Espinosa, tried to guess the answers on the other end of the line. There was no need to confirm them.

"Just because nobody's registered under that name doesn't mean anything. Let's go over there."

During their vigil inside the Meridien, they hadn't noticed the change in the weather. The sky was black, and rain was falling so hard that they could barely make out the buildings along Copacabana Beach. Instead of waiting for the car (the valet had gone to fetch it from God knows where), they got in a taxi that was discharging guests at the hotel. It took a little longer than normal to travel the distance between the two ends of the beach.

At the Miramar Palace they set aside professional courtesies and headed straight to reception. Espinosa flashed his badge and spoke simultaneously to the receptionist and the kid behind the computer.

"I called a few minutes ago asking for a guest. The name wasn't right, so we're going to have to find him by a descrip-tion."

"Officer—"

"I know what you're going to say—that it's Christmas Eve, that the hotel is full, that it's impossible to find someone from a description, et cetera. But it so happens that someone's life depends on this, and every minute counts."

"What information do you have?"

"He came in today, by himself, between ten and one. He's a little shorter than I am, very strong, short brown hair, roundish face, narrow, almost Oriental eyes."

"I know who it is."

"What?"

"I remember him perfectly. He came in by himself right after noon. I'm not completely sure which room he's in. Let me check."

After consulting the computer, the kid emerged victorious.

"Room 512. Mr. Mozart."

"What?"

"Mr. Mozart. That's his name."

After leaving Espinosa's apartment, Flor rehearsed a few variations of the conversation she was planning to have with Vieira. She didn't want to lay out all the details—it wouldn't sound natural—and besides, if the story wasn't convincing enough, she would always have recourse to seduction. Furthermore, she had faith in the cheesiness of the holidays. But she had no idea what Vieira had been up to since the day before. She knew she'd pushed him too far. It was the second time he'd answered her with silence; the men she knew had been more prone to emotional explosions. Magali had told her that he could rage, but she'd never mentioned him reacting with silence; for Flor, it was completely novel. And leaving didn't seem to be his usual reaction to difficult situations; he'd always preferred sticking to the comfort of his apartment. He wasn't a thinker: he was a man of action. That was why she was worried about his disappearance. Even worse, she couldn't find Espinosa either. Deep down, she worried that the two were plotting against her. But the officer seemed to have really enjoyed her morning surprise. It was Christmas Eve; they must be out shopping. Even cops had friends and relatives. And if neither was home, there was no reason for her to stay cooped up in her apartment, even with rain threatening. She needed to fix her nails and do something about her hair—the beauty salon wasn't far. The only thing she feared, more than anything in the world, was running into the guy who'd tied her up.

The fight with Vieira hadn't been that serious; there was no reason for him to hold it against her. Besides, she was convinced that she was right: the gunman was doing exactly as he pleased, and the two officers and the little detective couldn't do anything to stop him. It was three against one, and the guy, all by himself, was in complete control. She was already on the street, looking at the clouds and wondering if they meant rain. Anyway, she could learn something from the episode with her assailant, wherever he was. He'd shown her quite clearly that the best weapon was order, precision, and efficiency: the winners weren't the ones who made the most noise but those who controlled the volume. That morning with Espinosa, she'd been extremely competent, almost wordless. The other night, when she'd come to his apartment and immediately blurted out that she was there to seduce him, the guy had gone on the defensive, especially after that girl had shown up with the face that looked scared of dick. Her mistake then had been speaking. This morning she hadn't made any mistakes; he'd had nowhere to run to; it was like a rape. That was how it was done. Few words, good timing, and just the right amount of action. You couldn't fail. If the equipment was up to the task. And her equipment was a gift from God. For the few random details that needed a little fine-tuning, the hairdresser was more than adequate.

Even though he didn't have family in Rio, Maldonado didn't want to spend Christmas Eve working. He wondered if what he was doing was at all useful. If the murderers and attackers really were from the police, he and Espinosa couldn't do anything about it on their own. Stories about kids confronting corrupt cops in a big metropolis belonged to films, and the setting was usually New York, Los Angeles, or San Francisco. This wasn't a film, he wasn't a kid, and the city wasn't New York, Los Angeles, or San Francisco: it was Rio de Janeiro on a hot summer afternoon, with heavy dark clouds in the sky announcing yet another torrential Christmas.

Kika was all sweetness with Espinosa because he'd spent the night awake in the living room, protecting her against the hired gun. He, who'd also been there since the early-morning hours, was looked upon with friendliness but nothing more. If the guy barged in suddenly and popped a bullet between his eyes, he wouldn't be remembered for more than a week. After that, she'd have trouble pronouncing his name correctly. So it was better to shoot the guy before he had a chance to shoot one of them, or even all of them. He took his gun from the holster and placed it on top of the table. He'd never shot anyone. Well, he'd never shot to kill; he'd fired into the air and, even once, in a slum, in the direction of some fugitives, but he'd known the bullets wouldn't hit anyone. But if that guy came up the stairs ready to get the girl, he wouldn't think twice, because by the second thought he'd be dead; he had to get the guy before he could fire back. He wondered if there'd be two different sounds, one of the shot and the other of the bullet entering the guy's body. Surely not. The two things would be simultaneous, life and death. He wouldn't like to have to kill somebody, even though he'd thought about it thousands of times. Something told him the guy wouldn't show up. But that suspicion didn't put him at ease.

In the old house, there was none of the natural excitement of three young women on vacation. The medical student was on duty, having volunteered for the shift to keep her boyfriend company; he was interning at the same hospital. Kika and the other girl couldn't decide whether to accept invitations to friends' houses or to make a cozy dinner and go to bed early. Maldonado thought it seemed sad for two young women to spend Christmas without parents, boyfriends, or friends. And neither of them was a wallflower. He was thinking of inviting them to a Christmas dinner with some friends of his when Kika's beeper nipped his Christmas romance in the bud.

Maldonado accompanied her to a nearby shopping gallery with a row of public phones. Even though there were plenty of phones, there was a short line in front of every one. The wait was compensated for by the smile Maldonado saw spread over Kika's face as soon as she hung up with the girl at the answering service.

"What was it? Did Santa Claus leave you a message?"

"It wasn't him, but it might have been his idea."

"And?"

"And I'm going to have to fix my nails and do something about my hair."

Espinosa and Vieira looked at each other, hardly able to believe their ears.

"Room 512."

"But he's not in his room," said the kid at the reception desk.

"What do you mean, he's not there?"

"The key's on the rack."

"Call up there. If anyone picks up, say the hotel is offering a little Christmas present."

"But the key's on the rack."

"Fuck the key, damn it, do what the officer's telling you."

The kid called up and let the phone ring until Espinosa told him to hang up.

"You didn't see when he went out?"

"No, sir. Sometimes we get busy with tourists arriving and the guests just drop the key off. Today we got two big bus groups; the lobby was packed for at least an hour. He could have gone out then."

"And about what time was that?"

"Between three and four, more or less—right before you gentlemen arrived."

"We can't spend the rest of the day running up and down the beach. If our suspicion that he's going to do something tonight is correct, he'll be plotting something against one of us or against Kika. And I don't think he's going to try anything before ten at night."

"Why ten?"

"Because, based on his previous behavior, we are acting on a somewhat fantastic hypothesis: our suspect likes constructing scenes. We must therefore allow that it is plausible that he is going to build some sort of grand finale today, precisely, Christmas night. So far, nothing has contradicted our hypothesis. According to that logic, we must conclude that if he's going to try anything, he's going to try it at night, at dinnertime, at the Meridien."

"Goddamn."

"Goddamn what?"

"You talk so well."

"I'm being serious, Vieira."

"So am I. I think the way you talk is fucking amazing."

"Thank you. Moving along. If the guy checked into two hotels it's because he's going to use one of them as a perch and the other for the scene he's concocting. Here he's given a new name, there he's made a dinner reservation. Let's go back to the Meridien. What worries me is that the reservation was made for two people. Who's his guest?"

"Shit, Espinosa, even criminals fuck and celebrate Christmas. He must have found a woman."

"I doubt it. As meticulous as he is, he'll play only after his work is done, and I suspect his work's not yet done."

The rain was letting up, and the leaden gray of the sky had given way to light gray, offering hope that they could walk around the city that night unprotected. The manager of the Meridien didn't offer the brightest of smiles when he saw the two return. He would prefer a quiet thug to two loud cops. Until now, however, no one outside of the security staff had noticed Vieira or Espinosa.

"So, Officer, you didn't have any luck?"

"I did. And it brought me back to your hotel."

"Officer, you don't want to let my men take care of this? They know the house like the back of their hands; they've all been trained for emergency situations. It would save you gentlemen some work, and help avoid putting our guests at unnecessary risk."

Espinosa couldn't say he'd had a lot of rest in the last two days: he'd slept for a total of less than three hours, his few moments of pleasure had been tense and nerve-racking, he'd been running after a suspect who was always one step ahead, and he was worried that someone was going to die before the night was over. It could be someone very close to him; it could be he himself.

"Sir, the man we're after has killed, this month alone, two children and two men; he'd kill your pretty boys one by one and pile them up on the reception desk for you to distribute as Christmas favors to your foreign visitors. So stop talking nonsense and try to help us before I have to put someone from my team on reception."

The mere idea of a cop acting as chief of reception was enough to transform the man into the most cooperative being imaginable. Espinosa and Vieira returned to their post upstairs and one of the hotel's security agents stayed behind at reception; everyone had walkie-talkies. Since they could be in for a long wait, Espinosa ordered some sandwiches and fruit juice, along with a thermos full of coffee.

They were sitting only a few meters from the elevators. If word came of the man's arrival, they could intercept him without much effort. They were separated from the ground floor by escalators, and from the reception by only one flight of stairs. The man would have to pass through reception. When he requested his keys, the hotel security guard would identify him and warn Espinosa as soon as he picked up his suitcase and headed for the elevators. Espinosa had ordered them not to even think of doing anything else; the thought of trying to arrest him forcibly should not cross their minds. They were to leave everything to him and Officer Vieira.

The possibility that the man would arrive before dinnertime was remote, unless he'd decided to reconnoiter the area first. The receptionist at the other hotel had also been instructed to inform them immediately if he put in an appearance, but Espinosa considered that improbable as well. Should they split

up, each guarding one hotel? The idea passed through his mind
before he immediately discarded it. Vieira was determined to
capture the man for the sake of his self-esteem, but in a con-
frontation between the two the man could destroy Vieira.
Vieira might act impulsively and lose everything, including
his own life.

Espinosa didn't think of waiting time as time he could use
for mental activity. He was doing something specific, which
was waiting, and that meant that the time spent waiting was
spoken for until the awaited object arrived. Thinking, for Espinosa, wasn't a matter of articulating concepts logically; it was
a mortal clash between pure reason and a limitless imagination. His imagination accounted for almost all the action he
considered to be real mental activity. Though he knew that
people thought of him as a cold rationalist, he recognized that
in fact he was more of a semidelirious fantasist.

Vieira's mood visibly veered from excitement and anxiety
to near exhaustion. Sometimes he even nodded off. Vieira was
old enough to be Espinosa's father, and when Espinosa was
with Vieira he felt a kind of nostalgia for his own lost father—
which made the incident earlier that morning even more problematic. These ideas didn't enter his mind clearly; instead they
worked their way into his head vaguely, between confused
thoughts and feelings, while Vieira catnapped, trusting completely in his comrade's alertness—a trust that made Espinosa
even more uncomfortable.

He thought back to his encounters with Flor, wondering
what he'd done to provoke her latest offensive. No woman in
the world would offer herself that way, unless she was a hun-
dred-percent sure she'd get what she wanted. And she could
have that certitude only if he'd given her some unmistakable
hint. He couldn't recall anything in particular. Such signs were

not always obvious, he knew, and he was aware that women could pick up signals invisible to others—especially a woman whose ability to pick up on them served as the basis of her career. But still there was something else, something beyond good and evil: Flor's combination of beauty and sensuality. No man alive would have thought of his friend when a woman like Flor burst into his bedroom completely nude just as he was coming out of the shower. And she knew that.

The crackling of the walkie-talkie brought him back down to earth. It was just static. They had to pace around a little to keep their legs limber. They had enough space to stretch, and the innumerable cups of juice and coffee they downed often forced them down the short path to the bathroom.

Espinosa left messages for Kika at regular intervals, including the number of the hotel. The longer they waited, the more he felt that the whole thing was a delusion: there *was* no gunman staying in two hotels at the same time (itself an absurd idea). All they had was a name, which wasn't even the same at the two hotels. From there, his delirious mind had created a fiction that he was now trying to lure back to reality: the idea that there was a police plot against him was persecution mania, pure and simple . . .

It was nine-thirty at night when a kid from reception approached with a piece of paper. Beneath the printed word "Message" he'd written: "Dona Kika asks me to inform you that she will arrive at the hour agreed."

"What? What hour agreed? Why didn't you call me?"

"She said she was calling from a pay phone, that it was raining, and that it would ruin her hair."

Espinosa was completely mystified. Vieira, wide-awake, looked at him, at a loss.

"What happened?"

"Kika called saying she'd arrive at the time we'd arranged."

"Arrive where?"

"It can only be here. If she called here to leave a message like this, it's because she got the messages I left, and the fact that I was here didn't seem strange at all—Of course! *She's* the one the guy's made a date with for dinner!"

"What do you mean, made a date with? Kika can't recognize your voice?"

"She doesn't have a phone; she uses a beeper. The messages are taken by an answering service and transmitted by an operator. Anyone can leave a message. He must have gotten Kika's number when he was in my apartment. He had enough time to go through everything."

"What does the fucker want with her?"

"If it's what I'm thinking, we're going to find out within half an hour."

Judging from the evidence on the street, the rain had completely stopped; the night would boast a sliver of moon. After receiving Kika's message, the quantity of adrenaline in Espinosa's blood had increased considerably. Vieira paced in front of the leather chair. It was five minutes to ten when a voice came over the walkie-talkie: "Attention, Officer, the man just took his key and is heading toward the elevator; he didn't pick up the suitcase. Repeat, man in elevator, not carrying suitcase."

A single brief reply: "Understood."

"Let's go."

Guns in hand, they pressed the buttons for all four elevators. In his hurry, Espinosa had forgotten to ask which elevator the man had taken. All they could do was wait to see which door would open first. Two bells rang almost simultaneously, and the up arrows flashed above the doors of two facing elevators.

They were a two-second dash apart. At the first sign that one of the doors was opening, Espinosa and Vieira, wielding their weapons, ran toward it; the elevator right behind them made the same noise at the exact moment they realized that the first one was empty; they turned toward the second elevator just as a lone man took a weapon from his overcoat. The two officers had their shots lined up by the time the door began closing; the stranger still hadn't had time to aim. They leaped inside, the man pressing himself against the control panel while Vieira and Espinosa bumped into the other two walls, attempting to keep their guns pointed toward him. And then the doors closed completely and the lights went off. Espinosa heard the muffled sound of bodies falling onto the ground. The darkness was complete.

The floor of the spacious elevator, with enough room for another dozen people, was thickly carpeted and absorbed every sound. Espinosa was the only one still standing; Vieira and the man huddled in corners to reduce the exposed surface area of their bodies. Espinosa and Vieira couldn't shoot because there was a risk of hitting the other; the man didn't have to worry about that, but as soon as he fired he would announce his whereabouts. There were thirty-seven floors between the lounge and the restaurant, and Espinosa figured it would take less than a minute to reach the top floor. As soon as the elevator started climbing, the weak green light on the display, a coveted landmark in the surrounding murk, began to glow more intensely, but the light still wasn't strong enough for the occupants to make one another out. Espinosa tried to listen for Vieira's breathing. Nobody dared to move; the first movement any of them made would be to pull a trigger. The man was the safest of the three. If he fired quickly, he could get off two or three bullets, and the odds were good that he'd be able to take out the cops. In that case, Espinosa and Vieira would have to act with extreme speed and precision, because if they didn't the man would keep firing until he was certain he'd made both his targets.

In the darkness, smells—from bodies, textiles, metals—grew more intense, but it was hard to discern the sources. Espinosa felt something brush against his pant leg—a shoe, another pair of pants, perhaps even a breath. It was quiet, with the hum of the elevator blotting out all less prominent sounds—muscles contracting, hearts beating, mouths breathing. Espinosa was sure of one thing: before the doors opened, the unknown man would fire. Espinosa kept his gun pointed down toward a point he assumed was the corner, basing his assumption on the location of the little green light. As the elevator rose, the light became brighter and brighter, but still without in any way diminishing the darkness. The number 11 blinked in front of Espinosa's eyes, but he couldn't let himself be distracted by the tantalizing green light: he had to focus entirely on the other light, the light that would come out of the barrel of the man's gun before the number 37 flashed onto the display. His gun was pointing toward the corner where he'd last seen the man, but he realized that if he'd been the one who'd turned off the light he wouldn't have stayed in the same position.

Once again, he felt something brush his pant leg, this time a little more firmly. It had to be Vieira. The other man would have opened fire as soon as they made contact, sure that his first shot would hit his target, before firing into the rest of the car; Espinosa waited two, three seconds and there was no shot, which confirmed his suspicion. A few bodies could fit in the remaining area; if he fired blindly, the probability of hitting the man on the first shot was low enough that a misstep would turn them into sure targets. Number 19—more than halfway there. Espinosa figured he wasn't the only one looking at the bright numbers: perhaps the man had already decided which number would be his cue to start shooting: 30, 32—no higher than that. Espinosa and Vieira had ten floors to decide who would fire first.

The cold surface behind Espinosa's back chilled the sweat coming through his jacket; the contact with his pant leg disappeared and the smell of lubricated metal grew more intense, but he couldn't tell if it was coming from the weapons or from the elevator. He'd have to take at least one bullet. He didn't know where he'd get hit, or whether it would kill him; he didn't want to die. He could fire first, but he'd hit Vieira; in the small space it was as difficult to hit the target as it was to miss it; 26: the sweat on his forehead threatened to cloud his vision, and even though that didn't make much difference in the darkness, he hoped the shot would hit his leg; 29: he lightly increased the pressure on the trigger, taking it to the limit; 31, 32: a flash accompanied by a roar followed by four, five, six reports—no scream, only the thudding of a body against the metal wall. The elevator shaft rang with the noise of the shots; when the door opened at the top floor, the gunman's body fell onto the soft carpet of the hallway, his legs still inside the elevator, holding the doors open. In one of his hands was the pistol he'd stolen from Espinosa. Vieira, huddled in the corner of the elevator, was daubing at his face. Espinosa, leaning against the back wall, was covered with thousands of shards of glass; one of his legs was soaked with blood. The gunman had two holes in his stomach and one in his leg. There had been eight shots in all: one had hit Espinosa's leg a few inches below his knee, another had grazed Vieira's face and taken off a piece of his ear; three had hit the man; two had hit the metal wall; and another had broken the mirror Espinosa was leaning against.

A guest made a tourniquet for Espinosa's leg and another

was applying a wet napkin to Vieira's cheek and ear when the doors to one of the other elevators opened and out stepped Kika. From his seat on the ground, Espinosa looked up at her. It no longer mattered what the guy had planned to do. He was just happy they were all alive.

Early on the morning of the twenty-fifth, after the emergency room doctors at the Hospital Miguel Couto were through patching them up, and after the officers were through taking depositions, the three sat down to Christmas dinner: a few sandwiches Kika had picked up. Then the same taxi dropped Vieira at home and took Espinosa and Kika to the Peixoto district. It had rained again, the remains of yesterday's late-afternoon storm. They walked up the three flights of stairs, Espinosa grasping the handrail and leaning on Kika. They'd never been so physically close.

"You spent the night in my apartment to protect me, so now it's my turn."

At the hospital Espinosa's pant leg had been cut above his knee; there were bloodstains all over the clothes Kika had picked out for the dinner at the Meridien.

More than anything, Espinosa wanted to bathe. The doctors had left a hole in the cast, above the bullet wound. Kika wrapped the injured leg in a plastic bag, carefully closing it with masking tape. Then she undressed him.

The night was part pain, part pleasure, the latter predominating, even though the anesthetics wore off rather quickly. Espinosa awoke to find Kika snuggling against the part of his body that wasn't in a cast and the phone ringing in the living room. When he tried to disentangle Kika's leg from his own, she awoke, jumping up immediately, stark naked, and looked for the phone. It was Vieira.

"So, how was my buddy's night?"

"I don't know about him, but mine was marvelous." And she handed the phone to Espinosa.

"Vieira, how are you?"

"Like van Gogh."

There followed a silence, no more than five seconds, in which Espinosa heard only the old policeman's breathing.

"Vieira, I'd like to talk to you and Flor. The conversation might take some unpleasant turns. It's important for all three of us to be there; it wouldn't do to talk to you first, and it's best to get it over with as soon as possible."

"She called saying she wanted to see me. She's coming over. If you want, we can have our talk as soon as she gets here. Can you move around?"

"I'll see what I can do. I'll be there in less than an hour."

Kika came back from the bathroom wiping her face, wearing only panties and a frightened expression.

"Are you going out?"

"Yes."

"But the doctor—"

"It's not over yet."

"My God, Espinosa, something else is going to happen?"

"Not to us. You're out of danger."

"What's going to happen?"

"I still don't know exactly."

Espinosa began getting dressed. He called for a taxi; Kika helped him down the stairs. They said good-bye.

He didn't have any problems at Vieira's building. There were only two small steps between the street and the elevator. Flor opened the door without greeting Espinosa. It wasn't hard to guess that the two had been arguing. Vieira steered them to chairs arranged in a triangle and pushed a little footstool toward Espinosa, to support his leg. Flor sat with her back toward the bedroom door, Vieira in front of the living room's lone window and Espinosa in front of the door to the outside hallway. There was a moment of silence, during which they tried to figure out who would speak first, but all eyes were on Espinosa. When he started talking, his tone of voice made it clear that this was not going to be a friendly conversation. Espinosa spied the revolver used the night before on the table closest to Vieira. Perhaps it had been there ever since the officer had returned the previous night.

"The reason for this conversation, as you've probably guessed, is Magali's murder."

Espinosa's voice was slightly distorted by pain. His leg was throbbing.

"This is not an interrogation, and it's not even an official conversation; I only want to present a few conjectures based on clues gathered over the last few days. I want to see if they have the same meaning for you that they do for me."

Flor and Vieira glanced at each other and shifted positions. The heat in the living room was almost unbearable.

"Magali was killed between midnight and three in the morning. At that time of night, anyone who doesn't live in her building has to ring the doorbell. They can only come in if they're expected, unless they're with someone who lives in the building, in which case obviously they don't need to call the doorman. Everyone testified that on nights Magali went out with Vieira she didn't make other plans, so she wouldn't have been with a client at that hour. If the murderer came home with her, they wouldn't have had to ring the bell, which means that it had to be either Vieira or some other friend."

Vieira shifted in his seat, stretching his hand out and making contact with his gun with the point of his finger, moving it back and forth across the tabletop.

"The doorman stated that Vieira was so drunk he couldn't

even get out of the car when he arrived with Magali; and he said that he saw the couple leave in the car together with Flor, who had run into them at the entrance to the building. He didn't see any of them again that night. If that story is true, it's improbable that Vieira would have come back later that night to kill his friend. So let's eliminate Vieira, on that basis. But make no mistake: I'm not necessarily saying he's innocent. I'm just speculating. So if we suppose that Vieira's innocent, even simply because all the witnesses agree that he couldn't even stand on his own two legs, the only remaining suspects are Vanessa, who lives one floor above Magali, and Flor, Magali's best friend."

Vieira picked up his gun, moving it from one hand to other, not looking at anyone. Flor stared at Vieira and Espinosa, visibly agitated.

"I spoke several times with both of them. The only one who defended Vieira on every occasion was Vanessa, even though she didn't consider herself his friend. She really only knew him through Magali's stories."

"Shit! What does this guy want, Vieira?"

Vieira pointed the revolver in Flor's direction, but aimed the barrel at the ground. Espinosa slightly shifted the position of his leg, which was still throbbing painfully.

"My suspicion—since it's no more than a suspicion—is that Flor killed Magali."

Flor gave a cry and stood up. Vieira raised the revolver. Espinosa placed his right hand on his back. Vieira turned the weapon against him.

"That's right, Vieira, shoot the son of a bitch; he forced me to fuck him—kill that faggot, shoot him!"

"I imagined . . ."

"Shoot, Vieira!"

". . . the following course of events: Magali and Vieira leave the restaurant and go to her apartment. Upon arriving there, they meet Flor on the sidewalk in front of the building. The two women try to get Vieira out of the car, but he's sound asleep. Flor offers to help take him home. Upon arrival there—or rather, upon arrival *here*—the three of them come upstairs. Vieira, practically carried by them, at no time wakes up—"

"Shoot, Vieira! Are you scared?"

"In the bedroom, semilucid, he tries to take off his clothes, tugging at his belt, which falls out of his hand, and his pants fall to the floor. Flor and Magali pull his pants off, get him into bed, and depart, leaving him to sleep it off. Once on the street, Flor realizes that she's holding Vieira's belt along with her purse—"

"What are you waiting for, Vieira? Shoot him!"

"Going through the glove compartment or her friend's purse, she finds the Mace; she hears her friend tell her to be careful, that it's powerful, that even a little is enough to knock someone out—"

"Crazy! You're crazy!"

"Once back in Magali's building, the two go upstairs, probably to discuss the evening. In Magali's room, still holding the Mace in her hand, Flor decides, as a joke, to try it out on her friend, who passes out immediately—"

"Motherfucking faggot piece of shit!" Flor, standing, was shouting at Espinosa. Vieira kept the gun aimed at a point on the floor between Flor and Espinosa.

"Seeing her friend passed out, she tries to revive her; she doesn't know if she's alive or dead, and she panics. She remembers Vieira's belt, which she'd tossed onto the bed, sees the plastic bag within arm's reach—"

"Kill him! Kill the fucker!"

"She ties up her friend with clothes she gets out of a drawer, ties her feet with a scarf and Vieira's belt, and sticks her head in the plastic bag."

"Faggot!"

Vieira slowly turned the weapon toward Flor.

"Kill him, Vieira, kill him! Yesterday the son of a bitch forced me to fuck him, he said he was going to turn us in, that the two of us planned to kill Magali. I didn't want to do it...the gas came out...I didn't mean to...I didn't..."

Vieira's single shot hit Flor in the chest.

ACKNOWLEDGMENTS

I would like to thank my friend and attorney Marcio Donnici
for facilitating my access to Rio de Janeiro's police stations and
Forensic Institute, as well as for putting up with my telephone
inquiries about criminal matters.

The translator wishes to acknowledge the kind help of Luciane
Moritz Sommer of Rio de Janeiro in preparing this translation.

ABOUT THE AUTHOR

A distinguished academic, LUIZ ALFREDO GARCIA-ROZA is also a critically acclaimed, bestselling novelist; he lives in Rio de Janeiro. The first book in the Detective Espinosa series, *The Silence of the Rain*, was published last year by Henry Holt; the next will be published in 2004.